Breaking Nick

Sammy Rose Taylor

Cover Art by Eileen Jeannette Widjaja

To my littlest loves, thank you for being the sunshine in my life.

One

"I hate that guy."

The statement left Holly Truman's lips before she could swallow it back. Holly didn't think she'd ever hated anyone in her life, that her brain wasn't capable of the feeling. Yet, she peered at Nick Jones across the sun-bleached football field and watched him toss an empty can of coke into the trash. Aiming poorly, he missed, and the can clattered to the ground, left to glint in the sun. Staring at the can, Holly could tell he was mulling it over, judging how long it would take to make the journey, while his friends beckoned him. Nick decided it was too much effort. Holly ground her teeth.

Yep, she *hated* that guy.

"Who?" Tess glanced up, two bright blue eyes peering over her sandwich. She followed Holly's narrowed gaze and scoffed. "Who? Nick Jones? You don't hate Nick Jones. You don't hate anyone."

"I do. It's in here, like—indigestion." Holly clutched her chest and then sniggered. "I feel it with my soul. Nick is...ugh. Don't get me started!

Tess let a beat of silence pass, unfolding her legs and staring across the field. "Very dramatic. Too bad you've been stuck with him since pre-school."

"He painted Wilbur."

Tess covered her mouth and laughed into her palms, and Holly joined, unable to resist the sound of Tess's foghorn laugh. A ball skirted close to where they sat, both held up their palms as one of the players ran to retrieve it. A gentle breeze wafted under the trees, and Holly fanned her neck with the lunch box lid. The air was stuffy despite the breeze, Willowdale had been cursed with a dry July heat. The grass was yellowed and singed. The back of Holly's knees were damp, and the usually neat uniform they wore for school was crumpled. Tess rolled her eyes. "Wilbur was his first victim. Are you ever going to let that slide?"

Holly picked at grass on her skirt. "Not until I'm dead."

It *was* kind of funny. At least it would be if Nick Jones had grown into a semi-decent, likable, polite eighteen-year-old. Instead, he was...Nick. Someone she avoided at all costs. She ran indoors to avoid him if he was washing his car out front of his house. If he walked home the same way as her, she'd duck into the nearest shop to avoid the awkwardness of any kind of conversation. Nick never acknowledged Holly, she was too below him.

Despite sharing a bedroom wall, living next door to one another since they were three years old, he preferred to pretend she didn't exist and Holly liked it that way. Nick was sullen, rude, and hung out with Davey Thomas, Willowdale's young offender. Nick, Davey, Tyler, and Casey made an odd group of misfits. They existed outside the school boundaries, barely turning up for class, drinking, and walking around with their earbuds in. They weren't exactly disruptive, but they didn't engage, and Nick spent most of his time with his eyes on the ground. Nick was regarded as cool, even if he was standoffish. Holly wasn't regarded as cool, she doubted most people regarded her at all.

The glaring truth was Nick Jones hated Holly as much as she hated him. Wilbur was only the beginning.

Wilbur, a white, pristine, stuffed rabbit, was Holly's first day-of-school gift. She held him tight under her arm, clutching him hard as she bravely went in on her first day, wearing a pristine, pressed uniform and her chocolate-coloured hair in pigtails.

Nick first said to her, "That's an ugly bear." Then he flicked chalk at her board.

Tearfully, she'd ignored him as they stood side by side at their chalkboards. They were drawing rainbows. Holly's was as beautifully executed as a five-year-old could manage. Nick's was all scrawls and shapes, a splodgy mess. "You aren't doing it right," she accused. "The colours are in the wrong order." She dutifully sang him the rainbow song to prove it. *Someone* had to tell him.

He snorted in reply, waiting till she'd finished the last line of the song before he grunted, "Colours can go anywhere I want."

Stung from the insult he'd made about her bear, Holly peered down at him. Wilbur was soft and white, with round, button eyes. Holly loved him.

"What's that thing's name?"

He was eyeing Wilbur with interest, with a look in his eye that made Holly grip him harder. "Wilbur. He's my friend."

Nick snorted. "Loser."

Later, after snack time, a sticky smorgasbord of chopped veggie sticks, tomatoes, crackers, and soft cheese—the incident occurred.

Nick locked eyes with Holly across the echoey hall, a red crayon dangling out of his mouth. He stomped his heavy feet in her direction. Snatching Wilbur in his large, sweaty palm, he ran with him to the small play area outside. Holly let forth a shriek. A sound so high pitch it could only come from the mouth of a five-year-old girl. She chased him outside, spotting him in a corner with a tube of red poster paint. Wilbur was defiled, sticky with red paint as though he'd been eaten alive, and thus began the war. Nick and Holly were not friends.

Nick didn't share toys. Nick didn't like to take turns. Nick ate crayons and stole her snacks. Nick called her a boring, four-eyed swat with no friends when they went into year one.

When they got to high school, he flicked her with ink and teased her for all the clubs she attended. Laughing because she preferred hanging out with little kids to girls her age. Nick grew up, he got tall, lean, with biceps she couldn't help but notice. His hair was usually a dark, wavy mess, cut short around his ears but longer on top. Holly thought that perhaps if he weren't a dick all time, he'd be cute.

Nick also lived next door, and over the years, the insults faded, like he couldn't be bothered anymore, now he ignored her. Holly wasn't sure what was worse. They shared a wall, a garden fence, a driveway, and a deep mutual hatred.

Tess tapped Holly's shoulder, bringing her out of her melancholic state. Thinking about him made her sad. Why couldn't he be nice? She was nice. "Earth to Hols!"

"Sorry."

"Let's not talk about him. I bet you are excited. Two days and you are out of this town for four days."

Holly made a face, peeling her sweaty legs apart and tucking them under her. "I'd hardly call it a holiday. It's an Eagle thing."

Tess prodded her. "You've been excited for months. And now you only have to wait two days for your trip."

"I'm in charge of a bunch of Robins for a week—seven-year-olds! *But* I will get my award, finally!"

Tess smiled. "Ah, yes, the prestigious Gold Award. What's it for again? Being the best Eagle leader ever?"

Holly scoffed. "I'm the *only* leader Martha has. But yeah, kind of. It'll look good on my Uni application." She glanced at the pale blue, cloudless sky and wiped her brow.

The Eagles were a long-standing tradition in Willowdale, like the Scouts or Guides. An association going back years; it took boys and girls from age five to eighteen. Learning life skills like cooking, first aid, sewing, painting, and crafts, they collected badges for various activities and regularly went on hikes and camping trips. It suited adventurous, outdoorsy kids who loved nature. Holly began as a Robin and worked her way through the club. Now she was an Eagle and about to leave unless she stayed as a permanent leader like Martha.

It was sad, as over the years, numbers dwindled, and kids didn't stay long past Owls or Hawks. Holly, however, was a stalwart member, and Martha relied on her, maybe too heavily at times. The Gold Award was the pinnacle of achievement and would be a glittering seal of approval on Holly's already gleaming university application.

"Doesn't this freak you out? It's nearly over." Holly came back to the present. The idea of her time with the Eagles ending left her feeling jittery. Why did everything have to change?

"I'm not going to miss this place," Tess said, clicking her tongue. Holly and Tess had been friends since their first year in Primary School. This was their last summer before going their separate ways, and Holly didn't want to acknowledge the growing knot in her stomach. Tall, lean, and willowy, Tess Brant was destined for Performing Arts. She was pretty, with gleaming, tanned skin and a blonde mane of curls, which she wore naturally around her face. Tess examined her nails, painted a baby pink. "One more day and we're out."

Holly sighed, staring across the football pitch. In the distance, a bell rang, and they hurried to pack their lunch. "I can't get used to the idea that we're done. No more routine, no more classes—no more Willows High."

In two days, high school was over. The last two years at Willows High were spent studying for their final exams, leaving Holly with a raw, hollow sensation. She'd never walk these familiar halls again.

Walking side by side, Tess flung her arm across her face as a sun shield, squinting as they headed back to the main school building. Willows High was a massive red brick Victorian building nestled in the sprawling countryside, green fields, and on the brow of a hill overlooking the small market town of Willowdale. It was a small town with two pubs, a cricket pitch, a place where everyone knew one another.

"Well—for six weeks. Then it's college, and that'll be a whole new routine—you'll be back in time for the party, right?"

Holly pulled her fingers through her dark curls, swatting sweaty tendrils off her forehead, she pushed her glasses up her nose. Her stomach lurched at the thought of one of Tess's parties, but dutifully, she'd promised to go as her best friend even though she'd rather be at an Owl sleepover with a bunch of rowdy nine-year-olds. Tess beamed at her. "Please don't bail on me."

"I said I'd come!" She tossed her a pleading look. "But put me on snack duty. Let me stay in the kitchen—"

"Ha! You mean you want to hang out with Adam? You are so transparent."

Blushing, Holly looked at her shoes as ahead, Tess threw open the big glass doors to the sixth-form common room, a large airy space with couches, a small kitchen, and computer stations. Hanging out with Adam Brant, Tess's nine-teen-year-old brother, made a party more bearable. Adam was gorgeous, blonde-haired and tall, and the strong silent type. In other words, he was painfully shy. Bordering on monosyllabic shy. Holly thought he was adorable in a way that made her heart race and wanton thoughts sneak into her head at night.

Like her, he was a kitchen dweller, too socially awkward to leave the safety of the snack bar. He wouldn't say much, grunt a quiet hello, and read in a corner. Drafted in as the 'responsible' one, Adam's parents forced him to go mainly to keep his little sister in line. When he smiled, his cheeks dimpled, and Holly would swell with longing. Adam was worth the social anxiety of a crowded, stuffy house party.

Holly smirked, avoiding Tess's inquisitive stare as she stuffed her pack in her locker. She held up a pink, painted nail. "I see right through you, Holly Truman! You're wasting your time with Adam, trust me. He's a lost cause. He only likes girls in books— they're safe!"

I like lost causes...if they can be fixed! Holly snapped her locker shut, the sound of trainers and long trousers shuffling over the polished wood floor. She groaned inwardly.

Speaking of lost, hopeless, dead in the water causes...

Nick shuffled beside her, flinging his locker open hard enough the door banged her own. Up close, he smelled strange, Holly couldn't place it, but it was a mix of spicy shower gel and sweat. Boy smell. His hand brushed her shoulder as he went to slam his door, and Holly caught sight of a rose tattooed on the inside of his wrist, his thumb ring glinted in the sun, and nails were bitten down to the beds. Nick had a lot of tattoos. Holly guessed he must've lied several times about his age to get them done.

Dragging her eyes up his muscled forearm, she paused, flicking a careful gaze at his stony face, two pale eyes pulled in a permanent frown and turned down lips. Too late, he caught her staring, and she looked away.

"Hey, Truman." He sneered, looking down his nose at her. Holly was used to people looking down at her. At only five feet, she wished she were a little taller. "Isn't it time your hormones kicked in, and you grew four inches?" Nick's smirk lifted his eyes, brightening for a nanosecond.

Holly threw him an even smile, determined not to let him get to her. "Isn't it about time you grew some facial hair?"

Nick's smirk vanished. "How come you're always under my feet?" He slammed his locker, and the crash vibrated in her skull. She stiffened as he loomed over her, flicking a lock of dark hair out of his eyes. "By the way, your parking sucks. Have you got to pull in so close to my car every night?"

She sniggered. "Why don't you move it? Like onto your driveway? Oh! Wait—there's no room for your shitty Fiat next to your dad's cars."

"If you want to talk shitty cars—"

"I don't, though. I don't want to talk to you. *Ever.*"

Slamming her locker, she spun haughtily and wandered to the water dispenser, where Tess watched with interest. Holly puffed and flicked her brown hair. Tess smirked and took a sip from her plastic cup, licking her pink lips.

"What?" Holly snapped.

"Nothing."

Holly raised a brow, grabbing up her pack from the sofa. "What?"

Tess grinned. "He's staring a hole in your back right now."

"Shut up!"

"What do you do to that guy? He looks so mad."

Holly pushed her glasses up her nose, defiant and determined not to give Nick another thought today. She took a short breath, content that in two days, she'd be out in the woods, alone with her sweet group of Robins, sitting around a campfire, telling stories and roasting marshmallows. Not stuck having to listen to Nick's trash death metal through the wall they shared.

"We better get to English," Tess reminded her, hand on the knob of the common room door as a commotion broke out behind them.

The crash of metal on metal squeaked in her ears as she whirled around, in time to see Eddie Norman grab Nick by his denim jacket and slam him against the lockers. They rocked under Nick's weight and his face twisted in pain, his toes barely touching the floor.

Eddie was massive, all muscle and sinew, his round face clenched in anger as he banged Nick hard against the frame. "Do you want to explain yourself, loser?"

Holly hadn't been aware she'd even moved, but something in her snapped. Hurrying across the room, she grabbed Eddie by the back of his jacket.

"What the hell, Eddie? Leave him alone!"

Nick's eyes bugged in shock, and Eddie snapped his glare in her direction. He was well over six feet and towered over her. Holly wasn't budging. It wasn't the Eagle way to stand by and let someone get hurt. Even if you hated that person with every fibre of your being.

Eddie looked momentarily dazed, faced with her scrunched-up, freckled nose and hands-on-hips pose. He let Nick slide down the lockers and then shoved a small piece of paper in his face. "Why the hell are you sending my girlfriend drawings, Jones? Is this a weird way of flirting?"

Red-faced, Nick got to his feet and straightened his jacket, hardly able to look in Holly's direction. "It's not what you think." He rubbed the back of his head. Holly snatched up the paper mid-air as Nick tossed it away. Unfolding it, she saw an inky drawing of a small dragon woven between the initial V.

V for Violet, Eddie's girlfriend.

"Then what the fuck is it?"

"It's a tattoo," Holly answered, folding the paper and handing it back to Eddie. "It's a tattoo design." It wasn't hard to work out. Nick was obsessed with his tattoos, his fore-arms often adorned with inky scribbles, his face pinched in concentration as he drew in class when he was supposed to be studying. Holly didn't want to imagine how many he had over his body, even the parts she couldn't see. She'd spotted him washing his car topless from her bedroom window once. He had a bird on his shoulder blade. It was massive, and she guessed must have taken hours to complete. Holly shuddered at the thought. "That's all, right Nick?"

Nick stared at her, a mix of horror and humiliation that this five-foot, bespectacled girl child had rushed to his rescue. "Right," he choked out in mortification, turning to Eddie, puffing. "Violet asked me to design one for her—she saw a couple of mine and liked them. That's all—I swear!"

Eddie's sneer dropped, he screwed up the paper, and threw it in Nick's face. "Fine. But you stay away from her, Jones. She doesn't need any of your weird shit scrawled on her body. If she asks you again, you say no, understand?"

Nick scowled. "Isn't it up to her what she does with her body?"

Eddie balled his fist and grabbed a fistful of his shirt, and Nick screwed up his face, ready to take the hit. Holly stepped in between, adrenaline spiking in her veins. She grabbed Eddie's fist. "He understands." She swallowed. "You don't need another mark against your name for fighting Eddie. One more day and we're out of school for good."

Eddie stared at her petite, freckled face, his own full of grudging respect, because, of course, Holly was right. His lip curled in a sneer. "Little miss perfect, aren't you, Truman?"

Holly stepped back, allowing Eddie to saunter away, staggering as he bumped her aside. Holly's palms washed with cold, prickling fear, hardly able to believe she'd just stood between Eddie Newman and Nick Jones and why the hell she'd done it in the first place. Shaking, she turned when Nick grabbed her shoulder.

"Who the hell do you think you are? I didn't ask you to do that."

Holly blinked, stung, and words stuck in her throat. Inwardly she sagged, wondering if she should've let Eddie punch him. Anger boiled in her gut. "You're welcome."

"If I need a four-year-old to come to my rescue, I'll call on on of your little Pigeons to help me next time. I'm sure they'll hit harder."

Holly puffed. "They're *Robins*, not Pigeons. Dick head."

Lifting her chin, she turned on her heels and met Tess in the hall, standing with her mouth hanging open. "Holly—you little rockstar. You just—"

"I know!" Wandering into the hall, she went limp, her hands and feet like wood blocks. "I nearly got punched by Eddie Newman."

"No, I mean...." Tess grinned, her bright eyes shining as Nick stalked past, not daring to look at either of them as he hurried to class. "I mean you...you hate that guy."

Holly watched his figure retreat down the hall and didn't want to admit she sensed a small pang of sadness. He hadn't even said thank you.

Two

"Torch?"

Holly smiled at her mother, clicking on the small device in her hand. "Check."

"Water shoes?"

"Check."

Mrs. Truman scrawled another item off her list, neatly filed in her notebook. She leaned against the kitchen counter. "Sleeping bag? Bug spray?"

"Check, and check."

Holly's mother chuckled and shook her head. "I think we've exhausted the list! I need a coffee after that."

Holly drew the notebook across the counter and hopped off the barstool. Biting her lip, she scanned the kit list, mentally checking she'd packed everything she needed. It was her first trip away with the Robins as an Eagle Cadet, and she was insanely nervous and excited. Saturday morning, at eight AM, Holly and Martha, the Eagle leader, would travel to Tillbury Woods, a sprawling rural campsite deep in the heart of Suffolk, with a group of young Robins. Hopefully, to give them an experience of a lifetime and their first taste of camping in the woods. Holly loved spending time with the Robins. She loved their energy, enthusiasm, and bringing the best out of them, coaxing them to try new things. She remembered the day she'd been a Robin and the thrill of receiving her first badge. It was for sewing, and she'd beamed with delight when Martha, then a young Eagle Cadet, pinned it to her sash.

An Eagle is true in spirit and deed. They raise their wings to protect all those who shelter beneath.

The Eagle motto was imprinted in Holly's soul, it was part of everything she did. She carried it with her even when she was down. Holly knew her friends sniggered and thought she was probably a little insane to dedicate so much of her free time to helping the group's younger members. Spending hours thinking up activities, practicing recipes to teach them, and taking them on nature walks. But in a town like Willowdale, where everyone knew you and everything about you, Holly often caved under the stifling glare of eyes upon her. She was a teenager, and she wanted to be seen. The truth was, maybe she was a little different.

Holly didn't fit in like other girls, she didn't wear makeup, short skirts, or fashionable jewelry. She loved to learn, and sometimes it didn't go down too well. Tess Brant had been her best friend since they were five years old, and Holly suspected even she didn't get her most of the time. Teaching was the natural step forward for Holly and come September her dream would become a reality.

Holly glanced up and caught her mother watching her, a fond smile on her face. Holly screwed up her nose. "What?"

Her mother released a long exhale. "I just...nothing. It's nothing."

"What?"

"I...you will have some fun this summer, right?" Mrs. Truman said, arching a perfectly thin brow, overplucked in the nineties. "I mean...after you get back from camp?"

"Fun?" Holly scoffed. "This *is* fun."

"I mean with your friends. With Tess. Hang out...make some memories... even some mistakes."

Holly tutted, leaning her elbows on the countertop. "Do you mean like boy mistakes?"

"I mean fun. *Your* age fun. You're going to Bramston in September, and I want to see you enjoy yourself. You give so much time to the club—which is admirable!" She held up her hand when her daughter went to butt in. "But, you can let go if you want to. As long as you're sensible."

Holly hid her scowl. She was always sensible. Did her mother mean what she thought? That she should hook up with someone and fool around? There was only one guy Holly was romantically interested in, one person who kept her awake at night, and that was Adam. She shrugged. "There's no one...I mean, the only one I like doesn't know I exist."

Mrs. Truman chuckled. "You mean Tess's brother? He's cute but very shy. I doubt you'd get more than two words out of him, let alone...." Mrs. Truman raised her brows suggestively.

"Mother!" Holly burst into giggles. Holly didn't mind his silence, he was shy, sweet, and dreamy. "I like him."

Mrs. Truman exhaled briefly, choosing her words with care. "I want to see you have some fun. Please try and be more open-minded. And stop saying yes to every activity Martha signs you up for. I swear she'll have you running that club!"

Now that sounded just perfect.

Mrs. Truman patted her shoulder as she wandered past. "I'll be glad to have all this gear out of my hallway!" She planted a kiss on her daughter's cheek. "But I'll miss you for a week."

Holly gave her a snarky smile. "But you have Kit to hang out with."

Mrs. Truman rolled her eyes with a grin. "Speaking of the lovable teenager, will you let her know she has a pile of laundry to take upstairs?"

Holly nodded, hopping from the bar stool and passing the vast array of camping equipment in the hall. Dodging it, she spotted the box of marshmallows she'd forgotten to take to the clubhouse. "Damn," she said, biting her lip. "Mum—I have to run over to the clubhouse."

"Okay, but dinner is in an hour."

Skipping up the stairs, Holly raced to her bedroom to grab her sunglasses, pausing outside Kit's bedroom door. She peered around the crack sand and spotted a pair of DM-clad feet dangling off the end of the bed. Kit, finished home-schooling for the day, was lying on her back, chewing a pen-cil, staring at a blank notebook propped on her knees. Holly tapped the door, and her green liner-ringed eyes snapped up. Kit yawned. "Hey."

"Hey—your washing is done. Mum said to tell you to col-lect it when you...have a *spare* moment." Holly's lip curled in a grin, unable to keep the sarcasm out of her voice. Kit's eyes were bright green, heavily lined with kohl making them appear ethereal. Kit loved colour, her mousy hair was unrec-ognizable under the vast amount of pink dye she stained it with.

"You mean...*your* mum said to tell me my washing is done?"

Holly snorted. "Whatever. Yes, *my* mum. And yes, *your* washing. Which you could go pick up and help her out...you know...when you get the time?"

"But I'm slammed." With a grunt, Kit sat up, pulling her greasy pink locks into a ponytail. She grinned. "All ready for your trip?"

"I'm about to go over to the clubhouse. One last chore. But yes, I'm ready."

"Aren't you freaking out about looking after a bunch of three-year-olds?" Kit visibly shuddered. Holly rolled her eyes.

"They aren't three—they're seven."

"Can they wipe their own backsides?"

Holly burst out laughing. "Of course they can. Martha and I can manage a small group, we'll be fine." Nerves did a little dance in her belly. She hoped she'd be fine.

"It's a crazy way to spend a summer if you ask me."

"I didn't. But thanks."

Holly was used to the jibes. Kit's bedroom smelled like vanilla pods hiding a faint aroma of cigarette smoke. Holly was sure her cousin smoked out the window but wasn't about to rat her out. She'd been with them for six months, and getting Kit to settle had been a long, painful process. The daughter of her Aunt Issy, Kit moved in when life with her family wasn't doable any longer. Mrs. Truman was used to dealing with difficult teens, and when her sister begged for her to house Kit, she agreed.

Holly never knew her dad, and for years it'd only been the two of them until Mrs. Truman joined the foster programme. Over the years, Holly had seen this room used by several different kids. James was the last foster kid who'd lived here. Only meant to be a short stop gap, James fitted the Truman's like a glove, and for years Holly treated him like her very own older brother. But it all ended when she'd been fourteen, and even thinking about James made her ache.

Kit threw her legs over the side of the bed, smoothing out her wrinkled shirt, and she squinted as she peered into a mirror, pinching her pale cheeks. Spiky, solitary, and a little edgy, Kit was hard to get to know, and it'd taken Holly lots of mental energy to let her jibes roll off her back. Kit was nice but a loner, suffering from crippling social anxiety and outbursts of anger.

Kit shuffled to the wardrobe, throwing it open with enough force to make it slam, reminding Holly of Nick. Shrugging out of her old shirt, Kit rummaged for a fresh one when Holly spotted the remains of old Pokémon stickers on the wall mirror. Ice struck her heart, and she puffed, looking away. Her heart spiked out of nowhere and absentmindedly, Holly picked her nail at the edge of a faded Pikachu. "We should clean these off."

Kit made a face behind her in the mirror. "It doesn't bother me—a few kid's stickers."

Holly swallowed emotion, surprised to see her eyes were wet when she glanced at Kit in the mirror. "Dinner is in an hour."

"You okay?"

Holly shook her shoulders and fixed on an even smile. "Great."

She fled for the stairs, wiping the corners of her eyes, trying to force away memories determined to rise to the surface. Grabbing the giant bag of marshmallows, she headed out the front door, momentarily blinded by the bright glare of sunshine. She smelled soap and peered over the top of the bag, her glasses spattered by droplets of water.

Nick was washing his car, sleeves rolled up, and instantly retracted the hose when he spotted her. Huffing, Holly slammed the door shut so hard, she heard her mother yell. Nick ignored her, turning his back as she jogged down the steps. She froze the second she saw the second boy lingering by the car, Davey Thomas, Nick's friend. Davey had been Nick's best friend since the start of Willows High. Massive in stature with dull, greasy dark hair and a complexion to match, Davey took a wide step out of her way as she walked by the car.

"How are you doing, Holly, *tosis*?" he joked. Holly lifted her chin, her expression haughty as she clutched her marshmallows tighter. Taking a step, she ignored him, even if the insult stung.

Then, with a sharp cry, she was on the ground. Something caught her trainer, and she lost her balance, smacking the concrete. Yelping, the bag of marshmallows flew out of hand, split open, and spilled across the pavement. One rolled under the car. Holly cried in frustration, on her feet in seconds, fighting the urge to burst into tears. "You jerk!"

Davey had a length of hose in his hand, grinned, and dropped it. "Opps—how'd that get there?"

Holly growled, dropping to her knees and scrambling all the spilled unedible marshmallows into the bag, now wet and sticky. "Thanks a lot!" She briefly locked eyes with Nick, who looked away, while Holly burned with frustrated tears. "These were for the Robins. Why are you such an arsehole?"

Davey waved his hands, cackling, his dark eyes alight with mischief. "Why are you so uptight? Is it because you can't get any?"

Holly smirked. "Is that really the best you could come up with?"

Davey stepped closer and shoved her shoulder, his playful smile gone. Upclose he smelled like sweat and cheap deodorant. His fingers were hard against her skin. "I could think of plenty of worse things to say....how about a prissy, friendless, ugly little—"

"Davey!" Nick barked. "She isn't worth it."

Holly's heart dropped, staring at him in dismay. Nick flipped his hair, casually running a hand through his dark lengths before rolling down one of the windows to polish a smudge. His blue eyes flicked to hers. "How about you run along and deliver those to your little friends before they melt?"

Holly's stared in dismay at the soggy pink and white marshmallows in her arms. Then she puffed with anger, like a tiny baby dragon. "Oh, I'll deliver them alright!"

Stalking to the car, she elbowed him sharply out of the way and dumped the bag's contents through the open car window, watching in great satisfaction as they spilled and left sticky, slimy trails all over the leather interior.

Nick went wild-eyed. "Bitch!"

Holly stomped away, turning and flipping him a middle finger. As she strolled down the avenue, she heard him cursing and yelling, and she'd momentarily glanced up at the window to see Kit laughing.

Holly paid for a new bag of marshmallows at the shop in town, basking in the glow of the late afternoon sun. Hurrying to the clubhouse, she crossed Willow Green, a large expanse of field used for all the lower school matches and fairs that came to town. It was the village centre. Everything happened here, from festivals, matches, and outdoor cinema. Nick's father hosted the local boy's football team here. Nick volunteered to coach the holiday clubs in the half term, though Holly suspected it was under severe duress. Nick's dad was ex-army, and pretty strict, and she doubted Nick would ever get away with a sick day.

Stop thinking about him, she told herself. Her knee hurt from where she'd smacked it on the concrete, stinging almost as badly as his attitude.

The clubhouse was an old, dilapidated cricket pavilion with white cladding needing a fresh coat of paint. Breathing in humid air, she unlocked the clubhouse and dumped the snacks in a pile to collect on Saturday morning.

Inside she was still seething, rattled by Davey's aggression and Nick's dismissal. Catching her reflection in the glass window of the clubhouse door, she paused, slipping off her glasses and blinking away tears.

Was she just an upright know it all? A girl who, when she was mentioned, earned a snicker or an eye roll. Someone to be mocked and jeered. A loser. Holly combed her fingers in her unbound hair, letting it fall freely around her shoulders and pushing her glasses back on.

Was she really *ugly*? She was short, curvy, and freckly with a small nose and a mouth that looked like she was always pouting about something. Holly never thought she was ugly. Something ached in her gut, and she sensed the planted seed would nestle and take root. She locked the door behind her, determined to forget Nick or Davey and his nasty comment. She waved to Mr. Tanner, who was bustling up and down on the back of his sit-on lawnmower, the scent of fresh-cut grass permeating the air. Holly hoped by the time she tracked home, Nick would be done with his obsessive car washing.

Why'd he care about that crappy Fiat so much anyway? Lifting her chin, she didn't regret the decision to coat his interior with sticky marshmallows. He was a jerk, and he deserved it. Turning into the avenue, the sun was setting, casting a glow over the tree-lined street she'd lived in since birth. Holly's house was a modest, three-bedroom semi, joined with the Jones's. The house came into view, and Holly gulped, spotting Nick leaning on the bonnet of his car. The ugly seed sprouted and wound its way around her heart.

Holly's gut swirled as he hopped off, arms folded as he waited for her, his face pinched and angry. "What the hell do you think you're playing at?" Taking a wide step, he blocked her path, staring down his long nose at her.

Holly stuttered, "What are you talking about?"

He sneered and waved his hand at the car door. "This—*you* did this!"

Holly followed his gaze, her mouth open as she spotted the long, deep gouge in the paint of his door. "Oh my god! Who did that?"

Nick laughed, revealing his teeth. "Don't play me. *You* did!"

"I did not!"

Nick folded his arms, stepping closer, so she was forced to take a faltering step back. Edging around him, she fingered the paint.

"Don't touch it, you've done enough."

"I didn't do this. Surely you know I would never...."

"Like you dumped a box of marshmallows through the window? I know you did. Who else could it have been?"

Briefly, Holly glanced up at Kit's empty window. She was about to argue she'd never damage anyone's property, but that statement was void. She'd only just damaged his interior. "I swear I didn't do this, Nick."

He wasn't listening, just puffing in anger. "Do you know how much this will cost me to fix?"

Holly crossed her arms and said under her breath. "More than that piece of junk is worth."

"Excuse me? What did you say?" He brought his face closer, and she lurched backward. His eyes were so pale, sometimes he looked vampiric, glassy orbs with flecks of blue. Coupled with the dark hair against his tanned skin, he was intimidating.

"I didn't do this. You can't prove shit," she said, turning and stalking away. "Maybe you'll think twice about calling me ugly or a bitch...?"

"*I* didn't call you ugly. Davey did. You *are* a bitch Holly Truman. You have been since you were five years old–always looking down your nose at everyone because they aren't as perfect as you. You won't hear the last of this!"

Her eyes blurred, trembling as she unlocked the front door and hurried inside. Greeted by the smell of dinner, she sagged against the door and clutched her chest. Then she spotted Kit sitting cross-legged on top of the stairs.

"Did you do that? Did you key his car?" Holly hissed, as her cousin's face cracked in a mischievous grin.

"You're welcome," she sang.

Three

School was out.

Holly stared through her sunglasses at the giant umbrella twirling in the breeze. She dangled her hot feet in Tess's pool. Sighing, she leaned back on her palms and smiled.

Tess lived with her family on Maple Drive, a large, Georgian white townhouse with a fancy fountain in the sweeping driveway and six bedrooms inside. Holly loved the house, and Tess took full advantage of using it for parties when her parents left town.

Together, Tess and Holly had survived seven years of Willows High. They'd endured jibes, taunts, and tests and were ready to move onto a new beginning. Holly was off to Bramston to begin her Teaching Degree, and Tess to college to do performing arts. Together they had been unstoppable, Holly the short bespectacled know-all and Tess, the tall, willowy dancer. Tess grinned and passed her a glass of orange.

"We did it!"

"We did. I'm going to miss you, though."

Tess tilted her head. "Bramston is a bus ride away, and I might pass my test before then. We'll see one another."

Holly withdrew her foot and let it dry in the sun, the red paint on her toes twinkling. "I have to get going."

Tess yawned and made a face. "Don't tell me—Robin stuff."

Holly flashed her a bright smile. "Yes, Robin stuff. I've got to haul my camping stuff to the clubhouse for tomorrow. You could help me?"

Tess drew up a knee, wiggling her wet toes and sighing woefully. "Fine. Only because I'll be bereft without you for a week."

Holly laughed as they wandered inside Tess's house into the vast, sprawling chrome kitchen. "It's four days—I think you'll live!"

Adam sat propped at the kitchen counter, his nose in a book and his hand curled around a glass of orange. Holly fought a pang of nerves erupting in her belly, but they did a crazy dance when he glanced up and gave her a shy, sleepy smile. Adam was nineteen and didn't say much. When he did, it was like winning the lottery, to be caught in the shining light of his smile. Holly sighed, tilting her head as she paused to look at him from the door. Adam was solid, tall, and broad, with blonde, cropped hair and tanned skin, like Tess. Though his eyes were rich brown, not blue like Tess's, often fixed on his phone or anything else so as not to have to make conversation.

"Hey, Hols," he said, finally acknowledging her, scratching his neck and flipping his dark eyes back to the book he was reading.

"Hey." She lingered by the counter, drumming her fingers on the marble, as her tongue went slack, and she fought for something clever, sexy, or anything remotely interesting to say. "You cut your hair."

Nice one, Holly.

He ran his fingers through his blonde locks. "Thanks for noticing."

"Of course I noticed!" Holly laughed, a strained sound tinted with rising hysteria. "I notice things."

Adam met her gaze, confused. "That's good. I guess."

Maybe he likes me as much as I like him, and that's why he can't speak to me either...or I'm just an idiot.

Adam's phone buzzed, and he slid it towards him with his long fingers. Holly was still gazing at him when he glanced up and cleared his throat. "How's your housemate working out?"

"Who?" She blinked rapidly.

Adam blushed. "Your cousin...what's her name...Kathryn?"

"Oh, Kit?" Holly paused, growling inwardly. "She's great."

And a total vandal... Holly had yelled at Kit for what she'd done to Nick's car until Mrs. Truman came up the stairs and told her to calm down. She was still pissed about it today and avoided his accusing glare at school. Some small part of her hated he thought she'd damaged his property, more than just a bit of marshmallow easily cleaned. Actual, physical damage he'd have to pay for. He'd have to do extra shifts in the petrol station to pay to for it, and she knew he got up at six on Saturdays for his job. She could hear him through the wall, banging around, opening and closing drawers. So loud she'd be forced to get up when he turned on his shower, and the noise blasted through her wall.

But the other part of her thought he was a complete dick and deserved it.

"Is she coming to the party?" Adam's voice startled her out of her Nick haze.

"Huh?"

Adam smiled shyly. "The party next Friday. Will Kit come?"

Why the hell was he asking about...? Holly's stomach sank, and she ran her hand over the smooth marble worktop.

"Maybe. I mean, she's shy and an indoorsy type...but I can ask her...?"

Tess bounced into the kitchen and startled her out of her bleak mood. Of course, he'd ask about Kit. She was his age, pretty and mysterious in an unpredictable kind of way.

"Ready?" Tess asked.

Shoulders slumped, Holly waved goodbye to Adam, *the most handsome, kindest, thoughtful, and perfect guy in the world,* and followed her best friend into the street. As they walked toward the green, under the canopy of the tree-lined avenue, Tess tossed her a devious grin.

"What?"

"How do you manage to tell Nick Jones exactly what you think, and yet you turn into a babbling mess around my brother?"

Holly grinned and stared at her shoes. "Because Nick Jones isn't in the same league as Adam."

"Wait!" Tess ran ahead and twirled, walking backwards in front of her. "You don't think Nick's cute? Like, at all?"

Holly stared at her aghast. "Uh—no! Do you?"

Tess frowned. "He is *cute*, Holly. You'd have to be an idiot not to see it."

Holly laughed and held up her hands. "Clearly I need a new prescription."

Tess laughed. "Really? The dark hair, blue eyes...all the tattoos? He's hot."

"He's an arsehole. I prefer the strong silent type. The *non-tattooed*, short-haired, cute, and sweet-silent type."

"Adam is about as interesting as sour milk."

"I like him," Holly admitted, her cheeks turning rosy.

"Ew," Tess giggled, scrunching up her nose. "You can't date him, Hols. He has too many weird rules."

"Like what?"

"Like he won't go out with anyone who isn't interested in *everything* he's interested in. He's found fault with every girl who ever showed the slightest interest. Do yourself a favour and forget him. And he *won't* date anyone younger than him."

Holly lifted her nose in defiance. "Good thing I like rules!"

They detoured past Holly's house to pick up all the camping gear, and Holly breathed a sigh of relief when she saw Nick was out, and she didn't have to face his wrath. The gouge in his car shone in the afternoon sun, and she cringed. It did look bad. Holly wondered if Nick's dad had spotted the damage. Mr. Jones kept his cars immaculate. Surely, he'd have noticed the massive scratch in the Fiat by now?

Huffing and groaning, they hauled all of Holly's equipment through town. Holly's car was blocked in on the drive by her mother's, so they made the journey on foot. Sweating by the time they reached the green, Tess took a moment to rest by a lamp post.

"Hols...I was going to ask Nick and his friends to my party," she said. Holly tried to keep her face neutral.

"Oh...I mean. Do what you like."

"It would be mean not to. I've invited the whole year group. It would look like I'd left him out."

Holly grabbed her bags and hauled them over her shoulder. "It's fine by me."

"It's not, though," Tess said, biting her lip. "I can tell by your face."

Holly stared at her. "I don't care about Nick Jones. I don't want to think about Nick Jones for a whole week. I'll deal with that trauma when I get home. Can we please just drop how cute you suddenly think he is? I don't like the guy. I will never like the guy!"

Tess dutifully shut up and hauled Holly's huge overstuffed backpack into her arms as the dying sun beat their skin. "Sure."

They walked in silence across the green, and Holly couldn't fight the explosion of tension bursting inside her. Thinking about him made her seethe. She couldn't wait to be out of here and not have to see him every day or hear his trash music through the wall.

Tess stopped abruptly, letting the bag drop again. Her blonde curls were sweaty and stuck to her scalp. "Look, don't kill me for saying this...but...."

Holly braced herself. "What is it?"

"Adam...he isn't James."

Holly's brown-eyed went saucer wide, and her mouth dried up. "What?"

"If Adam reminds you of James...he isn't like him. Not at all."

Red-faced, Holly dropped her tent and bedroll. Panic exploded inside her and washed her palms with sweat. "Why would you even say that? I never felt like that about James—not ever."

Tess waved her hands. "I didn't mean that. I know you didn't. But I'm wondering if you're...you know...*projecting*? Because they have similar personalities."

"I...what...?" Holly spluttered. "James was my *brother*."

Tess took a deep breath. "No...he wasn't, Hols. And he's been gone four years."

Holly blinked away hot tears, her heart going into freefall. "Tess..."

"Don't you think it's time you let him go? And stop pushing yourself so hard?"

"I don't push myself. Why are we having this conversation?"

"You do push yourself!" Tess waved her hand at the clubhouse in the distance. "You work yourself into the ground for these kids, you give up all your free time. And you look down your nose at anyone who isn't toeing the line. Anyone not obeying the rules! James was a good person, but you don't need to push yourself to be like him."

Holly wrung her hands, her throat constricting. Images of James tried to flutter into her mind's eye, but she forced them away. Cold prickles erupted down her neck. "I don't want to argue with you. Not on my last night."

Adam was nothing like James. Unlike James, Adam couldn't string a sentence together without blushing beet red. James was like a beaming star, confident and charming.

And gone. She closed her eyes, struggling to take a full breath.

Forcing a close to the conversation, Holly grabbed up her bag and stalked away, leaving Tess to stare after her. Heart hammering, she wiped at her eyes with her free hand. It wasn't true. She didn't look down her nose at people. She wanted to *help* people. Okay, so maybe sometimes she was a bit pious...maybe a little self-righteous?

She recalled a couple of years ago, Nick had drawn her as a cartoon and stuck it to her locker. He'd drawn her with huge bubbly hair and round spectacles pointing her finger with the words under saying 'No, no, no!" It had stung at the time, and it still hurt now.

She shook her head and heard Tess groan and grab the bags, trailing behind. How could Tess say those things to her? She was supposed to be her best friend.

Not actually say what she thinks...god forbid you let someone tell you the truth...

She stopped abruptly, grass slipping underfoot, and gasped. Behind her, Tess cried. "Who did that?"

Holly gaped open-mouthed at the thick, black graffiti covering the white cladding of the clubhouse. Spray painted on the front was a giant round-faced girl with cross-eyes and a big pair of glasses. Holly's feet rooted, staring in horror at her caricature. Of course, it was her.

Hearing a scrambling noise and a loud curse, she glanced up to see a familiar shape running across the field. He turned and spotted her, flipping her a middle finger before running off.

Holly burst into tears and screamed after him. "I'm going to kill you, Nick Jones! Do you hear me? I'm going to make you so fucking sorry."

Four

"I'm *sorry*."

The words hit the air, tension fizzled in the room like bottled lightning. Across the immaculate cream sitting room, Mr. Jones, Nick's father, leaned in the leather recliner. It hadn't taken long for the inevitable knock at the door. Nick stared dismally at his palms. His hands were covered in black spray paint. It wasn't like he could hide what he'd done.

The last hour was a blur. He'd gone to take out his car, and his eyes fell on the deep gouge in the paint. So deep, it couldn't be buffed or painted over. She'd gouged her mark on it, as she did with everything, like a cat pissing up a back door. Nick's temper bubbled.

The car belonged to Nick's mother, discarded when she left, and his father hadn't minded when he asked to restore it. Over the last year, he'd fixed it up and took spare hours at the garage to pay for repairs. It needed new tires, and the brake pads were worn thin. It was *his* car, something he worked hard on.

He was going to make Holly miserable for this. And what did Holly Truman love more than anything? That damn club.

"How about you say it with feeling this time, Nick?"

Pinpricks of sweat grazed the back of Nick's neck, and he flipped his hair in an attempt to show nonchalance. He tapped his fingers on his thigh, his blue gaze wandering till he found Holly Truman's dark orbs boring a hole in his skull. Her full lips were pulled into that pouty frown, staring at him through round glasses perched on the end of her nose. Like an irritating, haughty barn owl.

Nick swallowed. "I'm sorry, I just...." *Lost my shit, saw red. Wanted to wipe the smug look off Holly Truman's annoying little face.* "I don't know what I was thinking."

True to form, Nick rarely knew what he thought when it involved Holly. Only when she tossed him *that* look, the one she was famous for, he wanted to do something bad with his hands. As he recalled, he'd done that the first day they'd met. Spotting her across the class, her hair in ringlets tied with ribbons, he'd been in awe. She was petite and like a doll, with cherry red lips. He remembered offering her candy at snack time, the stuff he kept hidden in his pocket. She stared at it, sticky and squished in his palm, and turned her nose up in disgust.

"No, no, no, Nick," she'd said, wagging her finger in his face. "Candy is bad for your teeth. Don't you know that?"

No, no, no. It was all she ever said.

No, no, Nick, don't pull my hair. No, don't use paint like that; you're supposed to colour in the lines. Don't draw on the walls. Don't run up the slide. Don't eat Crayons. Don't play your music, don't park your car so close to mine. She enraged him enough to want to smash crayons into the carpet.

Another woman in the room cleared her throat. Nick recognised her as Martha, the middle-aged Eagle Leader. She was a tall lady with red hair, a kind face, and eyes that always appeared wet or weepy. Nick did feel a tinge of guilt, he was pretty sure she used to babysit him.

"I'm not sure when we'll be able to fix this," she said. "We're leaving first thing tomorrow."

His father waved his tanned hand, and Nick wilted.

Here comes the hero. "You leave it with me. I can arrange to have someone come clean that garbage off the pavilion. I'm disgusted with his behavior."

Nick sank into the seat, his palms itching. Martha leaned forward. "That's kind."

"It's the least I can do. This is so embarrassing. I don't feel like its enough."

Something pricked Nick's conscience, and he glanced up, catching his handsome, forty-year-old father staring daggers at him. It was coming, he could feel it.

"Dad…"

"The car is off limits. You're banned."

Nick's mouth hung open. He rose out of his seat, and from the corner of his eye, he spotted Holly's mouth twitch. "Dad…please…"

Mr. Jones shook his head, waving his hand, floating his expensive cologne across the room. "No way, Nick! I've had about enough of you this summer. It's time you buckled down and stopped obsessing over that thing in the driveway. What you did—"

"I'll clean it off myself!" Nick jumped from his seat like a flame had gone off under his backside. Panic made him stutter, and he hated how Holly looked at him with that bemused expression on her face. "I'll go down there right now!"

He couldn't lose the car. The car was freedom. He could sit in a lonely field with his music going full blast, and no one could stop him. He could just drive and leave this place behind.

His father frowned, and Martha gave a slight cough across the way. They met eyes for a moment, and the redhead held up her hand. "I have a suggestion…if Nick would be willing. And maybe I wouldn't have to press charges. It is the last thing I want to do as Nick is about to go to college."

Mr. Jones leaned forward, and Nick stopped panting. "Sit down, for god sake, Nick. What are you suggesting, Martha?"

What was this lady going to say? Nick paced, seeing Holly staring at Martha's withered profile with interest. God, why was she even here? His father nodded for her to continue, and Nick sagged in his chair.

"Holly and I are leaving tomorrow for Robin camp in Tillbury Wood. It will be quite an undertaking as today I agreed to take another boy for the trip. If Nick came along and helped for the duration, I'm sure I can forget this whole thing."

Now it was Holly who leapt from her chair. Her face went stark white. "What? No! Martha...No, no...*no*!"

Colour drained from her face, and Nick was on his feet. "No, fucking way!"

"*Language*, Nick!" Mr Jones barked. "Sit down now!"

"I can't...don't make me...." A week with a bunch of seven-year-olds? *Camping?* With little kids? *With Holly?* Nick's vision swam. "Dad—I swear I'll do anything you want. Take the car. Don't make me go!"

"We don't need him!" Holly stared imploringly at Martha. "We can manage just us two."

Martha shook her head. "I don't think we can, Holly. We've got Tilly Grey coming, and you know how lively she is. I think it'll be a great idea to have a guy around, an extra pair of hands."

Holly shook and slumped in the seat, Nick saw her wipe her palms on her bare thighs. His brows rose, eyes traveling down her legs to those clumpy trainers she wore. She was rarely bare-legged, always trussed up in tights and her school uniform, her tie neat and pressed blazer. While he wore his uniform casually, his tie frayed, and his shirt covered in drawings. She caught him staring and threw a glare sharp enough to cut glass.

"I disagree." Her haughty tone made his blood boil. "We can cope. We don't need Nick. He'll get in the way."

Nick seethed inwardly. He was almost tempted to agree to go just to piss her off. "I agree with her disagreement."

"Don't be cocky," Mr. Jones fired from his chair. He nodded slowly. "I think it's a great idea. God knows you could do with the exercise and fresh air. It'll get you off your XBox for a while. And who knows, you might come back with a little more humility?"

Martha tilted her head as though something only just occurred to her. "I would need to check with the parents to make sure they were comfortable with Nick coming, but I don't see it being an issue. I mean—they all know him."

Fuck this stupid, claustrophobic small town. Nick ground his teeth.

"Well, he's already got a security check in place," Mr. Jones said with a clap of his large hands. "He volunteers with me every half term with football coaching, so he has to have one. Looks like you're all set." He tossed Nick a charming smile and he wanted to sink into the plush carpet.

The word *volunteer* was sketchy at best. More a case of Nick being dragged out of bed on a Sunday morning by his ankles to freeze in a muddy field while his father coached the local boys club. His father forced him into it years ago. Mr. Jones was ex-army, and had a voice that cut like a trombone, tough to ignore. Nick never minded the kids. He quite enjoyed riling them up and chasing them around. And it kept him fit.

"I don't have a tent," he went back to arguing.

Martha smiled. "I have a spare one you can borrow. Really, you need very little. I'm sure Holly can help you with...."

"No," Holly gasped. She turned to Martha, glossy-eyed, and looked like she was about to burst into tears. She knelt next to the older woman, lowering her voice enough to whisper. "Please...don't do this to me...."

Something in him snapped. Did she hate him that much? Enough to *cry* over him coming on their stupid trip? His chest flared. Well, now he wanted to go. If it made her day worse, if she shed actual tears over him. She was going to be sorry she touched his car.

Nick got up, towering over them before sinking to the carpet next to Holly, who scooted to get away. "I'm so sorry, Martha. I feel terrible about what I did." Holly bored holes into his profile, mouth gaping open as he took Martha's pale hand in his. "I do. And I'll accept my...." He locked eyes with Holly, and her nostrils flared. "...*punishment.*"

Mr. Jones rose from his seat, eyeing the teenagers with a confused expression. "Well...okay, that's settled. We'll get Nick organised and meet you at the clubhouse at...what time?"

"Eight AM," Martha said.

Fuck it, Nick snatched back his hand and rose to his feet. The first morning of his summer holiday and he was getting up at the crack of dawn.

Holly stood, breathing hard and rubbing her arms like she'd gone into shock. His heart spiked with glee, if this was what revenge looked like, he'd enjoy inflicting it on her for four days. So what if he had to spend the week with a bunch of whiny kids? He'd sneak in his phone. He'd lap it up like a greedy cat if it made Holly Truman's week worse.

Holly all but fell out of the front door into the afternoon sunshine. Nick leaned in the doorway and wiggled his fingers in a wave, a smile creeping over his features. When they'd gone, he turned and faced his father, whose composure had vanished.

"I don't know what to do with you, Nick." He stormed into the kitchen and grabbed Nick's phone off the counter. Nick cried out and jumped for it, but his father held him back with a hand. "*This* stays here. If you think I'm going to let you take a phone so you can text that lay-about friend of yours...."

Mr. Jones hated Davey. It wasn't a surprise. Most people did. Nick tolerated Davey's vile comments and socially unaware behavior. He'd even gritted his teeth the other day when he'd called Holly a bitch, inwardly cringing. Though that feeling quickly dropped the moment she vandalised his car. Davey was edgy and carried a slab-sized chip on his shoulder. They'd become friends in the first year of High School, and Nick never really minded him. It was better to be on the good side of Davey Thomas.

"You can't take my phone too," Nick argued. "I'll go insane."

"It'll do you good."

"I might end up in prison."

His father scoffed, and he wagged his finger. "For killing seven-year-olds?"

"No. *Her!*"

"This thing you have with that girl. Drop it, Nick. She's sweet and...."

"A total pain in the arse."

Mr. Jones sighed. "Is this because you think she keyed your car? Is that why you did this?"

Nick stormed around the kitchen, yanking open cupboards and pouring himself a coke. He glugged it, ignoring his father, and stared at him with a stinging expression. Why did everyone think they had him figured out? Why did his dad always have to look so disappointed?

When he didn't answer, his father carried on. "Holly *didn't* key your car. The other one did."

Nick blinked. "What? Why didn't you say anything?"

"Because I know Rachel had a hard time settling Kit and to be honest...you kind of deserved it. You let Davey trip her. I saw the whole thing from my office window." He relented. "But I will speak to Rachel about her behaviour."

Guilt tugged at Nick's gut. He had kind of done that. He remembered the way she'd hit the pavement, and he'd winced. The last two hours played back in his head, so intent on hurting Holly, a fine mist of anger dulled his thoughts. "Shit," he grumbled and scratched his chin.

"Look." His father leaned on the kitchen counter. "Since your mother left, I've looked the other way for a lot of stuff. The drop in grades, the tattoos...."

Nick rolled his eyes. "The tattoos don't hurt anyone."

"I understand you want to express yourself—your mum was an artist and I get it. But you are too young for them. You lied and forged my signature to get them. You lie and hang out drinking with that guy. I hate all the lying, Nick."

Nick slid onto a bar stool, holding his chin in his hands. "What can I do to get out of this? Seriously tell me. I'll do it."

Nick's father settled across from him, rolling up the sleeves of his immaculate white shirt. It baffled Nick how he'd ever gotten together with his mother, they were so different. But then, that's why she left.

Mr. Jones looked at him through his dark lashes. "Your mother emailed me."

Nick's chin jerked in surprise, flushing hot at the statement. "Oh?"

"She asked if you wanted to visit her in France for a couple of weeks this summer."

Nick scowled. "And you didn't tell me?"

"Well, you've been acting up so much this year I didn't think it was a good idea."

"To go and spend quality time with the woman who gave birth to me...no...I can't see how that's a good idea!"

"Nick you don't make things easy!" Mr. Jones barked. "Your grades have slipped. I only hope you studied enough to get through your exams. You lie and stay out late. Why *should* I let you go?"

Nick blinked, swallowing slowly. He missed her, the one person in the world he swore would get him. She was an artist, flighty, emotional, and romantic, and sat opposite was a man with whom Nick struggled to find any common ground. Uptight, strict, a lover of rules. It amazed him his parents married in the first place. "So...you're saying I can't go? Not only do I lose my car, but I lose the chance to go to see Mum."

Mr. Jones folded his arms. "Nick, you just vandilsed public property and have been offered a way out free of any charges. How about I make you a deal?"

Nick cocked a brow and leaned his forearms on the counter. "Okay...."

"Do this week with the Robins," his father said. "And...you can go to France."

Nick folded his arms, his brow raising in disbelief. "Really?"

"I want you to make the best of this trip. If I hear from Martha that you were whiny, you gave her *any* trouble, it's off the table. No car, no France, and you'll get the bus to college in September. Just go on this trip and be a good guy...for once. Stop this tough guy act. We both know it isn't you."

"You don't know me that well, do you?"

"I know you better than you think. I know this trip could be good for you."

Nick laughed, waving his hand. "Shall I draw you a map now of where I'll bury her body?"

His father's expression darkened and Nick flinched, knowing he'd gone too far.

"Don't say stuff like that...she is a sweet girl. And you've always had a thing about her."

"A *thing*?"

Nick's father laughed, tucking his phone into his jeans. "You know what I mean."

Nick wafted out of the kitchen, putting an end to the conversation, and if he had a camping trip to go on at some ungodly hour of the morning on the first day of his summer holiday, then he'd better pack.

Throwing open a case on his bed, he chucked in shorts, hoodies, and jeans that didn't have rips. Groaning into his palms, he turned on his music, letting the noise spiral him out of his dark mood. Metallica's The Four Horsemen blasted through his speakers, and he exhaled, waiting for Holly's reaction.

A fist banged on the other side of the wall. Then again. So he turned the music loud enough to drown out her pathetic attempt to annoy him. After an hour, he'd chucked in enough books and magazines to keep him entertained and closed the lid tight on his case.

Flinging himself on the bed, his thoughts traveled in time, remembering when she'd pissed him off in class or made a disgusted face at him across the room.

"*No, no, no* Nick..." he said mimicking her whiny voice. God she made him so angry, he itched all over.

Holly was his nemesis and had been since she was five years old. Part of him was looking forward to making her life miserable for four days. When it got late, he turned the music down, his ears ringing. A noise from the other side of the wall made him press his face closer to the wallpaper, listening carefully.

A wicked smile played on his lips. On the other side of the wall, he could hear Holly Truman crying her heart out.

Five

Slamming the door behind her, Holly screamed into the empty hallway.

Her mother appeared, her hands clutching a plate and dishcloth. She eyed her daughter warily. "I take it that didn't go so well."

Holly took the stairs two at a time and burst through Kit's door. Kit sat up in surprise, earbuds dangling around her neck. On her knees was an open laptop. "What?"

Holly pointed wildly. "You did this! Why did you have to key the jerk's car?"

Kit pursed her lips. "He let that *arsehole* speak to you like a piece of shit."

"It doesn't mean you get to vandalise his property. Nick is weird about that car—it's all he cares about!"

Kit raised a skeptical brow. "It's weird you know that."

Holly flushed, heat creeping up her neck and she broke out in a sweaty rash. She grabbed her glasses and wiped off sticky prints on her shirt. "What does that mean?"

An annoying smile curled on Kit's lips. "Nothing." She folded her legs, flicking pink hair out of her eyes. "Look—I lost my temper. What can I say? I react badly if I see someone I care about fall flat on their face."

They locked eyes, and Holly breathed in deep, trying to ignore that the room still smelled like someone she loved once. James living here seemed like a lifetime ago. She threw Kit a withering smile. "Thank you. I guess."

After the initial shock, the mindless weeping and sobbing into her pillow, Holly dialed Tess in consolation, needing to hear her friend's calm voice, even if only hours before they'd quarreled. Tess answered, and Holly shot a helpless glance at the wall. Nick's music throbbed so loudly she swore the wall breathed. She bashed the wall with her fist, tears springing to her eyes, and when the music only went up an octave, she banged again. It made her fist ache, so she stopped and took her phone to the top of the stairs, pressing her feet against the wall.

"What happened?" Tess asked when Holly bawled down the receiver. When she'd made quick work of her horrifying predicament, that she had to spend four days with Nick Jones on a campsite in the middle of a wood, the other end of the phone went oddly silent.

"Did you hear me?" Holly cried. "Do you know how awful this will be? I thought I'd be rid of him for a week and now he's going to be there, right under my feet. He's such an annoying, selfish, *loser*...are you laughing?"

Tess snorted down the receiver, the sound muffled as though her friend was covering her mouth. Holly's blood boiled red hot, and when finally Tess regained her composure, she blasted. "Why are you laughing at me?"

"Tone down that temper of yours, Holly," Tess scolded her. "I heard you. I think it's flipping hilarious—that's all."

Holly blinked away hurt tears. "How could you be so mean?"

"You and Nick were bound to collide someday. I, for one see this as an opportunity, don't you?"

Holly raised a brow. "An opportunity for what? Man slaughter?"

Tess laughed. "You love a challenge, Hols. There's nothing more you love than a good puzzle. You're a born fixer, even if sometimes the stuff you think needs fixing isn't actually broken. But Nick...this is the *ultimate* challenge." She let a beat of silence pass. "You could get him to like you."

Holly nearly dropped the mobile in her lap, her mouth hanging open. "I don't want him to like me. I don't want to be on his radar."

"But you have to live next to him. *Forever*. Or at least until one of you goes to university or moves out. Think how much better life could be if you two could at least tolerate one another?"

Holly grunted, shuffled on the top step, and threw her legs up the wall. "I'm kind of following."

"Imagine a *nicer* Nick. A guy who might think twice before he blasts his music through your wall till midnight. A guy who won't shoot you death glares over the fence? It wouldn't be perfect...but it could be tolerable."

Holly sat up, her cheeks pink, alive with the seedling of a new challenge planted within her. "It could work...I mean, I don't want to be his BFF, but I don't want to live like this anymore."

Tess sighed, and Holly wondered when she'd gotten so wise. "Precisely, Holly." Tess's long nails tapped the back of her phone. "Think of it as the 'Breaking Nick' challenge."

Breaking Nick? Holly would like to break him. Break his spirit and his soul. And perhaps his neck too.

Holly sniggered and wiped at the corners of her eyes. "What's my prize if I succeed?"

"Well...maybe a friend...or at least an acquaintance. Anything is better than all-out war." Tess paused. "Besides, you have a Gold Award to collect at the end of this trip. It's in your best interest to get through the trip without killing him. I think Martha might frown upon murder."

Holly snorted out a short laugh, imagining Nick accidentally tumbling to his early death off a bridge. Or an arrow landing in his backside. "I mean...they could design a new badge?"

They both laughed. "When did you get so insightful?"

"I've always been insightful!" Tess said playfully. "But Holly—do one thing for me? Give the guy an actual chance."

Haughtily, Holly straightened, her stomach already knotted at the prospect of seeing him tomorrow. "I will." She crossed her fingers.

"Like an actual, fighting chance. Don't write him off—"

"Like I do everyone else?"

Tess huffed. "Okay, well, I shouldn't have said that. You're a good, sweet person Holly. But you do tend to put people in boxes. And in Nick's case, the lid is nailed tight. Give him a chance to get out of the box."

Even though Tess couldn't see, Holly smiled, crossed her fingers tighter, and said. "I promise."

After they'd said their goodbyes, Holly hung up and let the phone dangle in her hands, her temples throbbing with the noise permeating the wall from her bedroom. What Tess suggested was a great idea, even though she was resigned. There wasn't a hope in hell's chance Nick would change. Could she put on an act convincing enough to get him to like her? She stood, twirled, and headed to her bedroom.

She yanked the band out of her curls and shook them free, staring at her creamy pale face dotted with freckles. When she was little, her Grandpa nicknamed her Flake. Her freckles resembled flakes of crumbled chocolate, dotted all over her nose, cheeks, and neck. She was covered right down to her belly in the damn things.

Could she make Nick actually like her? Did Nick like anyone? What did she even know about him?

"Well, you have a week to find out," she said to her wearied reflection as she changed for bed and put in her ear plugs as she crawled under the sheets. Tess was right about one thing.

She had put Nick in a box. Tess didn't know Holly had nailed the box shut, gaffer tapped it and then buried it six feet underground. Guys like Nick Jones didn't change.

And neither did girls like Holly Truman.

Sunshine streamed through the curtain, and Holly's eyes fluttered open. Instead of bouncing out of bed to the chirpy sound of her alarm, she lay there numb, her chest aching. This should have been her happy day, but she was weighted to the bed, hollow and numb.

"This is bullshit," she said and wiped her eyes. How could this be happening to her? The alarm buzzed ten minutes later, and Holly had no choice but to face the shower. Standing under the warm spray, she soaped up her hair, letting the water roll off her back, hoping to find some solace in the humid cubicle. Nick Jones would be waiting at the Cricket Pavilion, and she had to make the best of it.

She dressed and checked her luggage, throwing in an extra hoodie as outside the sky looked thick with rain. Pulling on her emerald green Eagle T-shirt, a polo style shirt with a dark orange collar, she wiggled into a pair of shorts. Lastly, she pulled on her cap and fastened her hoodie, covered in badges for everything from baking to first aid.

Stepping back to study her reflection for the first time, she connected with what Nick saw when he looked at her. God, she did look like a...square. Someone who didn't have a life outside of her beloved club. *But I love this life*, she thought, taking the silver whistle out of her bedside cabinet drawer and slipping it over her head. *This is what I love.* This is what *James* loved. Holly recalled James gifting her the whistle the night he'd left. James had been a Hawk Leader, part of the same club, and the whistle wasn't something he would need in his new life. The memory made her eyes prick, and she quickly shook her head.

"Make yourself heard, Hols," he'd told her. He'd smiled and hugged her tight, as though he'd never see her again. Firming her chin, she pulled on her socks and trainers.

She met her mother in the hallway, throwing her backpack over her shoulder. Mrs. Truman's eyes shone as she straightened Holly's white and orange striped tie. "I'm so proud of you, honey. You can do this. Don't let that boy get to you."

Holly sniffed and followed her mother into the grey morning. She wasn't going to cry anymore, not over him. Operation Breaking Nick Jones was about to begin.

Six

Mr. Jones's car rumbled into the car park of the Cricket Pavilion. Nick's stomach somersaulted when he saw the minibus parked, cutting a shape against the grey sky. Inside the car, his father switched off the engine as a few rain splatters fell on the windscreen.

Martha was out front, and so were a few of the club's younger members. She was ticking them off a register while their worried-looking parents loaded their bags and camping equipment onto the bus. He spotted three girls and one boy so far. Nick's palms were so sweaty he wiped them on his jeans and cast his father a horrified glance.

"I'll wash your car every weekend for a year....I'll do the shopping...mow the grass...."

Mr. Jones's eyes crinkled as he snickered. "Honestly, Nick. You aren't scared of a bunch of children, are you?"

He wasn't scared of the kids. Nick didn't mind kids, not at all. He liked kids, and enjoyed spending time with his little cousins. Swallowing, he wiped the sweat off his top lip as another car pulled into the car park, his blue eyes widening. Mr. Jones caught his expression, following his gaze, and sniggered. "Or maybe it's a certain girl you're terrified of?"

"I'm not scared of her," he gritted out.

Holly got out of the car, and he did a double take. What in god's name was she *wearing*? His mouth gaped as he took in her full Eagle attire. Dressed in shorts and an ugly green and orange polo shirt, her hoodie was covered in pins and badges, earned from no doubt all the do-gooding she did. The cap finished the look, and Nick was baffled she didn't realise what she looked like. Holly was like a walking target, and he recalled every mean comment he'd ever made, every jibe his friends flung at her over the years. He remembered comments other girls had made. Holly had always stuck out, she'd never fitted any group or clique. And he could see why. He cringed, imagining what Davey would say if he saw her. She practically had the words 'kick me' printed on her backside. Nick narrowed his eyes.

Oh my god. Is that a whistle?

Holly had a whistle around her neck. It swung against her chest, and his eyes flared. Something in him coiled, like a rattlesnake ready to strike. Did she think she'd use a whistle on him?

She was so earnest, so good. So irritatingly nice. His hands clenched again, reminded of the fateful day they'd met, her accusing glare and wagging finger. He swore right then if she dared wag a finger in his direction, he'd....

Okay...calm the fuck down. He was sweating under his jacket. It was the Holly effect. The sight of her did something weird to him.

Grinning, she greeted Martha with a hug and opened her arms to the younger members to welcome them. One of them, a small blonde girl, was crying, and Holly picked her up and squeezed her, rocking her around till she started to laugh. She stood there chatting and laughing animatedly with parents, reassuring them as they put their precious children in her hands.

Nick took a deep breath and turned to his father again. "I'll iron all your work shirts. You hate ironing."

Mr. Jones cackled and waved his fingers at Nick's battered hoodie. "So do you."

"Don't make me do this."

"Nick—you're eighteen years old." His father's expression turned serious. "You scraped through your exams and are off to college in September. This will be good for you. It's time you learned if you cause damage, you pay for it. You'll be fine. You might even enjoy yourself."

I'll enjoy strangling Holly Truman. It was worth one more try.

"I'll cook. I cook better than you, anyway. Please, Dad—"

"*Out*. Of the car. *Now*." He opened the driver's side door, and a rush of cold air wafted in and cooled Nick's burning skin. Groaning, he tumbled onto the wet pavement, following his father to the boot as he grabbed his camping gear. "Lucky we still had some of this stuff—and Martha had a tent you could borrow."

"Nick—come say hello to the Robins!" Martha's cheery voice floated across the carpark and he squirmed, his insides crumbling. On wooden feet, he crossed the car park, pulling up the collar of his fleece-lined denim jacket. His father slapped his shoulder, propelling him along. Holly glanced up from a conversation she was having with a little dark-haired girl and threw a glare acidic enough he felt the burn. "They're all waiting to meet you."

Six little heads turned in his direction as she said those words. A mix of redhead curls, blonde pigtails, and tight black ringlets. Six pairs of eyes gazed at him expectantly, shyly, and in wonder. Like they'd never seen a boy before, one his age, six foot and dressed in his ripped jeans, heavy boots, and beanie hat squished onto a mop of messy dark hair. Martha stood beside him and placed a hand on his shoulder. "Now, Nick will be an honorary Eagle for the week. He'll help you with your tents, cooking, and taking you to the bathroom at night...."

"I...what?" Nick spluttered but quickly shut up when he spotted the curious glances of the many parents standing behind their children. His father had put a hand on his other shoulder and squeezed it in a death grip.

"Holly and Nick are here to help me look after you, but I'm sure we'll all make him feel very welcome with us. How about we recite our motto for Nick before we leave? Holly?"

Holly, who'd been staring at him with barely concealed resentment, blinked. "Oh...sure. Right."

Nick let smile tug at his lips, watching with interest as a red stain coloured her cheeks, and she smiled at the children and stood behind them. "Say it with me." She cleared her throat, mortified as they all said in unison. "An Eagle is true in spirit and in deed. We raise our wings to protect all those who shelter beneath. We will stay true to our beliefs with kindness and courage and look after all those in need."

Well, that was a little cute. Nick winked at the little pig-tailed blonde grinning at him with an adorable gappy smile. "*Great,*" he said, clicking his tongue. He glanced at his father, who was staring at his shoes, trying not to laugh.

"Very good." Martha beamed at them. "You'll get to know them all when we reach camp. But we better hit the road. Say goodbye to your parents."

There were a few tears, some mumbling of goodbyes, and Nick felt his father's hand on the back of his neck. "Good luck."

Nick didn't reply, only lifted his chin and walked for the bus. He threw his luggage in the wrack underneath and nearly collided with Holly as they both went for the stairs. "Oh," she said, flustered. "Sorry."

"After you." Nick waved her ahead, and she brushed past him, and for a second, he smelled something floral and heady, a scent clinging to her hair. Trailing on the bus behind her, he stared quite openly at her backside, wondering why he'd never noticed her figure before. She was curvy and had a sloped waist and flared hips, which fit nicely in her shorts. The Eagle attire wasn't exactly fetching, the socks and trainers combo killed it.

Nick admitted he never looked at her. He'd never studied her or bothered to notice what lay under the uniform they wore for the past seven years. Throwing himself into a seat, he spread out, throwing his long legs over the seat next to him, as if he were on a school trip, while Holly opted for a front seat.

Of course, she'd take a front seat. Isn't that what all teacher's pets did?

He shoved on his sunglasses, huddling as close to the window as he could manage. The bus's engine revved up, and they pulled out of the car park, and he resisted showing his father his middle finger. There was some commotion and some crying, but Nick ignored it, staring at the scenery as the bus headed out of town.

An hour later, he couldn't ignore it any longer. A kid was sitting across from him, a girl with deep chestnut skin and tight ringlets. She sniffed and wiped her eyes on the cuff of her red Robin hoodie. Nick cast her a glance, groaning inwardly. Briefly, she met his eyes, big, watery, and wet.

Give me strength. Nick forced a smile. "You okay?"

She was hugging a bear to her chest, she wiped her nose and shook her head. "I miss my mum."

"We pulled away an hour ago."

"I want to go home."

Nick sighed and edged a little closer, folding his legs under him. "Want to come and sit here?"

Eagerly, she nodded and shifted, crossing the aisle and jumping in beside him. He gave her a smile. "What's your name?"

"Chloe Ford."

He patted her hand. "And this guy?"

She beamed, and looked down at the bear. "Socks."

Nick laughed. "Well...you have to be a little brave, Chloe. For Socks. I bet you were excited last night, weren't you?"

Her smile dropped, and to his horror, her eyes filled up again. "But I want my mum. I don't *want* to go now."

He knew the feeling. He'd wanted his mum since he was eleven years old. Since he woke up one morning and found out she wasn't downstairs in the kitchen. It made his gut ache to even think about it.

Thinking on his feet, he grabbed his backpack and took out his notebook and a black sharpie. Chloe leaned closer, her chin on his arm as he quickly sketched Socks and tore it out for her. She gasped. "Can I draw one? Can you help?"

"Sure," he said. Winding an arm around her, she took his notebook, rested it on his arm, and with his free hand, he guided hers until they'd drawn something resembling the old, ratty bear. Chloe beamed and pointed to his wrist. "You drew on yourself."

Nick chuckled. "They're tattoos."

"What's that one mean?" She pulled up his cuff to reveal the inky black pattern inside his wrist.

Nick blushed. "That's an arrow," he said, and then instantly, stiffened when a shadow loomed over the pair of them. Holly stood, leaning on the seat, arms folded and watching with interest. He flushed hot, avoiding her gaze. "Uh...I forget now why I had it done."

"Is it to remind you your right handed?" she deadpanned, and Nick glared at her.

Chloe giggled. "What about this one?"

She'd crawled on her knees, straddled his lap, tugging down his shirt collar, revealing the one he'd gotten a few months ago. It sat on the base of his neck, only visible if he wore a loose shirt. It was a set of woven loops. Holly cocked a brow, narrowing her eyes with interest.

"You two are having fun back here."

"She was crying," Nick said, letting Chloe slide back to her seat. He was clammy, and edgy and the way Holly stared at him made him want to flee the bus. Holly's eyes widened in surprise.

"Oh, well, it was nice of you to keep her company." Her voice was clipped; she didn't sound like she meant it. Nick snapped, darkness falling over what small lift of mood he'd had.

"What does it mean?" Chloe asked again, and Nick squirmed, his cheeks burning.

"It means mother," he said, swallowing a lump in his throat. "In Gaelic. She's Irish. And I miss her too, so you and me, we'll get along just fine."

Holly's lips parted, and before she could speak, he'd jumped out of his seat, barging her out of the way. He was stifled, his chest tight like he couldn't catch air. "Is there a toilet on here or anything?"

Holly made a face. "It's a ten-person coach. We'll be stopping in about an hour."

"Fine...great..." He barged past her and headed for a spare seat at the back of the coach.

She caught his hand, her fingers curled around his wrist, and for a moment, she stared at it, as if she were puzzled she'd touched him, but her eyes narrowed in concern. "I can get Martha to stop. Are you okay?"

He couldn't breathe. "I'm okay." Why the hell did she care anyway? Ignoring her, Nick threw himself into a seat and pressed his forehead to the cool glass, his pale eyes reflecting back at him. He didn't know what spurred that brief, temporary panic attack, only he couldn't stand the disapproving looks she threw him. When he glanced into the aisle, she was still looking, but not with anything other than concern.

Biting his nails, he settled and closed his eyes. Holly and Nick were fire and ice. She was a rain cloud in his blue sky, the colour the snow went when it turned to sludge when the fun was over. Staid, boring, sensible. Like his father. Not interesting enough to keep his mother in the home. Not fiery or passionate. Not enough for her to stay. Nick sensed the vines tightening around the muscles of his chest.

Four days and you'll be in France, he promised himself. He could last four days if spending time with his mother would be the prize at the end of it. Nick could hardly recall her last visit. She'd planned to come over last year, but there had been an issue at her gallery, a lost order, and she missed the ferry. And the time before, Nick was supposed to go for Christmas, and she'd canceled. She was unwell, and his father broke the news. When she'd first left, her visits were often cut short, she was unable to tolerate sharing space with his father. Nick was left with resentment towards him, so bitter it coated his tongue.

He dozed off, lulled by the hum of the bus and exhausted from panic clawing at his insides. How would he manage a week without fighting with her?

When he opened his eyes an hour later, his arm was dead, and something was tickling the back of his hand. Looking to his left, he saw Chloe tucked up against him, drawing on his hand with the sharpie. She'd drawn Socks, her bear, across his hand and over his knuckles. She gave him a toothy smile.

"It means friend," she said. "He can be yours too."

Seven

Holly gathered the children around her legs. "Okay, listen up, everyone," she announced cheerily as Nick sloped off the bus. "We'll do half-hour here to stretch our legs and have a snack. Don't wander off—stay in the playpark. When I blow the whistle, it's back on the bus!"

Holly caught Nick glaring at her, and her cheeks burned, her fingers playing with the silver whistle tied with cord around her neck. She dropped it, realising it was the whistle he was staring at. She didn't know why he looked so mad. It wasn't like she was planning on using it on him. Unless *absolutely* necessary.

The cool air wafted around her bare legs, and she was thankful to be off the stifling bus. About an hour into her journey, she'd craned her neck to check on Chloe, who'd followed Nick to the back. She couldn't help the smile crawling over her face. Nick didn't realise he had a fan, the younger girl curled against him while he dozed against the glass. It was cute. Holly shook it off.

Martha had driven the bus to a shady, open playing field about an hour out from Willowdale. It was grassy, had a vast wooden climbing frame, a short nature trail, and was dotted with picnic benches. Three girls, Lea, Bryony, and Sarah grabbed one, taking their picnic boxes with them. Jack, the only boy in the group hopped on another close by. Jack was Tilly's twin and had similar red hair, freckles, and glasses. Holly did a quick head count. One short, and her heart leapt.

"Ah...Tilly? Where'd Tilly go?"

Tilly—Matilda Grey was a runner. Lively, red-headed, and impish, the youngest member of the Robins was hard not to love. Holly often babysat for the Grey family, and Tilly was a sweet, funny seven-year-old. Her brother was quiet, painfully shy compared to his sister. Tilly was fast and dangerous. And a climber. Holly tried to keep the strain out of her voice, her eyes scanning the clearing. Her breath caught, and her gaze met Martha's. Surely, they couldn't have lost her already.

"Is that her?" Nick called, pointing to a red shape in the far distance, a child hanging upside down from the climbing frame. Holly released a caged breath.

"Yes," she sighed. Nick grabbed a table about as far away from them as he could. But he was joined by Chloe, who didn't seem to want to leave his side. Holly watched him open a juice carton for her, threading the straw and pressing it into her tiny hand.

Wait, was that...a smile? Holly's eyes widened. *Did he just smile at her?* Blushing, she looked away, stalking across the fields towards Tilly, pretending Nick smiling wasn't a thing. She didn't think she'd ever seen it in real life.

She followed Martha's gaze, and Holly took a few steps, cupped her hands, and called Tilly's name, which she ignored. Holly had the whistle halfway to her lips when a hand clutched her shoulder.

"Don't blow that thing." Nick's voice so close to her ear made her shiver. He ran ahead. "I'll get her."

Holly scowled. Since when did he think he knew how to handle Tilly Grey? "Nick...."

He jogged and turned, his dark hair whipping in the breeze. "It's fine. I'm used to my cousin—he's an escape artist too. I'll get her down."

Was it her imagination, or did he look pleased with himself? Holly let the whistle drop, and she nervously glanced back at Martha, who rummaged with something on the ground. It looked like one of the girl's backpacks. Martha stood, her hands ringing wet, a look of disgust on her face. It was Tilly's backpack, and there had been a juice explosion.

Holly's head snapped in Nick's direction, where he stood at the foot of the climbing structure, hands on hips, coaxing Tilly out from the netting. He held up his arms, and she flung herself into them with a giggle. Holly watched, fascinated, as he laughed, pretending to stagger and sway on his feet, swinging Tilly around before tossing her over his shoulder.

Okay...she wasn't expecting him to be *this* good with kids. Holly wasn't expecting a burst of warmth to spread in her belly either. Seeing him hauling a giggling kid around was touching all the cute buttons in her soul.

"Oh god!" Martha gasped from behind, startling her out of her daze. "Tilly ate two bags of skittles on the bus! No wonder she's hyper." Martha held up the empty packets, and Holly sucked in a breath.

She recalled the Robin Christmas party last year when they'd accidentally left Tilly alone with a box of Kripsy Cremes. Holly whirled in Nick's direction.

"Nick!" she cried. "Don't swing—"

It was too late. Tilly made a weird face, went a greyish colour, and then puked down Nick's back. Holly clasped her hands over her mouth, fighting a cackle of laughter. The worse part was he didn't seem to register it happened at first, not until he sensed the warmth seeping through his jacket. Making a face, he dropped Tilly like a dead weight and ripped off his jacket. "Oh...shit!"

Holly turned on her heels, giggles erupting up her throat. Tilly ran by at breakneck speed, quickly followed by Nick, who'd ripped off his jacket and shirt. "Gross...oh my god...Gross!"

"I could've just used the whistle," she called as he headed for the restroom. He ignored her, muttering to himself.

"Not helpful," he growled, stalking to the men's restroom. He was gone for ten minutes, and when he emerged, damp and his shirt tied around his waist, his face was as dark as thunder. "Don't you dare laugh!"

"I'm sorry." She pressed her fingers to her lips, catching Martha shaking her head. He rummaged in his backpack, tearing out a hoodie, and wrestled himself into it. Holly spotted the bird tattoo on his shoulder and averted her eyes. His fleece-lined denim jacket was ruined. There was a nasty, bright yellow stain down the back.

"I stink of puke."

"There's a shower block when we arrive at the campsite," Martha offered, helpfully, her face pained as Nick stalked past. "We should've kept a better eye on her."

"No shit," he grumbled, stomping onto the bus. When he was inside, Holly laughed into her hands, a near hysterical sound she'd been keeping in. She tried to control herself, but she kept recalling the look of horror on his face when he realised what Tilly had done.

Rounding up the group, Holly breathed through her nose, anything to keep the giggles at bay as they piled on the bus. Nick had stunk up the bus already, and she slipped into a seat near the front, covering her nose and mouth. Everyone complained, and it didn't help Holly's hysteria.

Glancing over her shoulder, she spotted Nick in his seat at the back, knees folded, staring hard out of the window. He'd even disgusted his number one fan, Chloe, who sat with Jack holding hands.

He was being helpful, and that's what he got for it. She knew it was awful of her to laugh, but she couldn't help but feel this was payback for years of name-calling and insults. Holly swallowed a laugh, but it spurted through her nose, erupting as a snort.

"Holly, for god sake," Martha muttered as she took her place in the driver's seat. Holly went red, catching him glaring at her from his seat. He flipped her a middle finger and then looked away, and she chewed the inside of her mouth.

Fuck him. Suddenly she didn't feel bad at all.

Eight

Nick stank of vomit. His stomach swirled, enduring another hour's trek deep into the countryside. Thatched cottages, old churches, and sprawling countryside bled into thick, lush forestation. The bus continued on a dirt track until the beaten sign for 'Tilbury Wood' appeared. Nick pressed his face to the glass, humiliation staining his cheeks an abrupt hot pink. God, he wanted to dissolve. Whenever he thought he might feel a little better, he thought of Holly cackling like a witch from the front seat.

He was planning revenge. He'd wipe that smug smile off her face before the night was over. It boiled inside him so violently his fists clenched. Nick swore he'd not let a bunch of cute kids chip at his usually bulletproof amour. He was over them already, and they hadn't even parked.

Martha rolled the bus into a woody parking area, and the engine went quiet. The kids piled off, giggling and nervous, and Martha dragged their luggage out of the compartment.

Nick lagged, his feet like wood as they trekked across a vast open field dotted with old campfires, and a sprawling woodland flanked them on the right. He'd noticed a small petting area with free-roaming chickens and goats near the entrance as they'd driven in. He wrinkled his nose. That would explain the stench.

Cow smell. Nick gagged. At least it covered the aroma of Tilly's puke.

Martha directed them down a bark-chipped pathway, winding through tall pines until they reached a small secluded camp. It was a small space, big enough for several tent spaces, and it was already set up with its BBQ area, fire pit, and picnic tables. Everyone puffed and dumped their equipment.

Martha, who'd avoided looking at him for the last ten minutes, turned in his direction.

"Nick, I feel awful. Did you see the shower block as we walked across the field? Why don't you get cleaned up, and we'll set up your tent?" She tossed Tilly a withering smile. "I think Tilly wants to help."

Nick grunted a reply but didn't turn down the offer of a shower and a chance to get the sour smell of child vomit off his body. He was pretty sure she'd got it in his hair. Grabbing his washbag, he stalked back through the woods towards the shower block, possibly the most miserable-looking brick building he'd ever set foot in. Like a set from a horror movie, inside it was a wall-to-wall wet room with toilets smelling faintly of urine and a couple of private showers with ratty plastic curtains. As he stripped and waited for the hot water to kick in, his hope dwindled, and he made a mental note not to come here after dark. Gritting his teeth, he jumped under the cold water as soap rolled down his body, taking the fastest shower ever. Shivering and with his teeth chattering, he shoved on his clothes and jogged back to the camp, determined to lay in his tent and ignore Holly Truman for the rest of the afternoon. Nick's hopes were quickly dashed.

"What the *hell* is that?"

Holly's dark eyes snapped in his direction. "It's your tent."

Nick's mouth fell open, and indignation boiled under his skin. "That's not a tent. It's a coffin."

Martha wiped her hands on her jeans, eyeing the small one-man structure they'd erected. Slowly, other tents were popping up around the small clearing. Martha had a small, albeit luxury-sized tent compared to his, and Holly had a basic domed two-man with a porch area for supplies. The Robins were sharing a six berth, but it fit them all easily and cosily. Holly stared at him from the ground as she nailed a peg into the dirt. "It's a standard single person."

"I won't fit. My feet will stick out!" Nick waved his hands. "I won't be able to sit up."

Nick walked around the tent, his pent-up frustration near boiling point. He stood at six feet tall, and there was a good chance he'd suffocate in that thing before the week was out. "I can't do four nights in that."

Martha stood up. "Sorry, Nick. It was all we had at short notice. We blew up your bed and put your bag in there. Not the jacket though...think we should air it out."

Holly hid a snigger, returning to nailing the peg into the dirt. Nick imagined nailing *her* into the ground. Her throat bobbed, and she pressed her lips thin. Was she still fucking laughing at him? He exhaled hard. "Fine."

Admitting defeat, he crawled into the tent, having to stoop so near the ground his back ached. Wrestling inside his coffin tent, he unrolled his sleeping bag and curled up on his side, taking out the ancient iPod his father had loaned him and sticking in earbuds. He pulled the sleeping bag over his head and pretended he couldn't hear the giggles and squeals from outside.

After a couple of hours of actively ignoring everyone, including little Chloe, who'd poked him in the ribs, begging him to come out and play, Nick was startled out of his sleepy daze by a high pitch squealing.

He sat up, too quick, and bashed his head on the roof of the tent. Pressing his hands to his eyes his willed himself to calm down. Then the squeal came again.

It wasn't a squeal. It was that damn whistle. Crawling out of the tent, he was surprised and relieved to see it was twilight. The sun had set over the trees, casting a pretty orange hue among the leaves. The Robins were playing a game in the field, and Holly was using a whistle. Walking closer, he saw it was a kind of traffic light game, where Holly was blowing into the whistle, and the kids were running around the field in fits of laughter. He watched as Holly chased a small blonde girl, throwing her around by her waist.

"Hey, you're up," Martha said, appearing behind him, her arms full of kindling. "Any good at making fires?"

"Uh, no."

"Then you can watch and learn." Martha beckoned him to follow her back to the camp. He followed with his hands in his pockets. Martha built a fire on her hands and knees and asked Nick to tear up some old paper to get it going. "Once the larger logs catch, we'll be able to keep it going most of the night. But we need to cook some dinner."

Great. His stomach rumbled. He half-heartedly gave Martha a hand and tried to ignore a blooming feeling of satisfaction when he managed to light a particularly twisted old log. Half an hour later, all the Robins were stuffing hot dogs into their mouths. Night quickly drew in, and the temperature dropped. Chilly air nipped at his skin as he sucked ketchup off his fingers. Chloe found a seat next to Nick on the log, and he didn't have the energy to tell her to get lost. Besides, she was warm, and he no longer had a jacket.

He leaned closer when he noticed a couple of tears spill over her lower lashes. "What's up?"

"I'm scared. I don't like the dark."

Nick patted her shoulder awkwardly. "It's not dark, not with the fire going. And you get to share with all your friends—and Socks!"

"What about you? Won't you be scared all by yourself?"

Nick looked at his miserable excuse for a tent and grimaced. "I'll be fine."

"I could bundle with you."

He laughed. "I barely fit in the thing as it is. But thanks. You bundle with Socks, okay?"

Holly wandered by where they huddled, and Nick couldn't resist taking a shot. "Maybe Holly will lend you Wilbur?"

She flung a glare in his direction. "Wilbur?"

Nick grinned savagely. "Yeah, the awful old thing you used to carry everywhere."

Holly blinked rapidly, licking the remains of tomato sauce off her lips. "I can't believe you remember."

Nick snorted. "It wasn't that long ago. Like twelve years?"

Holly puffed out her chest, the silver whistle glinted in the dark glow of the fire. Then she tossed him an even smile. "When it comes to you, Nick, I tend to block out any time we shared as kids. Like this week, it'll be just another blot on my memory."

Nick's temper rose the longer she looked at him with that churlish smile. Fluidly, he stood and prodded the patch on her shoulder with a stick. "What's that badge for? Bitch of the year?"

Holly screwed up her face. "It's for first aid, dick head."

"Guys...*language*!" Martha threw them both a look of disdain. But Nick wasn't backing down, he poked at another above the left pocket of her hoodie. "And this one? Little miss sunshine award?"

"It's for self-defence, actually." Holly balled her fist. "You want me to demonstrate?"

"Sure, I'd like to see your moves!" He waved his hands, knowing full well he was baiting her, and he could be risking a black eye. A muscle jumped in her temple, but it only spurred him on. "If you think you can take me....but then we know you're full of testosterone—explains why no one will date you."

Holly's eyes shone, and he knew he'd plucked a nerve. Inwardly he cursed, hating the brief flash of hurt in her eyes. He didn't even know why he'd said it.

"Nick, that's enough!" Martha hissed, and he was quickly reminded of the trip he'd been promised, and he shut his mouth. Holly leaned closer, her hair brushing his face as she whispered.

"Nice one, Nick. I can take your insults. Because we both know, in the end, that's all you have. "

They locked eyes, and he gritted his teeth. Why did she have to be such a bitch? Okay, so maybe he did steal her toy once and cover it with paint. But he'd been five years old, a million years ago. His parents had been fighting at the time, and he remembered sitting at the top of the stairs listening to them, little fists clenched. He couldn't remember a time when he wasn't angry. Wilbur had been one of many incidents, and it wasn't only Holly who caught the brunt off his wrath as a kid. Too bad she had an infallible memory.

Nick looked away as she stalked off, gathering the group around her like ducklings. Maybe he'd gone too far. Regret settled in his gut, recalling how she recoiled when he mentioned her dating life. He'd hit her where it hurt. He sighed. Why did she have to be so high and mighty? Holly always struck him as kind of a small robot, unfeeling and cold, and he didn't think she was capable of being hurt. She walked around with her nose so high she didn't see anyone below her. But that look in her eyes...his gut coiled.

Watching from the corner of his eye, resentment boiled under his skin. Holly was reading them a bedtime story, and they gazed at her in awe. She was so perfect. Nick paused, maybe perfect was a step too far. She *thought* she was perfect. So nice, so good, except when it came to him. She looked at *him* like he was a loser.

"Right, we better get you ready for bed," Martha announced. "Nick, can you keep the fire going while we take the kids to the bathroom for the last time?"

Nick plastered on his best fake grin. "Sure." He leaned on his knees, poking a stick into fire, like he knew what he was doing. Holly bit her lip, eyeing him with that dazed, confused expression before she huffed, herding the younger ones through the path in the dark. Nick kept watch, and he was on his feet when they'd cleared the camp. He kicked around the outside of Holly's tent, rummaging in the hoodie she'd left discarded by the tent door, and the silver whistle slipped out in his hand.

Bingo. He stalked deeper into the treeline, dodging spindly sapling branches and thorny brambles, and without pausing to think, he tossed the whistle into the bushes. A hot flush traveled up his neck.

Maybe this was a bad idea.

He exhaled. It was a terrible idea. It was going to backfire on him. She'd know it was him. But part of him couldn't wait to wipe that conceited smirk off her face when she saw her dog whistle was missing. He undressed and threw himself in the tent, zipping it shut as he heard them traipsing through the camp, churlish laughter and excited giggles.

Impatiently he waited for the shit to hit the fan, but when it didn't come, his eyes lulled, and he stuck in his earbuds and went to sleep.

Nine

Nick woke, with his teeth chattering and the wire of his earbuds trailing over his face. Rubbing his arms, he blinked awake, dry-mouthed, and achy. It had been a long time since he'd slept on the floor.

Holly couldn't have noticed her precious whistle was missing, and he ignored the part of his brain, like an angel on his shoulder, yelling at him for being such a dick. So what if she'd laughed at him? She was cute when she laughed. Nick grumbled and unzipped the tent, his bladder too full to ignore, and shivering, he jogged through the quiet, leafy campsite.

He did feel bad, it was becoming an itch too hard not to scratch. This was his problem, he acted before he thought things through. Like when he stole Wilbur all those years ago, like when he spray painted the clubhouse. Something about her irritated him.

Holly looked down at him, she thought she was better. Nick scratched the back of his neck as he pushed open the shower block door, greeted by the familiar scent of old pee.

Maybe she'll think twice before looking down her nose at me.

Nick rounded the corner and stopped short, his feet skidding on the tiles. Stood in nothing but an oversized t-shirt leaning over the sink was Holly. Her hands were submerged in soapy water up to her wrists as she scrubbed the bright yellow vomit stain on his jacket. Nick's jaw dropped, a rush of heat traveling from his sternum to his neck, staining his cheeks pink. His eyes dropped to her bare calves, the slope of her thighs disappearing under the shirt, and he went as hot as the sun. He must have made a noise in his throat because she glanced up and beamed at him sleepily.

"Morning."

"Uh...morning."

He took a wary step closer. "That's my jacket."

Holly held it up, it was wet, soapy, but the stain was nearly out. "Yeah. I wanted to see if I could work on it before you got up. I feel so bad we didn't warn you about Tilly."

Nick stood motionless, his mouth refusing to catch up with his brain, even if coherent thought wouldn't form. He was struggling not to look at...well, everything. Her hair was loose and messy, and her legs, smooth, shapely, and toned, and the way the shirt barely covered—

Nope, keep your eyes to yourself....

"Sorry...I wasn't expecting..." She gestured to her lack of attire.

Nick waved his hand. "That's okay...Uh. Thank you."

Why was she being nice? What was the play here? Last night, he'd been a complete dick to her, and she was washing out puke from his jacket.

Holly blushed, moving to step past him. "It's the best I can do. I'll hang it out by the fire."

Nick swallowed, his gaze following her as she walked by him; that heady smell, like wildflowers, still clung to her hair. He thought she must dose herself in it.

Eyes off her backside! He threw his gaze at the wall as Holly looked back. "Nick..."

"Hmm." He rubbed his eyes.

"You're good with the kids," she said. "It'd be great to have some more help with Tilly today, she's a handful. And you seem to have a way with her."

When he didn't reply, she hurried on. "And little Jack too. He's her twin, and I think he hides behind her because he's so shy. If you could spend some time with him...." She looked at her feet, curling her toes, perhaps embarrassed she was barely dressed. Then she looked up and gave him a pretty smile. "Not to mention Chloe loves you!"

Nick folded his arms, realising he still badly needed to pee, moving from one foot to the other. He didn't mean to look aloof, but if he made eye contact, he feared he'd go red. She looked good. Too good, *unexpectedly* good, and it was doing things to him. Finally, he flicked her a quick glance, clearing his throat. "Glad someone likes me."

Holly's smile dropped. "Don't say it like that."

Nick let out a chuckle. "I screwed up your trip. You don't want me here, it's fairly obvious." He struggled, clenching his fists as he uttered, "Last night—"

"I really don't want to talk about last night. Can we forget it?" Holly held his damp jacket closer, and the way her lip dropped made him flinch. "No matter what I feel, you are here, and I don't want to spend my week...tense and stressed out...and fighting with you. I'd rather we try and—tolerate one another."

Nick laughed. "Well...we aren't ever going to like one another, are we?"

"I'm trying to be nice here! Why'd you have to...?" Holly paused, biting her tongue. Disappointment creased her face, and she let out a long sigh. "I'll see you back at camp."

Nick huffed, finally alone to pee, leaning one arm against the wall as he gritted his teeth. He spotted her walking back to camp through the window, clutching his jacket, and his stomach dropped.

The fucking whistle!

Nick bounded out of the shower block and ran back to camp, but instead of passing Holly, he ducked into the trees, going around the long way, hoping she didn't spot him.

Shit, shit, shit!

Where the hell did he toss that stupid thing? He scraped through the dirt on his hands and knees, but it was impossible to tell where he'd chucked it in the daytime. He started to bake under his shirt, knowing any moment she'd discover it was missing, and then the shit would truly hit the fan. He could already imagine her face.

He kicked over leaves and bushes, whirling in a circle. Where the hell was it? Pricking his finger on a bramble, he winced and sucked away blood, his skin washing cold.

She was being nice. He didn't know why, but she got up early, took his stinky jacket, and scrubbed it with her bare hands and a washcloth just because she felt bad.

Nick stopped. A shrill cry made his skin prickle, and he rose to his feet. He could hear someone yelling for help.

Ten

Holly hung Nick's jacket out to dry, setting it a short way from the fire. She eyed her work critically, the faint outline of Tilly's vomit barely visible. Nick hadn't asked her to wash it out, and it wasn't her place to lend him a hand. But she'd woken with a need to put things right, even if he'd been mean.

Last night at the bonfire, it'd been a disaster. She'd poked the bear. The bear got pissed off and lashed out. Retaliating, he'd prodded her self-esteem, teasing her lack of a love life, something she was well aware she didn't have.

Besides a few drunken fumbles at house parties, Holly hadn't been brave enough to go further. Not that sex was all she thought about. She did think about it, sometimes. With a boy like *Adam*, someone nice and safe. Guys didn't see past the haughty, cold wall she threw up, and most of the time she didn't let them. What if she was no good at it? And they laughed at her? Willowdale was too small a town for random hookups. People talked.

Holly thought about Nick, last night, comforting Chloe, and it made her chest flutter. Nick was *trying*, and even she could see it. Then, he'd sloped off in a huff, and Holly couldn't help but feel a tiny bit sorry for him.

Stuck in the woods with a bunch of kids was about as far from Nick's thing as it got. Holly didn't know exactly what his thing was, but she guessed this wasn't it. She dived back into her tent and grabbed a pair of old jeans, wriggling into them, pausing when she remembered running into him in the shower block a few minutes ago.

Holly zipped up her jeans. Had it been her imagining or had Nick been checking her out? She'd sworn he looked nervous, casting quick, lustful glances at her legs as she stood at the sink, wrist deep in water. She shrugged it off, even though it had been so blatant. Adam wouldn't look at her like that.

Holly poked at the fire with a stick. Adam hadn't cast so much as a lusty glance at anyone she could remember. She wished she could sneak off and call Tess and discuss every detail. Behind her, a tent unzipped, and Lea, a little dark-haired Robin stumbled into the clearing.

"Good morning," Holly greeted her with a smile. Lea was the first Robin awake, and Martha wasn't in her tent, sneaking off for a shower while Holly was on the way back.

When Lea didn't reply, she twisted her head, kneeling before the fire. Lea was pale, her lips tinge a greyish blue, and she gasped for breath. "Shit...Lea, are you okay?"

Lea wheezed, tears leaking from the corners of her eyes as she collapsed next to Holly on the ground. Panic burst in her chest, and Holly gently took her shoulders, pressing a hand to her chest where she rasped shallow short breaths. "Where's your inhaler? Lea?"

Lea nodded to her bag inside the tent flap. Holly dashed across the camp and grabbed her pink and white spotted bag. She ran to Lea, crying over her shoulder. "Martha! Martha, help...please?"

She didn't know if Martha could hear her. Several other Robins had woken and sat tearfully watching from the mouth of the tent.

"Shush, Lea, it's fine!" Holly got on her hands and knees. "I'm going to help you, okay? I've just got to find the inhaler...*Martha!*"

Holly couldn't keep the panic out of her voice, strained and high. She dug through the bag with trembling fingers, while beside her, Lea gasped for air. "Martha!"

"What's wrong?" Nick's voice called as he jogged out of the trees. "What's wrong with her?"

Holly threw stuffed toys, night dresses, and clean underwear out of Lea's bag, but there was no inhaler. "She has asthma," Holly said with a gasp. "I can't find...."

Nick took the bag and shook it so hard everything tumbled into the leaves. He sat cross-legged beside Lea and pulled her onto his lap. "Hey...Lea. Relax...we'll find it okay. Just try to take long breaths through your nose. Like this." He demonstrated, and Lea nodded tearfully. Her skin looked paperwhite, and Nick rubbed her shoulders, pulling her back to his chest. "In and out, you can do it."

Holly rifled through all of Lea's little toys, her vision swimming. Trembling, she looked up and caught Nick staring at her. Going lava hot, she focussed and ripped open the front pockets of Lea's bag, and to her relief, the blue inhaler tumbled into her hand. "Thank god." She ripped off the lid and eased it through Lea's tight lips. "Make sure you hold the air in your lungs, Lea."

Nodding, Lea's head lulled, her silky dark hair spilling across Nick's arm. Holly gave her two pumps. Every muscle in her body was taught, every nerve on edge. She'd given Lea her inhaler before on Robin sleepovers, but never under stress, not during an attack when it mattered. When it could save her life. Holly knew she should have kept the inhaler on her. Martha hadn't signed it into the medical box. Lea's colour returned, her cheeks turned a rosy pink. But she was sweaty and crawled into Holly's arms for a hug.

"Lea, I'm sorry," Holly said into her hair. "Maybe the tent was too stuffy? Or something in the air irritated you?"

"Is she allergic to anything?" Nick asked, wiping his brow.

Holly slumped in relief. "I don't know, nothing new at least. We ask parents to sign a medical form."

Lea smiled sleepily, exhausted from the attack. Tilly was running around the campsite, and Chloe threw an arm around Nick's shoulder. "Is Lea okay?"

Nick grinned at her. "She's okay now. Holly came to her rescue."

Holly met his gaze, and for an endless beat, their eyes locked until she cleared her throat and broke first. Breathing hard, she stood and walked away, confused as to why she was burning hot. In those brief seconds, Nick had some kind of balming effect. She'd paused and gained focus. What would have happened if he hadn't come along? Nick calmed Lea, got her to relax, and listen to him more than she had managed to do. He brushed the dirt off his hands as she strolled towards him, cagey with her arms folded. Holly sucked in air.

"Nick..." she started, and he tilted his head, blue eyes narrowing, expecting an insult. "...thank you."

He pursed his lips, awkward. "What for?"

"For what you did for Lea. You were..." She didn't want to use the word amazing or brilliant, in case it made her look insincere. "You were great. I screwed up."

He made a face. "How?"

"I should've known exactly where her inhaler was. I should have been faster...."

Nick's brows rose in confusion. "There's two of you in charge...well, three if you count me. But I don't count."

"No, this is *my* trip. I was in charge of planning, and I should've...." Guilt iced her spine, imagining Lea gasping for breath. She visibly shuddered. "I'm here to earn my award, and I should have been more organised."

Nick shook his head as though he didn't understand. "It was an accident. She has asthma. You found her inhaler, and you stopped it in its tracks. I don't see..."

Holly held up her hand. "You don't have to be nice." The thought that he was being nice was weird enough. "Thank you for what you did."

Nick still looked confused. "You would have managed."

The kids ran back to the tent, and Lea rubbed her eyes. "This could've been so much worse," Holly said, wrapping her own arms around her waist in a hug. Nick's eyes drilled into her skull as she paced.

"I think you're being a little hard on yourself, Holly."

She paused, her feet digging in the leaves, shooting him a confused look. Was he trying to make her feel better? He'd said her name, not loser, not four eyes. *Holly.* It was nice, in a confusing way. She brushed him off. "Thanks anyway...Oh, Nick?"

"Hmm?" He'd been staring at the ground, and Holly couldn't see his eyes, couldn't tell if he was bored or irritated. He glanced up. "What?"

She tried to smile. "You do count. I'm glad you were here."

Nick shrugged in nonchalance. Martha returned from the shower, damp-haired. Holly made quick work of telling her what happened, and Martha groaned.

"My guess is the tent was too hot," she said. "I'd better phone her parents, see if they want to collect her? They might want to take her to hospital."

Martha threw on a hoodie and grabbed her phone, and Holly avoided her gaze. A sinking feeling clogged the pit of her belly.

She'd panicked. *Really* panicked. Martha tapped her shoulder. "Can you two organise breakfast and then maybe take them on a walk or something? We've got crafts planned for this afternoon."

Holly spotted Nick grimacing at the word crafts, and she nodded, biting back tears as she dashed to her tent. She rummaged around in her pile of clothes from last night, confusion furrowing her brow. She bit her lip, chewing it hard, checking under her pillow and sheets. Where was her whistle?

Holly stripped back her sleeping bag, upturning the inside of the tent. It was gone. A dragging sensation settled on her shoulders, and she glanced outside, spotting Nick perched on a log, biting his nails.

He took it. Holly didn't know how she knew, but she knew. *The little shit! That was why he was being nice!*

He felt guilty. She stood straight, fastening a neutral expression on her face. Inside, she boiled, she planned to ransack his tent when he wasn't there.

Holly gritted her teeth. *He wants to pick a fight. Well, that's not happening.* This was the Breaking Nick challenge, after all. Holly wouldn't react, even though losing James's whistle stung deeply.

Holly could kill with kindness, and she planned to bury him with it. Turning, he almost looked wary as she moved around the camp, dragging out boxes of cereal and milk from the cool box. He stood. "You need help?"

She flashed him a bright smile. "I'm good."

"You sure?"

"Absolutely."

He had her whistle alright. It was scrawled over his face like one of his garish tattoos. She only hoped it wouldn't be hard to find.

She didn't get a chance to rifle through his belongings. Nick had been oddly present all day, which she wasn't used to. He didn't complain when she set up a crafting table. In fact, he sat, cross-legged on the grass and helped construct lanterns with the kids. Later she spotted him wandering to the meadow with Jack to play football, coaxing the girls to join. Holly narrowed her eyes, watching keenly as he chased a ball over the field, weaving it around Jack and encouraging him to tackle. Red-faced and panting, Jack chased Nick across the field, and Nick swept him up, carrying him around on his shoulders, which Holly pretended wasn't the most adorable thing she'd ever seen. Jack was usually so shy, but Nick was a winner at drawing out his confidence.

What is this about? Holly folded her arms, unconvinced Nick was doing this from the goodness of his heart. Especially as every so often, Nick would glance up to check she was watching. Holly ground her teeth. *Thieving bastard!*

Lea's parents arrived at the camp to take her home, and when they walked her out to the gate, Nick came along, explaining to Lea's father what had happened. Holly side-eyed him in disbelief when he announced, "Lea was lucky Holly thought so quickly on her feet."

What was his game? She narrowed her eyes at his profile. *I know you took it, dickhead!*

His niceness irked her. She was keenly aware he kept watching her like a dog who wanted praise. It was all a well-executed act, and she swore to god if he'd lost...

Calm down, you've come this far...

As night drew in, the sky shone an inky black above them, and Martha entertained the kids with a campfire ghost story. There was a sharp chill in the air to match the story. Chloe clutched Nick's shirt tightly, burying her head in his neck. Martha let out a loud boo, verberating around the camp. Nick let her sit in his lap.

Holly sat across the fire, heat from the flame licking her skin. She watched him, boring holes into his skull, her gaze darting to Nick's pitiful coffin tent, wondering how she would look through his stuff without getting caught. Martha got out the Marshmallows, tore open the bag, and a few spilled onto the floor. Nick smiled to himself, then lifted his eyes to find Holly's.

He smiled at her, nodding at the marshmallows, the things that had gotten them into this predicament. Holly snorted, a smile tugging at her lips, but she looked away. Nick looked momentarily disappointed.

He knows I know. She furrowed her brow. *I'm so going to kick his arse for this.*

Roasting of the marshmallows was underway. Holly poked her stick in the fire, waiting for her pink one to crisp and turn globby. Nick was distracted, helping Chloe thread hers onto a stick, and Holly took her moment to bolt.

Taking her stick, she crept away carefully, and circled Nick's tent, which was partially hidden between two tall pines. Getting on her knees, backside in the air, she dragged out his sleeping bag, tossing over his pillow and the shirt he'd slept in. Nothing. She ran her hands through the tent in the dark, sweat beading on her brow. Nothing, nothing.

Damn.

"What are you doing?"

Shit. "Uh…" She backed out of his tent, arse in the air, whipping her hair out of her face as she stood up. He was too close, and they nearly bumped chests. "I saw a deer…."

Nick cocked a brow. "A *deer*?"

"Yes!" She hated that was the best she could come up with. "I saw it sniffing around your tent."

"Oh? Where is it now?" His smirk was driving her insane.

"It ran off…so…I was checking it hadn't eaten any of your stuff."

Nick pursed his lips, folding his arms in disbelief. But then he smiled, and it was dazzling. She didn't think she'd seen his teeth before, the two front ones slightly longer than the rest, even, white and straight. Her heart thumped. "Well…thanks for scaring it off. I'm going to the bathroom now. Maybe you'll keep watch for me in case it comes back for another go?"

She raked her hands through her hair. "I'll do that. You can count on me."

He smiled again, unsure, and she wilted. "Okay…"

Holly sagged, watching his outline vanish through the trees. Narrowing her eyes, she crept after him. Maybe he had it on him? Holly ignored the heat in her cheeks, the thought of how mortifying it would be if he caught her again. Suddenly he ducked off the path and into the bushes. Holly swallowed a whoop of triumph. *I knew it, arsehole!*

Taking care not to be seen, she tiptoed after him, keeping track of him ahead of her. He disappeared further into the dark, where it was thorny, and brambles caught her hair. He was hiding something. It was her whistle, she knew it!

God, she'd make him sorry. She knew him acting cute all afternoon was a rouse. She could pretend she didn't find it adorable when he hoisted Chloe onto his shoulders or tickled Tilly under the arms. Or that his smile was possibly the cutest thing she'd ever seen. *Maybe one down from Adam's.* She mentally tried to compare them. She couldn't remember her insides fizzing if Adam smiled at her. She shook her head.

This was the Breaking Nick challenge, not breaking Holly.

Holly craned her neck in the dark, admitting to feeling lost. Panic crept up her chest, but she pushed forward, using her arms to drag a branch out of her face.

In the dark, she collided with a hard, warm body, and he yelled. Holly screamed and toppled over him, landing face down in the mud. In the panic, she lost her glasses.

"Ouch! Shit...Holly, is that you?" Nick tugged her up by her wrists. Flailing, and her vision a blurry mess, she grabbed his arm. She spat out dirt and brushed dead leaves off her face.

"My glasses...I can't see without them...careful in case you...."

Nick crunched something underfoot, then ducked to the ground. "Oh...crap!"

He tried to slip them back on her face, but they were cracked, and she couldn't see. "Sorry."

"I can't see!"

"Yeah, I'm getting that. Why were you following me? Uh, wait, let me guess. Was I being followed by a *deer*?" Nick steadied her shoulders with his large hands, and she fought waves of panic, trapped and sightless in the dark. She still managed to scowl at him.

"I know you've got my whistle, arsehole!"

Nick's chest moved under her hands. Her cheeks streaking red, she snatched her hands away and balled her fists. She hadn't realised she was touching him. Was he laughing?

"Why would I have your stupid dog whistle?"

"It's missing—you took it! Admit it!"

His breath rustled her hair. How close was he standing? His fingers circled her wrist gently. "I didn't take it."

She wildly pointed a finger in what she guessed was his face, but she poked his chest instead.

"Ow!" Her finger throbbed. "You are *lying!*"

"Why would I take it?"

"Because you hate me." The words floated between them, and for a second, she prayed he wouldn't answer.

Out loud, those words sounded awful. She didn't know any reason why he would hate her.

"*You* hate me."

"I don't," she said too quickly. "I *despair* of you. You make me mad. I don't hate you. I don't hate anyone. I'm an Eagle, for god sake—we're nice to everyone!"

Nick tutted, and she imagined him rolling his eyes. "So fucking righteous, aren't you?"

"I'm not." She wiped the corners of her eyes. "I make mistakes all the time. I screwed up today."

"Oh, come on. How long are you going to beat yourself up about that? You acted fast, and the kid was fine. Is that why you've been watching me all day? Because you think I stole your whistle?"

You did steal it. She sniffed. "I haven't been watching you!"

Nick laughed. "You have. What's so important about a stupid old whistle anyway?"

"It's not stupid." Emotion welled in her throat. "It belonged to James—my brother."

She waited for the statement to hit. Nick would have to be a complete idiot if he didn't remember James, a guy who'd lived next door for years. James even babysat him once. She heard him swallow in the dark, and she swayed, unsteady without sight. He caught her shoulders. She noticed how he didn't correct her. Technically, James wasn't a brother. He'd just felt like one for a long time.

"Oh."

"So...I need it. He gave it to me before he...." She didn't want to say the word out loud. It was still too raw to admit he was gone.

"I get it," Nick said. "Look, I don't know about your whistle, but I'll help you look. I'm more worried you can't see anything."

"I have spare glasses at the camp."

"Let's get you back, then."

He took her wrists and twirled her carefully. Holly lost her balance and tripped, stumbling into his shoulder blade. "Ow."

"How about this?" He folded her arms around his waist, so she could lean against his back as they walked. "Just don't go too fast and trip me up."

Holly's cheek smooshed against his broad shoulder, the other working senses in her body going into overdrive. He was warm, smelled faintly like laundry detergent, a smell she liked, and he was firm to touch, and her arms snaked around his narrow waist. "Okay..."

Now she was sweating. Beads of perspiration broke out under her arms as Nick guided her back through the dark, step by step, her chest smashed against his back. He swore a lot, there were a few exhales and sighs and some missteps where she trod on his heels.

"Ow!"

"Sorry...but if you slowed down a bit...."

"So now you're criticising me for helping you? I can't do that, right."

"I wouldn't even *be* out here if you hadn't stolen my whistle!"

Nick growled. "Holly—you are really starting to piss me off. Do you want me to leave you here in the dark?"

He stopped, and she dipped her chin. Even though she couldn't see clearly, she sensed the heat of his gaze, his ire. She mumbled a grudging, "No."

"Then shut up for once in your life, hold onto me and let me get you back. And please watch where you put your big clown feet."

"I do not..."

"Holly!"

To her surprise, she didn't trip once, helpless as she put her trust in him. Glowing embers from the fire sparked in her blurry vision. "We're here."

"I know," he said, sniggering. "Where are your glasses? I'll get them."

"In the front pocket of my pack, in my tent." He guided her to the log, where Martha studied her curiously. Sitting on her bottom, Holly was powerless as he jogged away, returning a few moments later. In relief, she slipped on her glasses and blinked back to clarity. "Thank goodness."

"Uh...what were you two up to in the dark? You were gone ages," Martha asked, her smile curious and teasing as Holly fanned her hot skin. She wasn't sure if it was the fire causing her to sweat, or being tightly close to Nick.

Nick stood over her, grinning devilishly. "Holly fell on her face—saving me from a deer."

She smiled, his grin so infectious it was impossible not to return it. Martha shook her head and waved to the empty camp. "The kids are asleep. I suggest the two of you do the same."

A little shaken, Holly rose, casting him a shy smile before heading to her tent. Ducking to her knees, she opened the flap, glancing at him, where he stood watching her by the fire. He gave her a wave and winked. Holly's heart fluttered, but she shook it off, pretending he wasn't having any kind of effect on her. That being pressed up close to his strong, muscular back in the dark hadn't sent her dreams of finally losing her virginity into a complete spin. What was happening?

Undressing, she slipped into her shirt and tried to get comfy under the covers, though she was hot and her skin burned. And something was prodding her head. Sitting up, she yanked up her pillow and found the whistle underneath.

That fucking arsehole...

Holly grinned, clutching the whistle to her chest.

Eleven

The sun rose the next day, piercing through the canopy. Holly got up early, showered, and tried to push away thoughts of Nick and their shared moment in the dark. Last night the moment dinner was over, he'd helped wash up and trekked across the dark field to the toilets with the kids. Off duty, he sloped off, moody and cross, leaving Holly to worry any progress they'd made was shattered.

She ran to the shower block, armed with her toiletries. Holly had to give him props for his brazenness, he'd managed to return the whistle, and that was a huge leap in progress. Nick wasn't boyfriend material; she was sure he thought the same about her. She'd never fit in with his crowd, with his friends. With a sinking stomach, she recalled all the moments they'd laughed at her, cajoled her, and for some reason, now it hurt more than ever. Staring at her reflection in the dirty mirror, she studied her freckles, her wide dark eyes staring out from behind a pair of glasses. What must they all think of her?

You never cared. You are better than that.

Nodding to herself, she ran back to camp. She was Holly Truman, short, spectacled, and a born Eagle. She loved her life, her close friends, and her Robins. So what if she maybe felt a tiny spark between them? He made things clear. She was a firm, square peg, and he was a round hole. They'd never fit together.

Holly debated why she was suddenly interested in what he thought. Just because she'd been so closely pressed against him in the dark and for a nanosecond, she thought...

You imagined it, she told herself, deflating like a balloon.

When she reached camp, the fire dwindled, and she hurriedly cleared the debris, piling on logs and kindling to get it restarted so Martha could sort breakfast. She was responsible for today's activities, and Holly planned a mini beast hunt and nature art. She went to the supply tent and dragged out a cardboard box, unloading it onto a picnic table. She had spent weeks collecting jars for the kids, decorating each with ribbons. She'd added stickers and glitter for effect and pressed on white labels so they could scribble their names. Holly planned to take the jars with them on the hike this morning, so they could collect flowers, leaves, stones or twigs, anything they could use for art later today.

Holly placed the jars on the tables with a few coloured sharpies for the children to write their names. And then she got the pre-printed mini beasts charts ready for the trip. Sounds were coming from Nick's tent, a low rumbling snore, and Holly glimpsed his bare feet sticking out the end of the tent flaps. Snorting with laughter, she crept closer, careful not to step on twigs to wake him up. Holly made a face, his feet were massive, and she spotted a tattoo curled around his right ankle, running up his calf. Squinting, she leaned nearer. It was a lizard.

With a mischievous grin, Holly took a long twig, kneeling a good distance away from him, and ran the pointy end over the lizard, till his hairs stood on end. He jerked and snorted inside the tent, and Holly had to bite her cheek to stop herself from laughing. Gritting her teeth, she tickled him again, and this time he yelped, and both feet shot back inside the tent so fast she nearly toppled backwards.

Darting back to the picnic table, she pretended to look busy and uninterested as Nick squirmed out of his tent in nothing but his boxer shorts and flung his clothes, bedding, and pillows outside.

"What are you doing?" she called breezily. Nick tossed her a glare, his hair stuck up on his head in a way that made him look boyish.

"There's a spider in there!"

Holly chewed on her lip, even though giggles threatened to expose her. "Oh, no. You have a phobia?"

"I hate them!" he yelled, grabbing a rock. "I can't sleep in there if it's crawling around waiting for me to get comfortable again."

"It's probably gone."

Nick looked at her, wagging his finger. "They aren't *ever* gone. I swear I'll bash its head in!"

He took all his clothes, shook them out with enough gusto to rustle his hair, then found a hoodie and pulled it on. Holly sighed dramatically. "Shall I check your tent?"

"No it's fine—you're right it's probably done a runner." He upturned his shoes, shaking them out and checking the insides before stuffing his feet into them. Lifting his chin, he joined her at the picnic table. "What are you up to?"

"I'm prepping for the mini beast hunt."

Nick visibly shuddered. "Great."

His lack of enthusiasm rolled off her shoulders. "It'll be fun," she breezed. He picked up a coloured jar, studied the glitter decoration, and snorted.

"Your artistry?" He wasn't being mean, more poking fun in a gentle way, and she rolled her eyes at him.

She took the jar off him and poked out her tongue. "Not all of us are fine artists you know. I happen to love glitter."

"I can see that." He sat down, took up another jar and then pulled up a sharpie. "Who is this one for?"

Holly was marking the mini beast fact sheets with the kid's names. "It can be anyone's. I left them blank so they could pick and write their own names."

Nick made a face. "That's no fun. Tell me their names again."

Holly scoffed, annoyed he'd managed to forget half the group already. "Tilly, *Chloe*, Sarah, Jack, and Bryony."

Nick poked out his tongue in concentration, and Holly darted a curious look over her shoulder as he got to work. By the time the girls emerged sleepily from their tent, Nick had completed their art jars. He'd decorated each label with their name and a drawing. Sarah's name was written in a beautiful calligraphy scrawl. The S in her name extended, so it flowed into a pretty flower. Holly picked up the jars and studied them one by one. "Nick these are so pretty. They'll love them."

He beamed, pleased with his handy work. He stood over her shoulder, admiring the one she was holding. He'd decorated Bryony's with butterflies. All the labels were personal: Tilly's was a baby dragon, and Chloe's had a picture of Socks, her bear.

Holly glanced up at him, her heart fluttering anxiously as she met his gaze. "What would you draw for me?"

Nick awkwardly swung his arms. "I'd have to think about it."

Holly cocked a brow with interest, knowing full well he was squirming and she was putting him on the spot. "All these years of living next door to me, and you can't think of anything you'd draw for me?"

Nick shrugged, trying to look nonchalant as he grabbed up the page of spare black labels and quickly scrawled a picture of a cartoon bee with a pair of glasses. He slapped it on her shoulder. "There."

Holly looked down at the bee, her heart sinking. "Right." Warmth rushed to her eyes. *Oh my god, do not cry!* "Of course."

Nick spluttered, his cheeks pink and flustered. "I mean if I had more time..."

"No, I love it!" She faked a smile and patted the bee sticker on her chest. Spinning on her heels, she rushed to the fire as Martha emerged from her tent, sleepy-eyed. She caught Holly's gaze, and her face fell.

"Are you okay—"

"I'm good. Just getting breakfast." She plopped next to the fire, using the sleeve of her hoodie to wipe the corner of her eyes, then scolding herself for reacting. Swiping up a stick, she poked the fire, keenly aware of Nick lingering behind her.

Who was she kidding? A bee. An annoying, buzzy insect. Of course that's what he thought of her. Nick wasn't going to change and she never could.

Twelve

A bee? A fucking stupid bee? Nick growled as he stomped to the shower block, determined to wash the cold sweat off his body. "Stupid," he muttered, his insides tightening as she recalled the look in her eyes.

One word. Disappointment. He could have drawn *any-thing*. A flower, a tree, or anything pretty. But no, he went with a fat bumblebee with a pair of reading glasses. He threw on the shower and stood under the cold spray gritting his teeth. "Idiot." Nick cringed, recalling the massive bespec-tacled face he'd graffitied on the clubhouse wall. The 'art' which had gotten him into this situation in the first place.

Truthfully, he didn't know what he would've drawn. She had put him on the spot, staring up at him with those doe eyes, made even larger and woeful with the glasses. Nick sniffed, stepping under the spray, rigid as the cold water hit his body. The eyes were getting to him, she was cute, *very* cute, and somehow, she was working her way under his skin.

Lathering himself, lost in thought and his idiocy, he didn't hear little footsteps till a head poked around the shower curtain.

"Nick..." Chloe wailed, her eyes full of tears. Nick yelled and grabbed his towel, hurriedly trying to cover up.

"Chloe! I'm naked in here. What's up?"

"Tilly stuck gum on Socks." She broke into sobs, and Nick groaned, turning off the shower and wrapping himself in a towel.

"Calm down. We'll sort it out."

"It's really stuck."

Nick muttered curse words under his breath, faced with her puffy, red eyes and the bedraggled bear. Ten minutes of scrubbing and picking with his short nails, he'd scraped all the sticky gum in Sock's white fur. "That'll have to do." He knew something about ruined stuffed toys, after all.

Chloe sniffed and wiped her eyes on the edge of Nick's towel, which nearly unravelled at his waist. Was he allowed privacy with all these little women around? He gave her a short smile and pinched her chin. "He looks better. Now, bugger off so I can get dressed."

Chloe stomped away with a pleased and contented look on her face. In case of further mini intruders, Nick threw on his clothes and dashed across the clearing back to camp. Holly seemed brighter, even gifting him with a small smile, and he hoped maybe she'd forgiven him for his fuck up. She still wore the bee badge he'd made, but he suspected that was more out of bloody-mindedness.

Martha scanned the sky. "We should start on the hike. Holly are you good to take the lead?"

Holly rounded up the girls, who gathered around her like ducklings. She explained the morning activities and then produced the box of glittery art jars. She tossed Nick a smile across their heads. "Nick personalised these all for you, so make sure you take good care of them. Fill them with flowers, leaves, or anything you want to use to make some forest art later."

Nick folded his arms, forcing down waves of pride as they all *ahhed* and *oohed* over his handy-work. Scratching his neck, his skin broke into a rash, turning away before Holly caught him blushing. He wasn't sure why compliments got to him, he guessed he wasn't used to hearing them.

Holly lead the way, taking a leafy dark route through the forest. It took about half an hour to get to a tall meadow filled with bright violet borage flowers. There was lots of starting and stopping, collecting of supplies as each Robin decided they absolutely had to have a particular leaf from a tree only he could reach.

Holly fell into step behind him, as he crouched to help Sarah with her bug-hunting sheet. She'd spotted some woodlouse under a log and was keen to record it. The sun peaked through the trees, hot enough for him to tear off his sweater and tie it around his waist. He stood up abruptly as Holly went to walk past him, and he knocked her elbow with his. Holly toppled and Nick caught her waist, and they tussled for a second, both breaking apart and laughing.

"Sorry," Nick said, letting his hands slide to his sides.

Holly pulled away, slightly breathless, but her face creased in pain. "Oh!" she gasped. "Oh, *crap*."

"What is it?"

Holly fell to her bottom on the dirt path. Behind her, borage seed rose to tower over her head. Holly's eyes watered, as she tugged off her right shoe, followed by a sock. "I stepped in nettles."

Nick ducked to his knees as bright red welts appeared on Holly's calf. She hissed through her teeth. "Holy crap it stings!"

Nick looked about, and Sarah watched with interest. "What can we do?"

"Uh, nothing much," Holly said, grumbling as she got to her feet. Nick reached for her gingerly, but she batted him away. "It's fine."

"Doesn't look fine." He took her wrist and she slid out of his grip. "Holly..."

"I'm fine, Nick. Ow....shit!..*Shit*"

Nick covered the kid's ears with his hands as Holly cursed. Finally, he and Sarah locked gazes, and the canny seven-year-old yelled, "We need Doc leaves!"

Confused, Nick wandered behind her while Holly fell on her bottom, wincing and clutching her ankle. "That would be great, Sarah. Good thinking! You remembered the training we did."

Nick scoffed, finding it amusing that even in eye watering agony, Holly was still trying to be a good Eagle. She caught him rolling his eyes and hit him with her infamous pursed lip pout. The look on her face was legendary, only now it didn't irk him. It only made her more adorable.

Nick had no idea what he was looking for. Most of the group had wandered ahead with Martha, while Holly sagged in the dirt, looking more stricken as the seconds ticked by. A thin sheen of sweat broke across her brow. Sarah huddled over a patch of weeds and yelled a triumphant 'ahha' before dashing back to Holly with a palm of large, veiny green leaves. She dumped them on Holly's lap before tearing down the dirt path to find her friends, and Nick snorted.

"Some bedside manner," he joked, sitting cross legged in the dirt opposite her. "How does this work?"

Holly panted lightly, the sting clearly becoming stronger. Her ankle looked puffy, and red welts travelled up the underside of her calf. Nick made a face, taking her leg and placing it in his lap. "Does that hurt?"

"Umm," she grimaced, puffing through her nose. "Rub my calf." She squirmed in agony, the corners of her eyes leaking tears, and Nick looked abashed and ran his hand over her bare calf with vigorous friction. "No!" she yelled, nearly kicking him in the ribs. "With the fucking leaves!"

"Oh. *Oh!*" Nick's face went hot, and he snickered, turning the leaves over in his hands and rubbing them over the swollen welts. "Sorry!"

She choked out a laugh despite the searing agony she was experiencing, leaning on her elbows and allowing him to get to work. After a minute, they locked eyes, and both exploded in laughter, the absurdity of the situation not lost on either of them. Nick stopped. "Any better?"

"A little better," she said, then added a grudging, "thanks."

Martha circled back with Chloe and Sarah in tow, and her face narrowed with concern. "You better get back to camp. I have antihistamines in my pack."

Holly rolled to her side and then scrambled to her knees. "Good idea." Nick took her hand and tugged her to her feet. She swayed and fell into him, and he caught her shoulders. She took a few steps, wincing and hissing in pain, the underside of her leg still a red, spotty mess. Stumbling off, Nick thought she looked pretty pathetic, and Martha touched his shoulder.

"See her back, will you?" she asked, and he mumbled an incoherent 'alright' under his breath. Holly hopped ahead, squealing as she tried to walk on her stinging leg.

He caught up with her along the dirt track, waist high borage on their right and the sun bearing down hard. The skin on his neck tightened, and he was sure he was burning. Holly's curls were damp and stuck to her forehead. "Can you walk?"

"I *am* walking, aren't I?" she huffed in annoyance. "It just stings like a bastard, that's all."

Without warning, her hand landed on his bicep to steady herself so she could wipe the sweat off her top lip. Nick placed his hand on her lower back and grimaced, his palm damp. Holly really needed medication.

"Nice."

"Then don't touch me!" she yelled, flushing. "I can manage."

Nick guessed she hated her vulnerability, and she hated it more that it was in front of him. Sighing, he steadied her spine with his palm again. "I can put up with your gross sweaty back."

Holly hopped, then let out a reedy breath. "I'm not sure...."

Nick looked up. Okay, this was it. It was his time to shine, to prove he wasn't the complete waste of space she thought he was. He could be useful. "Not sure of what?"

"I'm fine...I can do this." She forged on, ignoring him, and he wondered if the sting was so bad she couldn't string words together. He'd fallen from his bike once into a patch of nettles, and he remembered the burn and the aftermath as it wore off. Like spiders crawling under his skin, and he winced on her behalf.

He stopped and knelt in front of her. Holly's face fell in horror. "If you think...."

"C'mon. Climb on."

"I'm too heavy."

"Don't be ridiculous, you're tiny. How heavy could you be? Get on!"

Holly groaned, her cheeks bright red and shiny, as she wound her arms around his neck. Nick took her weight and heaved. Okay, she was a *little* heavier than he'd expected, but he wasn't exactly regular in the gym. The only part of him that got a regular workout was his right forearm. He grunted, and she slid off shamefaced. "I told you!"

Nick laughed it off making a big deal of flexing his shoulders. "You're fine. Climb on. We can do this!"

Holly wasn't seeing the funny side, not at all. Puffing, she tearfully climbed on his back, and he almost growled as he straightened, grappling with her thighs around her waist. He tried to ignore that he could feel every part of her pressed into his back, and it wasn't setting his hormones alight.

"Jesus, Hols. Maybe lay off the smores for one night?"

Now she laughed, only because she probably felt useless, and half hysterical. "You're such a dick."

"Ah, but at least I'm consistent. No surprises here." He took a few paces, and with the sun blazing down on them and the uneven ground, he admitted this may not have been his best plan ever. But he'd already teased her enough and forged on, knowing she was in pain, and humiliated.

It was a sweaty, long trail back to the camp meadow, and the muscles in his upper arms were wailing. Nick adjusted to her weight, stopping to jerk her up his body as she slipped.

"You know, I think I'm probably fine now," she said, right in his ear, her breath tickling his neck and sending shocks down his spine. Every nerve in his spine pinged, went taught and he shuddered. "I can walk."

"Uh, don't do that!" he cried rolling his shoulders.

"What?" More shocks traveled down his back and he wriggled. It was unbearably ticklish.

"Don't keep talking so close to my ears. It feels weird!"

Holly snorted, her arms linked around his neck. She leaned in closer. "What—like this?"

"Stop it!" Nick laughed struggling to keep hold of her thighs around her waist. Holly hoiked herself up higher, and blew straight in his ear and he yelped in hysterical agony.

"Glad you're enjoying yourself back there."

Her reaction was to blow into the other one.

"At least I'm consistent!"

Nick was glad when he could finally dump her off at the picnic table in their little camp clearing. Holly hobbled to Martha's tent and found the medical bag. She popped some pills from the plastic film and chased them with water, it dripped down her chin and onto her shirt. She watched him with interest as she gulped back the liquid, and finally, she screwed the cap back on.

"Thanks." It was grudging, but she'd said it.

"Does it still hurt?"

"I'll be fine."

His brows rose. "You can say it hurts, if it hurts. You don't have to put on an act."

Swinging her arms, she looked a little lost for words. She hobbled to the table and sat with her leg up. Nick couldn't get a hold of her. One minute she was laughing and blowing in his ear, and the next it was like she couldn't look at him. It was like she threw up a giant stone wall only an army could bring down.

Didn't she see he was trying? But then he asked himself, what did he expect from her? Years of insults, every mean comment or thing he'd ever done to her came back to haunt him. Nick was fairly certain he'd once drawn her as an unflattering cartoon and stuck it to her locker. He noticed she still wore his sticker, probably because she didn't want to admit he'd hurt her.

Why did he even care what she thought? They only had two nights left here and this would be over and he'd be off to France.

Holly dragged herself to her tent, offering a small wave. "Thanks Nick." She turned her back but paused. "It does hurt," she said over her shoulder.

For some reason, he didn't think she meant the nettle sting.

Thirteen

Nick woke up incredibly horny. Frustrated, he lifted his head, wondering how he would solve the problem that had arisen under the covers. It wasn't like he could have a moment's privacy, and the last time he'd gotten up early for the bathroom, he'd run straight into Holly.

With her hair loose. Wearing nothing but a shirt.

Nick groaned and rolled onto his stomach, determined to think unsexy thoughts. Which was difficult now he knew what she felt like, her body pressed against his back in the dark. And when he'd carried her through back to the camp. Why did she always make him want to do bad things with his hands?

Unsexy. Thoughts.

He hoped she'd found the whistle. He suspected she had. He'd made it easy for her to find, and maybe that smug smile had vanished for a second before she returned to hating him. Holly nearly foiled him. Nick had waited all day for his chance to escape and was flooded with a cool wash of relief when he'd found the thing in the bush, tangled around some vines. In the dark, as she'd thrashed around without her glasses, it had been easy to slip it into his pocket.

Nick rolled onto his back, rubbing his bleary eyes. He wasn't sure what was happening. Was it possible the nice girl was cracking him? Daydreaming, the ache under the covers worsened, wondering if she'd ever slept with anyone before. Nick doubted it. Holly didn't date, that he knew of. He didn't think there was much time for casual sex in between the various clubs and commitments she had.

Its not like you're in double digits. Nick scratched at the early morning stubble on his jaw. Nick had slept with exactly two people. One he'd rather forget, a drunk friend of Davey's one night after a boozy evening. The other was someone he'd met on holiday; it wasn't love or anything special. He'd been seventeen and just wanted to do it. Nick wasn't unattractive, tall, lean, and dark, it hadn't been hard to meet a girl under the Mallorca sunshine. It was over embarrassingly fast and, again, not an experience he wanted to repeat anytime soon.

So why was he lying here wondering about Holly's sex life when he should be getting up and helping with breakfast?

The thought of more crafts made him grind his jaw. But his France trip loomed like a lingering threat if he didn't tow the line.

Remember all the times she shot you that look. The one that makes you want to hurl yourself off a building? The pompous, overbearing way she says your name, the way she rolls her eyes. Remember that.

Nick got up, too hot to remain in his sleeping bag and unzipped the tent flap, allowing cool air to douse his skin. Proximity, it had to be. Too close proximity and he hadn't had any for a while. He stood, stretching, and spotted Holly sitting by the fire, hand on fist, poking it to make it come alive. Her hair was loose around her shoulders and she was wearing a spaghetti-strapped camisole and a pair of jeans.

Nick swallowed hard. The sun was already streaming through the trees, and it was warm.

She held up a cooked sausage on a fork and took a bite. "You hungry?" she said around a mouthful.

He scratched his head, suddenly awkward, and worried anything he might say would come out tangled, so instead, he mumbled. "I'm okay."

Holly made a face and chewed her food as Tilly flew out of her tent behind her. Tilly ran into her back, tackling her to the ground and Holly laughed and captured her in a hug. "Good morning. Someone is full of energy!"

"Are we going on the boats today?"

Holly wrestled the cute pig-tailed girl to her feet, wiping a smear of dirt off her cheek. She beamed, peering into her face. "Yes, but only after we've had breakfast and completed our lanterns—you'll want them for tonight!"

Nick cocked a brow. "What's happening tonight?"

Holly straightened and let Tilly slip out of her arms, brushing back her mass of curls. "It's Campfire Joe night!"

Nick smirked. "Campfire Joe?"

"He owns the campsite, comes along, tells spooky stories, and we have smores." Holly shrank, under Nick's scrutiny, shrugging and reaching for her hoodie. "It's fun."

"Sounds riveting."

Holly pulled on her hoodie, fanning out her hair, a pink flush staining her cheeks, and he felt marginally guilty for making fun of her. "You don't have to join us." Then she smiled, and he was struck by her prettiness. When she smiled, her whole face changed, lightened, and creased, and the dimple on her chin deepened. Nick stretched his arms, pretending he hadn't noticed. "But," she said with a mischievous twinkle. "I can think of at least two or three girls who'll miss you if you don't come."

Nick cleared his throat. "I take it that doesn't include you."

Holly turned, giving him another nonchalant shrug. "Do what you like."

True to Holly's strict schedule, they sat at a picnic table in the woods and threaded and stuck the last of the paper lanterns after breakfast. Nick sat crossed-legged, tongue poked out in concentration as he threaded wire through Chloe's garish pink and yellow creation. He was covered in PVA glue, his hands tacky, and his thumbs kept sticking together.

Tilly marched across the clearing and planted a blank square of paper in his lap along with a sharpie. "Can you draw me a dragon?"

"Huh?" Nick grinned, and Tilly pressed closer as if he couldn't hear.

"A dragon—like the one on your arm!" She yanked up his t-shirt to reveal the baby dragon tattoo on his right bicep. Nick gave her a side hug and pulled her down next to him on the leaves.

"You like it?"

Tilly held out her pen. "I want it to go on my lantern."

Nick took the pen and quickly sketched out the inky outline of a baby dragon with long eyelashes. Tilly giggled when he added a bow between her pointed ears. "I love it!"

"You're welcome Tilly Dragon," he said, bopping her on the nose with the end of the sharpie. As she waltzed off to finish her creation he glanced up, catching Holly eyeballing him across the clearing. Was she watching him? Nick's chest swelled, anxiety pricking under his skin. She didn't have the look on her face that made him want to hulk smash. Instead she looked interested.

Martha jogged through the clearing, clapping her hands. "Are we nearly ready? It's a ten minute walk to the lake."

A few of the girls groaned, but most got eagerly to their feet. Nick rose in one motion, brushing leaves and diet off his jeans, casually tossing a glance in Holly's direction. But his stomach sank.

The whistle glittered in the sun, hanging around her neck. He tried not to notice it, but it was there, loud, sharp, and shrill, an instrument of torture. Why did she have to bring that thing? Stuffing his hands in his pockets, he fell behind the kids as they walked through the woods. They crossed the camp and took a grassy route across a meadow on a public footpath. Holly glanced over her shoulder and lagged, allowing him to catch up with her.

"The drawing was so cute," she said, her smile earnest. "Is that what you want to do?"

She was starting a conversation with him. This was a first and Nick swallowed back the immediate defensiveness he often felt when anyone asked him about his art. His father tolerated it, but often jibed he'd never earn a living. When he applied to college, he guessed his father was relieved he'd chosen something, *anything* to keep him out of trouble. "Kind of."

"Are you going to college?"

Nick eyed her profile as they walked. "Yeah, Bramston."

Holly beamed. "Me too! What are you taking?"

"Art and Design," his reply was gruff, mumbled. He was trying to be civil, even though he was nervous. She looked up at him with interest, and he sensed he needed to fill the silence. "What...what about you?"

"I'm doing a degree in Teaching."

"Of course you are."

Holly rolled her eyes, but surprisingly said nothing. No, come back this time. Nick bit his need to tease her about something, wondering why he was compelled to test her.

Keep a lid on the sarcasm, he told himself.

Undeterred, she ploughed on. "Do they hurt?" Frowning, he peered down at her, and her eyes were fixed on the tattoo on his neck, exposed in his t-shirt, and he rubbed it without thinking.

Nick cocked a brow. "What? The tattoos?" He laughed. "A little."

She was staring at the dragon on his arm. "I mean...it looks like it would hurt. I don't think I could stand it."

"That one was quick. It took about an hour. But others have hurt like a bastard."

"But you design them yourself?"

Nick's lips curled into a smile. "Yes, mostly."

"Do all the girls you date have tattoos?"

Nick picked up a twig and dragged it along the path behind them, suddenly bashful. He wondered where that had come from. "I don't really...I mean...a couple have." He sniggered. "It's not a requirement to date me."

Why was she interested in who he dated? He hated to envision what the girls he'd dated thought of her. He was well aware of what they'd think. His friends laughed at her behind her back, and god, if they'd seen her with the whistle and the socks and trainers...and all the badges. Holly wasn't cool, or sophisticated. She was...Holly. But he always thought she never cared about what they thought, and it was something he grudgingly admired. He glanced at her sideways, her button nose covered in freckles. Nick wasn't sure if it was the heat or the confinement, but she was growing on him. And he still couldn't shake the image of her standing there in nothing but a t-shirt.

"So..." Holly paused, taking his arm, running her fingertips over the dragon on his bicep. His skin broke out in goose bumps. "What one hurt the most?"

They'd stopped, alone in the woods, and the group marched ahead, oblivious to them lagging. "Uh," Nick rolled down the neck of his shirt, revealing the snake on his collar bone. Holly gasped and touched it gently, so light it tickled, like breath on his skin.

"It's incredible. You designed it?"

She got closer to have a look, and her hair brushed his chin. The tattoo was a snake, but it appeared coiled around his collarbone. The head appeared at one end and the pointy end of the tail at the other. Holly's dark eyes widened in fascination. "That's so clever...it's just part of the snake like it's looping around...."

"It hurt a lot...right on the bone."

Holly shuddered and rubbed her arms, lifting her eyes playfully to his. "Can you do me one day?"

"What?"

Holly went crimson. "I meant...oh my god...."

"Can I *do* you?" Nick burst out laughing. "I mean...that's quite an offer."

She punched his arm on the Dragon's nose, her face adorably pink. "I meant the tattoo, idiot." She smirked. "I really liked the one you designed for Violet. Even if Eddie wasn't too happy!"

"Eddie is a dick." Nick gestured they ought to keep walking. "You don't strike me as the type."

Holly walked beside him. "The type of what?"

"I don't know...the type." He tossed her a grin and poked the whistle around her neck. Holly scowled.

"Oh right? Because I'm so uptight?"

"No," he drawled. "Because...you're Holly. And you don't seem...the type who'd get tattoos. You like rules and school and Robins."

Holly jogged a few steps ahead, turning to walk backwards. "So I don't qualify? And that's all you really know about me? We've been neighbours since we were kids, and all you know about me is I like school...and Robins."

Nick halted abruptly, feeling like he was being led into a trap. "I'm getting to know you more. Let's face it. What do you know about *me*? Really?"

Holly smiled. "You want to play this game? Okay." She looked thoughtful, folding her arms. "I know you paint, draw and sketch and have done since you were five. I mean, you ate half a box of Crayons in front of me once...."

"I ate one Crayon—Jesus." How did she even remember? He'd puked red that night.

Holly waved her hands, a smarty pants smile dancing across her mouth. "I know you have a bird or something winged on your left shoulder."

He smirked. "Been watching me have you?"

"You're always out the front washing your damn car—of course I've seen you. I also know you listen to heavy metal, Metallica is one of your go-to's. Your middle name is David. I know you have a massive problem with authority, you failed science last year and had to retake it. I know you help your dad coach football, and I know you have nephews and cousins you take the park, and you work twenty hours a week at the petrol station."

Nick let out an exaggerated sigh. "Anything else?"

Holly squared her shoulders. "I know...." She bit her lip carefully and lifted her chin as she chose her words with care. "I know you miss your mum."

Nick ducked, picked up a twig between his fingers, and threw it, hot around the ears, mostly because of the way she eyeballed him. "Are you done?"

Missing his mother wasn't exactly hard to work out. He'd had *Mum* tattooed on his neck for god sake, but in Gaelic, a secret he'd allowed to slip out on the first morning on the bus. Holly was razor sharp, seemingly she missed nothing. Nick's skin itched, vulnerable under her scrutiny

"Can you do better? I mean...more than I like *school* and Robins. You don't know the first thing about me."

Embarrassed, Nick stalked past her, irritated she'd called him out. Ashamed, he admitted he didn't know anything, years of living next door and he hadn't cared to know more about her than he needed to. She quickly caught up with him, catching his shoulder. "Nick."

"What?"

She stood in front of him, earnest and open. "Can we call a truce? For the next couple of days? Don't throw it back in my face if I say something nice."

Nick crossed his arms, the idea sparking a grain of interest. "I can do that. If you promise me one thing."

"What?"

It was his turn to square his shoulders, looking down at her through dark lashes. "Stop riding me. Looking down your nose at me...like I'm some kind of...."

"Felon? Vandal?" Holly filled the gap, a grin spreading across her face, and when he only glared at her she relented. "Okay, sure. You have a deal."

Nick took her hand and shook it. "We both want to get through this trip without killing one another."

Holly nodded thoughtfully as though she didn't believe he could bite his tongue and keep every errant thought inside his head. Maybe she was right. "I agree—so that's something."

She spun on her heels, stalking down the track the Robins had trodden, leaving Nick to stand and watch her go and wondering if there could ever be such a thing as a truce.

Fourteen

A truce? Holly shook her head as she edged down to the river side. She wondered how long it would be before Nick cracked. Sighing, she stood on the lake's edge, quickly catching up with the group. Martha was assessing the rowboats with a look of concern on her face.

The river was an offshoot of a canal, joining a larger body of water a few miles upriver. It was wide, murky, and deep, used by rowers, canoeists, and larger boats out on day trips. Either side was dotted with trees, lazy willows dragged their branches through the water. The Robins crowded around two boats moored on the jetty. A tall man with thinning brown hair waved them all nearer, jubilant and friendly. His name tag read Geoff.

"Ah," he said, eyeing the group. "There's more of you than I expected!"

Martha folded her arms, doing a quick head count as Holly appeared by her side with Nick lagging behind huffing and out of breath. "I didn't think of that. Shall we split up?"

"It's fine," Geoff said with a wave of his hand. Holly didn't miss the way he was eyeballing Martha and she hid her smile. "How about you and me take a boat with three of them? And then these two take a boat with two?"

"Oh?" Martha's usually pale cheeks coloured pink. "If you're sure you don't mind..."

"I don't." Boy, Geoff was eager, and Holly coughed into her hand. To her surprise, Nick snorted, picking up on the single dad vibes Geoff was shooting poor Martha. She tossed him a look over her shoulder. "Can you row?"

Nick shrugged. "Can *you?*"

"Of course I can."

Nick wandered to the boat, muttering, "Of course I can," in a whiny tone under his breath, which only made her stiffen in irritation. So much for the truce, that lasted all of thirty seconds. Wringing her hands, Holly let him go ahead. She peered at the dank water and hid her shudder. Holly could row and was a good swimmer, but she wasn't a fan of deep water. The choppy current made her shiver, and she rubbed her arms. Anything could be down there, and she blamed her irrational fear on a documentary about London canals she watched once. She also hated rats and knew the river bank was packed with them.

Nick hopped in a boat and held out his arms for Tilly and Chloe. Chloe jumped at him, and Nick caught her solidly, laughing as he settled her next to him. He whispered something to make her laugh, and Holly's heart pulsed harder. Why did he have to be so cute with kids? Holly approached the jetty, and Nick watched with interest as she stood rooted to the wooden boards.

"Are you getting in or planning to stand there all day?" he called as Chloe and Tilly waved for her to join. Gritting her teeth, she took a wobbly step into the boat.

Water splashed her legs as the boat rocked. She cried out, unbalanced, but Nick caught her hand. "Thanks," she muttered, sinking into the seat opposite him. Tilly crowded in beside her, and Holly wrapped her in tight for a cuddle.

"You look a little...." Nick narrowed his eyes. "Peaky."

Holly lifted her chin and refused to meet his keen blue eyes. "I'm fine," she said airily. "Shall we go?" She stared at the oars in his hands, wishing she could take them. At least then, she'd be in control of the boat, and she wouldn't be dwelling on her jittery nerves.

"Truce, remember?" Nick's brow arched so highly she thought it would run off his forehead, and her throat tightened as he grabbed the oars.

"Of course." She didn't say a word more, knowing he was waiting for her to grab the oars and prise them out of his hands. To her surprise, he flexed his arms, a soft grin escaping his lips as he swept the boat into the middle of the river. The edges grew farther away, and Holly's nerves kicked in. Tension built in her temples, and she shielded her eyes from the sun. Laughter floated from the other boat, and Holly guessed Geoff was doing his upmost to charm Martha. Sarah, Bryony, and Jack waved from the boat, and Nick grinned, the oar slipping out of his hands.

Holly jerked so hard the boat rocked, and her nails dug into the wood.

"Careful!" Nick laughed. "You look like someone died, Holly."

"I'm fine," she said through clenched teeth. "Maybe we should row a little closer to the edge...you know... in case...."

"In case of what?" he argued. "I capsize us? Don't you trust me at all?"

Holly swallowed, willing away the flutter of apprehension, working its way into her chest. She puffed out a breath, giving him a fleeting smile. Did she trust him? He'd carried her all the way home with an injured leg. He led her back to camp through dark woodland when her glasses got smashed.

Because he stole your whistle, she sniffed, fingering the object around her neck. "Yes, I trust you," she admitted after a long silence. Nick nudged Chloe's shoulder.

"You trust me, right?"

She beamed up at him. "Yes!"

Holly's gaze was drawn to his long fingers gripping the oars. He tickled Chloe with his free hand, letting the oar rest on his knee. Holly wished she were sitting next to him, she might have felt a little safer.

"How about we row under this willow?" Nick suggested as Chloe clambered onto his lap and rested her hands over his. "Can you help me steer?" Chloe grinned, and Holly's jittery nerves quelled as Nick did as she asked, taking the boat closer to the edge.

Swept up in darkness, she relaxed as Nick rowed the boat under a huge willow draped across the water's edge. Tilly jumped and picked off a few leaves. Out of the glaring sun, Nick found her eyes across the boat and looked away shyly. Holly's mouth went dry, and she licked her lips, unsure of what was happening and why her stomach did a crazy dance whenever she locked eyes with him.

You know what's happening, a voice tormented her. *You like him. A lot.*

The sun glinted as they drifted out of the willow's shade. Tilly made excited noises beside her, continually standing and pointing. "Careful not to rock it too much!" Holly warned.

A dazzling, mischievous grin spread over Nick's face as he grabbed either side of the wooden frame and rocked it side to side, with enough force it tilted. Both the girls yelled in delight but Holly's heart flew into her mouth. "Don't do that, Nick!"

"Do what? This?" He rocked it again and she squealed, clutching the boat's sides. His blue eyes flashed playfully, throwing her a wolfish smile. "You scared, Truman?"

"No," she lied, trying not to look too closely at the murky depths. Geoff rowed Martha and the other three Robins into the centre on the far side of the river. They were all chatting and laughing while Holly clutched the boat as the sun beat down.

Nick was watching her, and he snorted and glanced away. "What do you think I'm going to do? Drown you?"

"I'm not scared!"

"Such a liar," Nick tutted. "You can swim, can't you?"

Holly scoffed. "Of course I can swim."

"Then you won't mind if I do this?" He cackled and rocked the boat again, and water spilled in the sides.

"Nick!"

He stopped the moment Chloe bleated something in his ear, and with a sigh he hoisted her on his lap, letting her have a try. They drifted for a while, both girls chatting while Holly took a moment to close her eyes. She could feel his boring into her, and after a brief silence, she met his gaze.

"I'm not scared," she said. "I just...like being in control. That's all." She let out a long exhale of air, not wanting to look at him if he laughed at her. He tapped her knee and handed her the oars.

"Well that's something I've learned about you today—you want them?"

Holly firmed her chin. "No. You can row, I'm good."

"So..." Nick drawled. "To be clear, you're handing me the control—for now."

"For now."

"I'm not sure you should. Who knows what this vandal and future felon might do?"

A knot tightened in her throat when she looked at him, sitting across from her, in ripped jeans and a t-shirt, his hair reflecting the sun. The sweet ache in her chest swelled, and she fiddled with her hands. He looked so good that Adam Brant was a blip on the landscape right now. His hands wound tightly around the oars, his shoulders flexing as he pushed against the current, and she remembered how he'd held her in the dark last night. Her hand strayed to the whistle around her neck again.

She folded one hand under her bottom, the other wound around Tilly's waist. "Then I'll just have to trust you."

Conversation dwindled, and Holly bristled, trying to think of something to say. Chloe and Tilly were deep in their own child like banter, and Holly's mind blanked of anything clever or witty to say. Nick grinned, sheepishly, as if he sensed it too.

"So what's so important about this *gold* award?" he asked, looking at her carefully. "Does it come with any special benefits?"

Holly smiled, amazed it was him who initiated a conversation. "No special benefits...it's just something I've worked for a long time. It looks good on CVs and on University applications."

Nick choked in mock dismay. "You mean you don't even get any discounts to waterproofs are us? Or camping warehouse?"

His attempt at a joke, a nice one, not laced with any kind of malice, made her chuckle. "Nope, not a single penny off."

"You'd get into Bramston regardless of an award. You know that, right?"

"Yes, but...it's a community thing. It shows commitment and perseverance, and I've been part of this group...." She didn't want to talk about James. "I like being part of something. I can make a difference, and help. These kids will remember this trip for the rest of their lives, and I love it."

She waited for the retort, that she was wasting her time, and one day they'd love their screens more than being a Robin. Instead, he nodded, deep in thought. "I kind of get it."

Holly brightened. "Well you do play football with kids every half term."

Nick laughed. "Don't you hear my screams of protest through the wall? He forces me to be there, cold, rain or blistering heat. I don't *love* it. Not like you love this."

Part of Holly deflated, maybe he didn't get it at all. He went on and she looked up in surprise, shocked he was suddenly opening up. "Davey and Casey ride me for it."

"Why'd you care what they think?"

He scowled. "They're my friends."

Some friends, she puffed through her nose. "Tess sometimes teases me for spending my time with the kids, but she gets it."

Irritably, Nick scratched at his chin, his lips pressing into a line. "Well my friends aren't your friends, Holly. They don't do any of this uncool shit."

Stung, she dipped her chin and stared at the water. "Okay..."

Nick didn't reply, only peered at her through his thick lashes, staring out over the river, when his expression changed. Holly followed his gaze, and her jaw clenched. "Oh...no."

Nick waved to Martha across the water, twisting to stare at the eight-foot bow rider heading up the river, making a strong ripple of waves as it gained distance. "They see it coming, right?"

The boat ploughed through the murky water towards Geoff's boat. He seemed distracted, chatting to one of the

Robins sat by his side, and Holly's mouth went sandpaper dry. "I don't think he does!"

Time slowed to a crawl, and Nick pushed the boat to the far side of the river, the side of the boat brushing the grassy bank. Holly stood, wobbly on her feet, her eyes fixed. "They won't see it!" She cupped her hands around her mouth. "Martha! *Geoff!*"

"Holly..." Nick caught her hand. "I think he's spotted it."

"No...he hasn't!"

Geoff was laughing at something his little companion said, waving his hands, the oars loose in his grip. Sweat broke out on Holly's palms, real panic exploding in her chest. The bow rider neared closer, a massive, destructive vessel compared to the tiny row boat. It gained distance, and her vision swam. She panicked, heart throbbing, dizzying panic made her flush lava hot. "He can't see!"

"Holly!" Nick laughed, and she went from hot to ice cold. "He's spotted it—look, he's turning."

But Geoff wasn't turning. He wasn't watching, he wasn't paying attention. He'd get her Robins killed. Why wasn't Martha looking? "Geoff!"

"Holly, for god sake...." Nick sounded annoyed and embarrassed, but she shook with fear. If anything happened to those children... Dark thoughts raced ahead, she imagined the looks on the parent's faces when she broke the news. The stress was palpable, so strong it coated her tongue, and she was aware through greyed vision of Chloe and Tilly looking up at her in terror.

Holly grabbed the whistle. Nick grabbed her hand. "Holly don't you blow that thing—look he's turning, it won't hit them!"

"They'll be killed, Nick!"

"What the hell are you talking about...*look!*"

Holly wobbled on her sea legs, and both Tilly and Chloe burst into tears. Her fear made her voice tight and strained, so high and shrill she hated the way she sounded. She blew into the whistle hard and Nick's head dropped between his shoulders in embarrassment. She let out several long shrill blows through the silver whistle, and it sounded across the river.

Make yourself heard. It was why James gave her the whistle before he left to live with his biological father. *Make yourself heard.*

The whistle attracted Martha's attention. The older woman's furrowed gaze found her across the river as the boat sailed right by. Cold relief flooded Holly's system and she dropped the whistle with trembling fingers. Numbly, she glanced at Nick, staring at her like she'd grown eight heads. He held up his hands, flustered. "What the hell, Holly? A little overreaction, don't you think?"

Holly went dizzy. Both Tilly and Chloe were scared and crying.

You did that. The boat tipped as she went to sit down and her belly lurched, her knees trembling. "Crap!"

"Give me your hand!" Nick's palm shot towards her, but she batted him away as if she were swatting a fly.

She went white and wobbly. "I'm fine!"

"Holly for fuck's sake..." Nick stood up, taking her trembling shoulders. It only made the boat judder under their feet. "Let me help you!"

The boat swayed and bobbed, and both grabbed the other's shoulders. Top heavy, towering over her, Nick was losing his balance. "I don't need help!" she yelled, trying to struggle out of his arms, locked in the blue of his eyes. They grappled and struggled while both the girls screamed.

Holly lost her fight, and Nick grabbed her arm, falling backwards as the boat dipped under him. His fingers closed around her wrist as he dragged her overboard with him. Holly shrieked as everything slowed to a crawl, and the next thing she felt was the cold shock of water.

Fifteen

Holly's shoes squelched as she tracked to the shower block, hot and shivering at once. Humiliation boiled under her skin. God, she could kill Nick Jones. She decided right then she'd had enough of this challenge. She wanted to break Nick, alright, break his legs.

She'd been trying to warn Martha! What part did he think she'd overreacted to? Geoff and Martha weren't looking, they weren't keeping watch. They weren't protecting...

"Holly!"

Stamping into the shower block, her wet feet slapped the tiles, closely followed by Nick. Martha had taken the girls back to camp for a snack and to play. She ignored him as he tailed her into the echoey shower room.

"Get lost! I'm showering."

Nick jumped into a spare cubicle, yanking the thin plastic curtain closed. "Then you'll have to close your eyes!"

Holly groaned aloud. "Can't you wait five minutes?"

"No!" Nick flung on the shower, and it filled the room with steam. Then to her horror, he stripped off his clothes. "This is your fault."

"My fault?"

Bare-chested and stepping closer, Nick narrowed his eyes as she shrank, folding her arms. "Yes," he breathed out. "You *massively* overreacted. What the hell was that about?"

"I was trying to warn them!"

"You scared the shit out of Tilly and Chloe," he shot back, a blow that hurt. She didn't want to dredge up the image of their confused faces. On the boat, she hadn't been a calm, composed Eagle, she'd gone into fight mode. Holly chewed the inside of her cheek, hardly able to meet his accusing stare, recalling how seconds before the boat passed safely by, the world spun and went grey, rendering her useless.

Nick flicked the whistle around her neck. "I should have left that bloody thing in the bushes!"

Holly's eyes flew wide, indignation making her lip curl. "You bastard! I knew it. You took it!"

Nick rolled his eyes. "Of *course* it was me. You've come to expect no less haven't you? But I gave it back...which I'm regretting!"

They stood inches apart, both breathing hard and staring the other down. Then Holly stripped off her soaked t-shirt, leaving her in her bra. Nick's resolve wilted. "What are you doing?"

"I'm covered in river water because of you. I'm showering...maybe you should close your eyes?" She stamped into the cubicle next to his and yanked the curtain closed. She stripped off her bra, underwear, and shorts, tossing them out of the cubicle where they landed at his feet. She yanked the faucet on with a blast of cold water and stepped aside as it warmed up.

Inside the cubicle, she ground her teeth, squeezing her shower gel it into her hands. She lathered violently and thoroughly, scrubbing dirty water and residue out of her hair. She couldn't see his shape behind the curtain, so guessed he'd ducked into his cubicle, and moments later, she smelled the fresh pine of his shower gel. Rinsing out her hair, fat, hot tears escaped under her lashes, making her eyes sting. She gave an almighty sniff.

He was right. She'd acted like a complete moron. She thought...

I don't know what I thought...I thought they'd get hurt. I was trying to help.

"Holly."

The way he said her name made her shiver under the hot spray. His shower was off, and steam evaporated from the tiles. She held the wall, crying into her fist and ignored him.

"Holly. Turn off the shower and talk to me."

With a trembling lower lip, she took the faucet and turned it, shutting off the water. She reached for a towel and wrapped it around her middle, holding it tight against her chest. Nick's curtain rings jangled, and he poked his head out. "Will you come out and look at me?"

"No," she mumbled against her hand. Every time she shut her eyes, she saw Chloe and Tilly's confused expression. The adult in charge, someone they trusted, had behaved like a lunatic, unhinged. They put their trust in her, and she was failing them. She hadn't even been in control when Lea had her asthma attack. What was wrong with her? Sobbing into her palms, she came to the realisation that the only reason she'd handled the situation was because Nick had been beside her.

"Holly." She shuddered again, and rubbing her stinging eyes, she poked out her head, grabbing her towel. Nick's face fell, his cheekbones pink and hot from the shower. "Look—you don't know everything about me, okay?"

Confused, she blinked. "Okay...."

"The whistle." He nodded to where Holly tossed it along with her wet clothes. "It bugs the shit out of me."

Holly sniffed. "It's just a whistle, Nick."

"It's not the object...it's the rules...the routine...you know my dad is ex-army?"

"Of course." Everyone knew Mr. Jones had been a staff sergeant in the army years ago and fought in Iran.

"He likes routine, rules, and it's *stifling*. My mother couldn't hack it, so she left him. She was like me—an artist too. And she didn't like the routines he clung to. So now she's in France, and I see her barely once a year, if I'm lucky. And I..." His face creased, and he couldn't look at her. "I'm so angry...all the time. I don't remember a time when I didn't feel angry. I guess...I'm trying to explain...I shouldn't have taken it and gave it back the minute I found out it belonged to James. But it does something to me. I hate control. I don't want to be boxed in. Ever."

Stepping out of the shower, she leaned against the tiled wall, as he emerged too, with the towel around his waist, and she tried to ignore the heat creeping up her neck. She sniffed. "I understand."

Nick hated authority. He hated rules. He actively went against everything Holly loved and held dear. She sagged inwardly, hit by the startling clarity that she was everything he hated.

It all made sense.

They stood there for a moment, both awkward and half-naked, and when she glanced up his eyes were hot on her bare, freckly shoulders.

"I'm glad you told me."

He gave her a crooked smile. "Guess that's something new you can add to your list of things you know about me." His voice cracked a little and for the first time he didn't look cocky or arrogant, he just looked sad, and tired.

Holly bent to pick up her wet things. "Nick..."

"Yes."

"Don't yell at me if I say this...but...your mother leaving..."

She chose her words carefully, as she guessed this topic was eggshell fragile, and he already had his brows raised towards his hairline. "Go on."

"Well...I get she couldn't cope with your dad. But the fact you don't see her more than once a year is nothing to do with him. You know that, right?" Holly didn't want to hurt him, for the first time in as long as she could remember, she didn't want to inflict misery on him. But he was wrong, and there was no way she was going to agree with him. Nick folded his arms across his broad chest, his walls drawn up and his mouth downturned.

Bravely, she continued. "Maybe it *is partly* his fault she walked away. But it's not his fault she stayed away...and maybe you shouldn't lay all the blame on him. He's a good dad, and he loves you." Her thoughts rarely dwindled on the father she'd never known, and sometimes she wondered what he would think of her. Holly long since resigned her heart when it came to him. She couldn't miss what she never knew. Not like James.

She bundled her wet clothes into her arms, shivering, and then pressed the whistle into his palm, watching as his fingers curled around it. "What's this for?" he snorted.

"I get why this upsets you. So if we're going to remain civil, you keep it for now." Her hand curled around his as he closed his palm, and for a moment, she froze, wanting to link her fingers through his, to feel them close around her own. When she looked up, he was breathing hard. "But please don't throw it in the bushes. It means a lot to me." She paused, running the pad of her thumb across his knuckles, tracing the bones of his hands. "And it means a lot to me that you returned it."

Holly left him to gape, stuffing her feet in her damp shoes and jogging across the grassy field. When she was safe in her tent, she released a caged breath. What was happening to her? For a moment there, she'd wanted his hands on her. Equally, she'd wanted to wrap him in a hug, tell him he didn't need to be angry all the time, and she *wasn't* those things he thought she was. Stuffy, uptight, a bore.

Quickly, she dressed, yanking on her underwear and clean dry socks, revelling in their warmth. Who was she kidding? She was all the things he hated. Nick wouldn't change, and neither would she. They were both opposites: fire and ice, sunshine and grey skies.

Holly bit her lip, terrified to admit something dangerous was brewing inside her, he was getting to her, wearing down her barriers as quickly as she constructed new ones to climb.

What had her mother said? Make a boy mistake. Nick would be the biggest boy mistake she'd ever make. They were too different, and even if she was on fire right now, he'd say something dumb to douse the flame and make her feel more of an idiot than she already did. Holly groaned, throwing herself on her back, clenching her fists, her frustration building.

She told herself a mistake with Nick would be a really bad idea. *A bad...kind of exciting idea.*

She wasn't ready, and Nick would surely already be experienced. He was gorgeous and must have a few notches on his belt, no doubt with girls she knew from school, which made her chest ache with jealousy.

So you think he's cute after all.

Her attraction to him was becoming hard to ignore. Holly didn't know where all these errant thoughts had come from.

But maybe it might feel good to let go. Holly covered her eyes, groaning and wishing she had Tess to talk to about all this. She'd tell her she was nuts, Nick wasn't a keeper, he wasn't good boyfriend material. He'd even said it himself, he was a free spirit, an artist like his mother, and everything she was irritated him. Holly would have to change to fit into his world, and she didn't want to.

It had been a trying day, and all she wanted was to forget the last twelve hours and concentrate on the girls, have some fun tonight, and prove she was an outstandingly capable Eagle leader and not a panic-stricken lunatic who seemed to turn insane the moment she got within a few inches of Nick Jones.

This was supposed to be the breaking Nick challenge, but right now Holly felt like she was the one who was cracking.

Sixteen

Nick wanted to kiss Holly. Like, really, *really* kiss her.

Standing in front of him, wearing nothing but a towel, he'd been unable to keep his eyes off her bare shoulders. His throat knotted, imagining tracing the path of every chocolate freckle on her collarbone with his fingers.

Heavy limbed, he ran to his tent and wrestled on clean, warm clothes once inside. He barely fit in the thing, his feet peeping out of the end, nearly braking the flimsy poles

She'd acted crazy this afternoon. The moment she'd blown into the whistle, his good mood evaporated. Once she'd calmed down, the look on her face was so distressed it was enough to pull a heroic, protective response out of him. When he heard her sobbing through the shower cubicle wall, he wanted to make things right.

He didn't want her to hate him, even though he thought she probably still did. A spike of pain touched his chest, and he sat rigid in his coffin tent, alone, frustrated, and angry with himself. He hadn't exactly been easy to like over the years, and he admitted he'd done some pretty crappy stuff to her.

Sighing, he knew this was fruitless. Holly detested him, she'd told him with her stark, stony gaze since the day he stole Wilbur. He lay on his pillow, scrubbing at his face with his nails, drowning out the sounds of giggles and playing just inches away from the tent flaps. Throwing on his earbuds, he closed his eyes and let Metallica deafen him until his stomach growled from hunger, and he sensed he'd avoided everyone for way too long.

You only have two days left, he told himself. *Two days of this crap, you can go home, have alone time in the shower, and forget this ever happened.*

But Nick really wanted to kiss her.

Unzipping the tent, the light outside had faded, twilight peeking through the densely packed trees, and Tilly came running full thrust at his knees. Air whooshed through his teeth as he sailed backwards, and she landed on his chest. Her face was gooey with chocolate, and Nick eyed her warily. "You seem excited."

She thumped his chest. "Campfire Joe is coming!"

Nick grinned and fought an eye roll. "Well, that *is* exciting."

"He's gonna play guitar, tell stories and give us smores...."

"I think someone has already helped herself to enough smores." Martha appeared overhead, peering over Tilly's shoulder at Nick, lying prone on the ground. "You okay down there?"

Nick struggled to his feet, groaning with Tilly in his arms. "Sure."

"Fancy playing with the kids for a while? Holly and I have something we need to do."

Nick glanced up, his curiosity ignited. Was this something to do with Holly's behaviour on the boat? It was odd, even for her. "Oh?"

Martha helped him to his feet, dragging him up by an arm. "Nothing serious. Can you keep them occupied for half an hour?"

Nick dragged his heels, following Martha across the field where several of the girls were tossing a frisbee to one another. Tilly jumped up and down, catching the purple flying disc with ease and Nick ran in and grabbed her around her belly, before turning her upside down. The little redhead squealed and pelted his arm, and it wasn't long before all of them were jumping on him, demanding a ride on his shoulders or to be swung upside down. All except Jack, who was sitting cross-legged under a tree, picking at daisies. Nick wandered over and crouched by his feet.

"You aren't going to join in?" Nick prodded his toe playfully and Jack turned his big, soulful eyes on him, brimming with unshed tears.

"I'm not very good. Tilly always beats me—she says I'm too little!"

Nick tugged him to his feet. "Rubbish. We've got to stick together, you and me. All these girls ordering us around! I bet we could take them."

Jack wiped his nose on his sleeve, and Nick hauled him onto his shoulders. Ten minutes later, he was exhausted, chest tight as a rubber band after running around the field chasing a frisbee with Jack on his shoulders. It was worth it. Jack managed a few catches, yipping in delight.

Out of breath, he talked them into a game. Holly wandered into the field, arms crossed and chin down. She looked miserable. Nick was so preoccupied he narrowly missed the frisbee flying at his skull. "Hey!"

"Nick loves Holly!" Tilly squealed, and Nick went beet red, waving his hands at her, but this only made her shout louder. "Nick *loves* Holly. He can't stop looking at her!"

"Tilly," he growled. "*Be* quiet."

Holly wandered to a picnic table, where Martha sat waiting for her. Mercifully, they were out of earshot, and Nick hoped to god she hadn't heard. Deep in conversation, Holly sank onto the bench next to Martha, occasionally wiping her eyes, and Nick's insides clenched. It had to be about the boat incident, about Holly's bizarre reaction. He rummaged for the whistle in his jeans pocket.

A chorus of tiny voices broke out in song behind him. Sarah and Tilly sang, "Holly and Nick, sitting in a tree...K I S S I N G...."

Nick glared at them. "Tilly...*quiet!*"

Nick caught sight of Chloe staring at him, eyes like daggers. She stamped her foot with a pout to rival Holly's. "I *hate* Holly."

Nick ruffled her hair. "Ah, don't say that. You don't hate her."

"You're *my* boyfriend, not hers."

Nick laughed, but this only made her lip tremble, so he got on his knees. "Jealous?"

"Nick love, love *loves* Holly!" Byrony and Tilly chanted. Chloe's eyes filled up, and Nick gave her hand a squeeze.

"Don't take any notice of them...Tilly's only being silly."

"I'm not!" Fired up on adrenaline and sugar, Tilly scrunched up her face and Nick's patience wore thin. Why had Martha put him in charge? He kept glancing at Holly and Martha, in deep conversation and was glad they couldn't hear much. "Holly and Nick are going to kiss and have babies."

"Oh, my god. You are so annoying!" Nick said through his teeth, trying to keep a tight smile on his face. "Will you shut up?"

"Don't tell me to shut up!"

"Okay...shut up, please?"

Chloe clicked her tongue, shaking her head in disappointment. "That's bad manners, Nick."

"Oh, don't you start."

Nick's temples throbbed, he was close to losing his temper, and now he was surrounded by four nagging little women. Tilly stamped her feet. "You are so mean to her!"

"What? I'm not...!"

Chloe's eyes filled with tears. "I hate you, Nick!" She shook her dark curls. "You're the worst boyfriend ever."

"You're not my girlfriend, Chloe. I don't date little girls." He knew it was possibly the lamest comeback when it left his mouth, and guilt hit him like a hammer the second he saw her little face crumple. "Oh...Chloe!"

She burst into tears and kicked his shin. Nick yelped as pain exploded up his bone. "Holy *fuck*!"

Chloe stalked off. "Language!" she screamed, cuddling her bear tightly and crying into his fur. "Socks isn't your friend either."

Clutching his shin, he fell to his bottom, his irritation at a critical level, wondering how he'd lost control of a group of children so quickly. Tilly stomped up about two feet behind him.

"Hey, Nick!"

He clenched his jaw, his temper fraying, and he didn't think he could take another second of Tilly Grey. "What?"

"Duck!"

Martha sank onto the bench opposite Holly, and brushed her hand with her warm one. Holly's throat knotted and she looked away. Martha had known Holly since James first dropped her at her first Robin meeting when she was five. Holly's shoulders squared automatically, and Martha gave her a sad smile. "Are you okay?"

"I'm fine." She smiled, hoping it reached her eyes. Across the field, Nick played with the girls, tossing them into the air like dolls. It made something flutter in her stomach. They loved him, really loved him. He was a complete natural with them. When she glanced up, Martha was following her gaze.

"Is he getting to you?"

"What? No!"

"I know you two have been...."

"Sworn enemies since we were five."

Martha chuckled, something mischievous twinkling in her eyes. "For sworn enemies, you two can't keep your eyes off one another."

Holly's mouth dropped with embarrassment, unaware she'd been so obvious. "Martha!"

"I'm only saying it how it is. I can tell. Now, why you two can't put your differences aside...."

Holly slapped the table with a laugh. "That's just it. Those differences are giant chasms. We don't, we can't and never have gotten along. Besides...I like someone else."

Holly hid her gaze, peeking a gaze at Nick over her shoulders and Martha scoffed.

"You mean Adam Brant? The boy who doesn't say much."

Holly bit her lip. God, did everyone In Willowdale know about her crush on Adam? A crush which somehow didn't seem as urgent as it once did. News travelled in the town. Her gaze wandered yet again, and now Nick was running up and down with Jack on his shoulders. Jack was hysterical, laughing as he caught a frisbee his sister tossed him. Holly tilted her head, loving how windswept Nick looked, worn out and red-faced, but having fun.

"Look. I'm not going to pry." Martha settled a hand on her arm, pulling her out of her daze. "I'm more concerned about your reaction today on the boat. When I glanced over...you looked like you'd seen a ghost."

Holly's fist balled at her side, her chest fluttering with her breathing. Across the field, Tilly was yelling something at Nick and stamping her foot, but it looked like he had it handled. "I'm not sure. I'm sorry. I just—panicked."

"I'm not angry with you. But I'm worried, Holly. You take everything so seriously...so to heart. I'm worried...."

"You don't have to worry!" Holly was shaking under the table. Martha's eyes creased in concern, Holly's shrill tone indicating it wasn't fine.

"I was thinking," Martha started, holding up her hands. "Just hear me out. You don't talk about James, not nearly enough as you should...."

"Martha...I don't want to talk about it."

"...he was special, a big part of your life, and I'm concerned you haven't really processed what happened to him...."

Holly's temper spiked, cornered, hot, and angry like a cat. Her nostrils flared. "Martha..."

"Fuck!"

Both women jumped as Nick's voice broke across the field, and Holly's head snapped up in time to see him stumble to the grass and blood spurt from his forehead.

Martha put her arm around Tilly. She sobbed hard enough to send birds scattering out of the trees, snot and tears mingling on her pink cheeks. Martha walked Tilly to the picnic table, where Nick sat, arms crossed, while Holly dabbed at his forehead with an antibacterial wipe. He hissed and she hunched her shoulders.

"Sorry," she muttered, wiping away the last traces of blood. They shared a wooden bench, knee to knee, and Nick was puffing through his nostrils like a dragon while Holly did her best to swallow back a giggle.

"Now I think Tilly has something she'd like to say to you, Nick," Martha said, easing Tilly out in front of her. Nick glared at the kid, his jaw bunched. Holly guessed he was on the verge of letting something acidic tumble out of his mouth, so she poked his knee, shaking her head. Nick pressed his lips closed.

"S-Sorry I hit you with the frisbee, Nick." Tilly wiped snot on the sleeve of her hoodie.

"At point blank range," Nick added. Holly glared at him, then after a few moments, his lips twitched. "You've got a good arm."

"Tilly knows what she did was wrong. Now can the two of you make up and get along?"

"Hmm," Nick grumbled. "I think I can forgive you."

Tilly tumbled forward, and Holly paused with her administration, watching as Nick's grimace melted into a smile. He held out his arms, and Tilly threw hers around his neck. Holly's chest swelled, sighing as Nick hugged her then ruffled her hair.

"And maybe we can have less of the language, Nick?" Martha added. "They're seven after all."

Nick shrugged helplessly, as Tilly disengaged and ran across the field to join the group. Holly thought that might be too much to ask. He was barely managing to keep a lid on it. Asking him to button his lip for the remainder of the trip might be a step too far.

Martha tossed them both a withering smile, locking eyes with Holly. "Please think about what I said."

Nick turned his gaze on her, and she ducked her eyes, picking a plaster out of the packet and unpeeling it with her fingers. "What did she mean?"

"Oh, nothing," Holly breezed, unravelling the plaster. It was a Marvel design, a cartoon likeness of Captain America. She tipped Nick's chin with her fingers, and slid it over his graze. "She really has got a good arm."

"You could have at least picked Thor." He touched his wound carefully and winced, flicking his curious gaze back to her. "What did she mean?"

"It's nothing. She was worried about me, that's all. Martha worries." She hoped he would lose the scent, but the way he was staring at her made it difficult to concentrate. "Why were you and Tilly arguing?"

Nick chuckled as if sensing her evasion of questioning. "She was teasing me about being Chloe's boyfriend...all dumb stuff." He glanced across the field, where Chloe was sitting under a tree, crying into Sock's fur. "I think we might have broken up, though."

"That's adorable," Holly laughed. "I'm sure it won't last long before you charm your way back into her good books."

Holly suddenly realised they were still sitting knee to knee, the first aid kit open beside them on the picnic bench. The trees swayed in the breeze, and it was peaceful, and she liked sitting alone with him with no kids distracting them. She was blushing, furiously hot under the collar, and quickly remembered, no matter what, Nick wasn't interested.

"So...why was Martha so worried?"

Holly snorted. "You aren't letting this go are you? Fine—she thinks I push myself too hard."

"Do you?"

"I don't know. Probably. Everyone tells me I do. My mum, Kit, Tess..."

Nick butted in. "You do seem to react...." He closed his mouth and chose his words carefully. "Strongly to things. I mean, you have a lot of rules and I know you hate making mistakes. And you do say no...a lot."

"No, I don't!"

They both laughed, and Holly leaned her elbow on the bench. "Okay...maybe. But you don't know what I'm capable of, Nick Jones. Who was it who vandalised your car?"

Nick made a face. "Your cousin."

Holly crumpled with laughter, leaning her chin on her fist, tilting to look up at him. "Right again."

Nick slapped the table, his eyes lighting up. "See? I do know some stuff. I should've guessed you weren't capable of actual damage to someone else's property. And for what it's worth...I'm sorry I let Davey speak to you like that."

Holly's heart raced. He was apologising? Had she broken him after all? "That's okay. I'm sorry I dumped all those marshmallows through your car window."

Nick scratched at his chin, his smile a little melancholic. "I have a thing about my car. It was my mum's and to me... it's freedom."

"You do wash it—a lot." She was tempted to lay her hand on his arm, it was right there, and she was itching to touch him. Make a mistake. But what if he pulled away? Her heart clenched tighter in her chest, and she curled her fingers around the table's edge. "I'm sorry about Kit."

He was staring at her lower lip, and muttered something under his breath. Heat crept up her neck and she was desperate to flee, feeling like a bug under a microscope. She had her hand on the bench, her fingers inches from his. Nick poked her first aid badge on her shoulder.

"Good job you were here," he said. "I might have died."

She laughed. "Death by frisbee. I hardly think so, but I do come in handy."

He prodded the badge by her pocket. "And what's this one for again...?"

"I told you! Self-defence."

Abruptly, she stood and nearly kicked the first aid kit off the bench. She was hot, her heart racing. "I better go. Campfire Joe will be here soon. It's getting dark."

She bolted, keen to be away when Nick jumped up and grabbed her around the waist. Holly laughed as he wrestled her to the cool grass, surprised and a little embarrassed. Holly screamed and kicked, his fingers finding her ribs. Paralysed, tears ran down her cheeks as he tickled her. "What the hell are you doing? I'm not a seven-year-old! " She laughed, wheezing as he pinned her shoulders.

"Come on, Truman! Defend yourself!"

Holly giggled uncontrollably as his blunt fingers poked her ribs, tickling her so hard she nearly wet herself. "Nick, stop!"

His face was inches from hers, their breath mingled, and she locked onto his blue eyes. Her heartbeat spiked, her pulse thudding in her ears "What good is a badge if you can't defend yourself when the time comes?"

Holly wriggled under him. "I wasn't prepared."

"There is no preparation for a sudden attack. Come on!"

An oof of breath left his mouth, rolling away as she kneed him in the stomach. Laughing, he rolled onto his back, and she followed, straddling his hips and pinning his shoulders. "There!"

Twilight crawled into the clearing, bathing the trees in an orange glow, and out here alone, she swore she could hear the beat of her blood thundering around her body. Breathless, she leaned to roll off him, but he caught her around the waist so she couldn't escape. "I think I won." She grinned, hair falling in her eyes. "Very effectively."

Nick cocked a brow. "Maybe I let you win?" he countered. "Maybe you are exactly where I want you?"

Holly went liquid hot, her breath hitching as she jumped off him; embarrassed and shaken, she'd let her guard drop.

He said nothing, only rolled to a sitting position. Holly dashed through the trees, her breathing rapid and shallow. What was happening here? She looked back and watched as he headed back to play with the kids over the field. Being close to him was too much. His presence, his stare, she was caught, drawn in, and she didn't want to be anywhere else.

Seventeen

Fatigued from chasing five kids around a field, Nick sloped to camp, with Jack on his shoulders and Chloe dragging behind with a grim pout on her lips. Wandering through the woods he spotted a golf buggy parked near their clearing, and he wondered if the infamous Campfire Joe had finally arrived. Nick was all too happy for another guy's company, especially if it earned him a break from the kids. Jack jumped clear and chased Chloe through the clearing.

Peering through the trees, he heard a guitar and a voice singing, and Nick snickered, recognising the old Beatles classic 'Yellow Submarine' and laughed as little voices joined in. Hands in pockets, he leaned against a tree, content for the older man to entertain them a while. Holly jogged by, with a box of bread rolls in her arms. Nick straightened and cleared his throat and for a second their eyes met. Heat crept into his cheeks and he glanced away. Something was seriously wrong with him. All he could think about was kissing that pout of hers. Holly grinned, ducking through the trees towards the sound of the music, and Nick tilted his head, watching her retreat, a little forlorn.

A hand slapped his shoulder and he jerked in fright. "Shit, Martha!"

"I could do with some help hanging up the kid's lanterns around the camp...if you're not too busy," the older woman joked, and Nick huffed and pushed away from the tree trunk with his foot.

"No rest for the wicked," he muttered and she cast him a wry grin.

"You're here to work, Nick," she chided.

"Into the ground."

Martha tossed him a frown, shooting him a frosty glare that reminded him he had France to look forward to. "I'm not busy," he added quickly.

He followed Martha through the trees, the bonfire already glowing, firey embers dancing up into the air on a fine breeze. Then his jaw dropped as his eyes drifted to the sound of the voice singing and the man strumming the guitar. The children and Holly sat crowded around him. Holly wore a dreamy, glazed expression on her face, her elbows propped on her knees as she listened.

Nick stopped, his shoes digging in mud. "Who the *hell* is that?"

Martha paused, her face creased and her watery eyes followed his gaze. Holly was sitting next to the hottest guy Nick had ever set eyes on. An athletic man with sun kissed blonde hair hanging around his face, with deeply tanned skin and deep green eyes. The guy was *stacked*, and on his knees rested a guitar, his long fingers strumming gently at the strings.

"Fuck."

"Nick, for god sake—language!" Martha gasped. "That's Campfire Joe."

"*That's* Campfire Joe! I thought he was...like eighty!"

"Um, more like twenty-two. He took over from his father and runs the camp." Martha tossed him an interested grin. "Is there a problem?"

Campfire Joe was singing to the kids. He had the voice of an angel, and Holly had a strange, hazy look on her face. Nick stuttered. "Uh...no."

Yes there was a problem. Campfire Joe was a *ten*. He was more than a ten. Built like an action hero, muscular, and toned, Joe's biceps were the size of turkeys, glazed and golden, while Nick's skin resembled cold, cooked chicken. He flung his eyes skyward. Why was Holly sitting so close to him? Did she like him? A wave of jealously caught him off guard, and he stared hard at the ground as Martha shoved the box of lanterns in his arms.

"Come on."

Nick groaned, eyes down as they walked around the campfire.

"Nick, this is Campfire Joe!" Holly beamed, and Nick grimaced inwardly, forced to a stop. Willing a neutral expression onto his face, Nick turned and smiled.

"Hey."

Campfire Joe smiled, and it was blindingly white. "Hey!" Placing the guitar on the ground, Joe rose and shook Nick's hand. Nick stared miserably at the paw-sized hand encompassing his. "I've been meaning to come to say hello. It's nice to see another edition to the Eagle club."

Without meeting his eyes, Nick grunted out a grudging. "Uh... I'm not in the club."

Holly jumped up, grinning as she took Joe's arm, raising her brows playfully. "Nick is here as punishment. He's in hell right now."

With the flames heating his skin and his hand firmly gripped in Joe's, Nick thought hell seemed about right. Joe looked disappointed but waved his hand. "Still, it's good to see the group expanding. And with this little crowd, Martha needs all the help she can get."

Nick ground his teeth. So, he was nice. Nick met his eyes and wished he hadn't, it was like looking in two green pools of light. He blinked, even he was pulled in by Joe. No wonder Holly looked enamoured. Shuffling backwards, Nick shoved his hand in his pocket, while clutching the box. Joe narrowed his eyes and pointed at Nick's forehead.

"You have an accident?"

His stomach plummeted, a hand slapping on the Marvel plaster still stuck on his forehead. "Oh..." He wanted to sink into the ground. "Um..."

"Nick had a little run-in with a frisbee," Holly teased, and both she and Joe laughed.

Campfire Joe smiled when he recovered. "Glad to meet you, Nick. You sing?"

"Uh, no." Nick croaked, both his ears going red hot. When would this end? Couldn't he slope off and lay in his tent? Suddenly he couldn't give a crap about France. Nick wanted home, a hot shower, and his bed; weirdly, he missed his dad.

"Too bad. Guess I'll have to sing louder for the two of us. What are those?"

"Lanterns." Nick pointed his chin at the box under his arm.

"You want a hand getting them hung and lit?"

"No, no...I'm good...you keep on..."

His voice trailed off when he spotted Holly's smirk, and his jaw clenched. "I better..."

He stalked into the woods, where Martha was hogging a step ladder, stringing the lanterns from tree to tree. Nick stretched and hung a few from the branches, taking his time placing the tea light candles inside. They made a pretty, brightly lit display when strung up. Nick found himself smiling at his handywork, lighting Tilly's lantern, her baby drag-on glowing from the inside. Distracted by Holly's laughter from the fire, Nick peeked around a trunk, his heart snapping as she gazed at the hulk-shaped intruder. She kept touching his forearm. Was Holly flirting? He wished Joe would fuck off and fall down a hole in the dark somewhere.

"He's engaged."

Nick's brows rose, not expecting Martha to be standing so closely behind him. "What's that? Who?"

Martha's eyes creased and she squeezed his shoulder. "Campfire Joe. He's engaged—if you were wondering."

Nick cleared his throat. "I...wasn't...I don't care...."

Martha pressed her lips in a thin smile. "It's okay. You've been watching her all day. I can tell."

"Tell what?" Nick snorted, his irritation rising, not with Martha, his ire directed at the gorgeous, blonde Viking sat way too close to Holly, who didn't seem to notice or mind.

"I can tell you like her. And I think you two would be good together."

"Ha! That's where you're wrong." Nick scratched his neck, blushing, trying to ignore the hope reigniting in his chest. "We don't get along. Or if we do, it doesn't last."

"Ah, but sometimes you can blend ingredients to make something special."

"Why are we using food analogies?"

"Uh, Nick. You might not see it, but I do. You balance one another."

"She also has rules," he said, "Like a *lot* of rules."

"Which *you* like to break. Sometimes opposites make an exciting combo...and I love her, so much. She does so much for those kids and everyone. It'd be nice to see her have fun, let loose and maybe break rules from time to time."

Nick said nothing, too afraid of this older woman's insight. He lit more lanterns sending bursts of colour through the dense woods.

"You know...she does like you."

Now it was his turn to choke, he twisted so hard he nearly fell into a tree. "Excuse me?"

Martha's wicked gleam was hard to miss, as she stood there, lighter in one hand, studying him for a reaction. "Has all that heavy metal left you a little hard of hearing?"

"You're joking...she doesn't...." Nick went hot all over, casting a shy glance at Holly, sat oblivious through the trees. "That's just not true."

"Oh I don't know. I've lost count of how often she's turned up at the clubhouse, moaning or frustrated by something you've done. She tries hard but can't ignore you, and you have a habit of catching her attention...almost like you want it."

"No, no!" Nick waved his hands and lowered his voice to a hiss, not that Holly was even looking, too busy eyeballing the god of fire and song. "I frustrate her because I piss her off."

"*Or* because you've been crazy about her since you were little?"

"I'm done with this conversation!" Nick whispered, the look in her weepy eyes really starting to grate on his nerves. He was hot and uncomfortable and fought the need to escape into the tent and put on the earbuds.

Later after dinner, he listened to Campfire Joe telling the kids stories. They sat glued to him, eyes bugging as he relayed the tale of the headless witch of Tilbury Wood. He clapped his hands at the right moment to earn a brief yelp of terror out of them, and Chloe darted from the blanket and huddled on Nick's lap. He squeezed her. "You know it's pretend, right?"

He was back in her good graces once more.

She shook her head, and Holly eased out of her position next to Joe, finding Nick's eyes across the fire. His chest flared, a tight ache spreading from his stomach upwards, and looking at her, he could hardly breathe. So he left. Shaky and wanting to be away from the flames, Nick found a mossy log, planting himself on its damp surface.

He whistled out a breath. Okay, this was getting out of hand. Where could this go? His friends.... He dreaded to imagine what they'd say if he confessed his crush. Footsteps crunched on leaves behind him, and startled, he jerked as Holly appeared out of the shadows.

"I wondered where you went," she said, apprehensive as she edged closer.

Nick shuffled aside, letting Holly share the log seat with him. "Maybe we should wrap up the scary stories for the night?" she suggested.

"Unless you want to have your tent invaded by children at two am," Nick said with a wink, nodding to his coffin. "I'd offer to share you mine, but it'd be a tight fit."

Holly blushed, dipping her chin, and a part of him wondered if anything Martha had said was true. Did she look at him that way? Even a tiny bit? Nick admitted he'd not exactly made it easy to like him. In the moonlight, she looked pretty, her curls falling around her shoulders.

Holly's knees drew up to her chest, and Nick dug around in his pocket for the whistle. He planted it in her lap, and she frowned. "Why are you giving it back?"

"Because I don't want it. You don't need to tone it down or change who you are." He sighed. "I was being a dick."

She fingered the whistle in her lap. "Thanks."

They sat in silence, the fire behind crackled, and embers danced on the breeze. Finally, she glanced at him over her shoulder, looking at him through thick dark lashes. "It belonged to James."

Nick folded his arms, huddling next to her, their shoulders touching. "I got that."

"He gave it to me before he left. To go back to his real father—James was an Eagle too."

Nick pressed his lips together, one half of him listening, the other half pressured not to say anything snarky or rude, his brain in a fog. "I remember him."

"He was great," Holly said with a weary smile. "We had him with us for five years, and he was my big brother. I mean..." She rolled her eyes. "I know he wasn't. People like to remind me he wasn't, and I should forget him...but...."

"He meant a lot to you," Nick answered, and her eyes twinkled with understanding, glossy and wet.

"He meant the world to me. He took me to my first Robin meeting. We were close, and I loved him like a brother, and when he decided to go home to his biological father it broke my heart. He gave me the whistle." She nodded to the shiny object in her lap. "I understood why he went. He was so hopeful and his father was ready. But being an Eagle was going to be a thing of the past. So he passed it to me and told me to make myself heard. To never stop being me."

Nick chuckled. "Well, you certainly do." Inwardly, he winced, mentally scolding himself, but when he glanced up, she wasn't scowling at him. Instead, she laughed, but her eyes grew ever filmier, and she sniffed.

"At first, we'd have weekly phone calls, and things were going okay. We missed him a lot. Then he started college, and we'd see him once a month; once he started driving, we hoped he'd come over more often. He got a girlfriend, and she was nice. He brought her over a few times." Holly choked and wiped at the corner of her eyes. "One day, he'd visited as I was about to graduate to Hawks. He wanted to come and watch, and for some reason, I was so bashful I didn't want him to come. I was fourteen then and full of anxiety, but he brushed it off and said he was meeting friends in London anyway."

The whole time Nick listened, for once, laser focussed on her. He couldn't remember a time in his life when they'd ever sat this close, where he could count the freckles on her nose. Why had he never talked to her? Why had he been so closed off? Swallowing, he narrowed his eyes, waiting as she continued.

Holly blinked skyward and caught a tear on her sleeve before it fell. "James met his friends in a pub. Something happened, and James got between two guys who were fighting, and one of them shoved him out of the way—he fell and hit his head, and it was over. This good person, who only ever wanted to help people—was gone. Mum never fostered again, she was broken. He left a giant hole that won't ever be filled."

Nick shuffled closer, his heart thudding as he lay his hand over hers on top of the whistle. Holly drew away, embarrassed, and wiped her eyes. Nick knew she was fragile, she was nervous and edgy. He was filled with an urgent, protective need to wrap his arms around her. But she'd probably run screaming. "So...maybe that's why you're so hard on yourself?"

Holly sniffed and straightened up, as if she'd come to her senses and realised who she was spilling her emotional secrets to. "Tess says I'm too hard on myself. But..." Her eyes were wet again, and her cheeks. "If I'd have let him come to the ceremony...he *wouldn't* have been in that pub. He'd still be here."

"Whoa! Holly—it's not your fault he died," Nick cried, his brow drawn, and she looked up at him doe-eyed. "Do *not* blame yourself."

"But it's true," she said. "He was proud and wanted to be there for me, and if I'd have let him...."

Nick suddenly saw her clear as the sun. Everything about her sparkled into luminosity, the strength of her need to be the best, her incessant rule-following, and her overwhelming need to fix broken things. The panic on the boat, blaming herself for Lea's asthma attack. She was living under the guise of a ghost, trying to save a person who was no longer there.

"Holly...." With a gulp, he took her hand and linked his long fingers through hers. She stared down at their joined hands as if she couldn't understand the gesture, but she didn't pull away this time. This was his moment to say something meaningful and smart, but his brain went woolly, and he was overwhelmed by how much he wanted her and how wildly inappropriate it was after what she'd just revealed. An emotional knot clogged his throat. Finally, he uttered out. "I didn't know James...not well. But I know he was a good person, like you. And he'd be so proud of you."

Whatever he said, because he couldn't think straight right now—he must have nailed it. She was leaning closer and looking at his bottom lip, hands linked. Nick could close the gap and kiss her, he thought he might go stir-crazy if he didn't. Instead, he said, "You're so good, Holly...so kind...and I've been such a dick to you."

"Nick..."

His breathing shallowed out as she edged nearer, and he could smell her hair. He dipped his chin and closed his eyes. "You're so good."

Holly's bottom lip brushed his, and he made a noise in his throat, overcome with heat. His mind raced, like a horse galloping to the finish line, and he was thinking ten steps ahead, wondering if there were any way both of them would fit in his coffin tent and if anyone would notice if he dragged her out of the way of prying eyes.

Of course, they'd notice, but would he even care right now? Their lips were barely touching, and he couldn't think in a coherent fashion. She had broken him in half, her breath tickling his skin.

"Help! Please someone help!"

Nick's eyes sprung open, and they stared at one another dumbfounded as a shrill, urgent voice intruded into their blissful bubble. Pulling apart, Nick blinked back to reality as Holly jumped to her feet. The strung-out voice belonged to Martha, who ran into the clearing, sweat beaded on her brow. "Help, please!"

"What is it?" Campfire Joe jumped up, tossing his guitar aside, and Holly crossed the clearing, with Nick following behind.

"It's Tilly!" Martha wailed, her watery eyes wide with terror. "I thought she'd gone to the bathroom by herself...but I've looked everywhere...and she's gone!"

Eighteen

Holly's feet turned to wood, like two logs wedged in the ground as she tried to move. Her tongue went sandpaper dry as her eyes whirled about the clearing. "What? How?"

"How long has she been missing?" Campfire Joe piped up beside her, his hand landing like a concrete slab on her shoulder. "Five minutes? Ten?"

"About ten," Martha answered, fluttery and breathing shallow. Her hands strayed to her sternum as if she could physically keep her heart beating straight out of her chest. Then she sagged and Holly caught her, making her sit on a log. "Oh...my god...."

"We'll split up," Joe said, kneeling in front of her, taking both of Martha's thin hands. "She won't have gone far."

Nick and Holly exchanged a look. This was Tilly Grey they were talking about, she could have crossed a road and river in the time she'd been gone. Holly's heart shrank and she went cold. She tried to blink, but it was slow and deliberate, panic shrouding her thoughts like a blanket. Joe grabbed his walkie and spoke into it with a mumble, and when he clicked off, he turned back to the group. "I'll have my assistant ride out here and sit with the kids while we look. She'll be here any minute. Why don't we split and look for her? Martha, you and I can head out to the meadow and back to the river?"

The river.

Holly washed cold, swaying on her feet. What if Tilly made it to the river, back to the boats? What if she fell in? Alone in the dark without anyone to hear her splashing or crying. Rigid, Holly allowed darkness to crawl in, and for a second, the world tilted. This was her fault, she should have been watching her more closely. They knew Tilly was a risk. A warm hand found hers, and her head snapped to see Nick thread his fingers through her own, and she swallowed a rock-sized ball of anxiety. "Come on," he said. "We'll find her."

Was it just moments ago she thought he would kiss her? Or was it the other way around? Holly remembered the un-deniable pull, an invisible force making her lean close, his blue eyes shining cerulean in the light of the fire, and she'd wanted to feel his mouth on hers. Shaking her head, she ran after Nick as they jogged into the woods, a flashlight in his hands. The thin beam of light danced in the dark, across the paths and dense woodland. In the distance, another golf buggy rumbled into the cleaning and Holly guessed Joe's girlfriend had arrived to watch the kids while Joe and Martha went back to the lake.

Following closely behind Nick, Holly panted, her hand still firmly locked with his. "Nick...you're going too fast."

He turned to her, his face white and jaw tight enough to crack a nut. "She could be anywhere, Holly. Jesus...that kid is a flight risk!"

She couldn't argue with him. They trekked further and further into the dark. Brambles scraped her bare legs, and she fought the prickles of fear tickling her palms. She willed away visions of Tilly laying somewhere unconscious, her thoughts rapidly firing from one gruesome outcome to the next. Then she envisioned James lying dead on a pub carpet, and her vision whited.

"Stop!" she begged. Nick threw the beam of light in her direction, both silent, breathing rapidly. "I can't..."

Nick took her shoulders, forcing her to look up at him. "Stop it right now, Holly!"

"Stop what? Stop being shit scared?"

"No, blaming yourself. I can literally hear you doing it. Tilly going missing is on all of us, not just you!"

His hands were warm, either side of her face, her breathing rightened, and the thunderous blood rushing in her ears dulled to a whisper. Nick brought his forehead to hers, and they paused a moment, breath mingled. His hands trembled, and she guessed he was as scared as her.

They spent the next few minutes screaming out for Tilly till their voices cracked. Holly aimed the beam of light ahead of her, darting it in and out of bushes, behind trees, and through brambles, praying she'd catch sight of a lock of hair or a flash of a red hoodie. And Tilly would jump out and boo at them; it had all been a game. But as the minutes ticked by, Holly sweated under her t-shirt. "How long has it been?" she said, chewing her lip raw. "It's got to be an hour...."

"Ten minutes," Nick answered, and she was floored. Time slowed to a crawl. Holly's phone went off in her hands, and she fumbled to answer it, her heart rocketing when she saw it was Martha.

"You've found her?"

"No," Martha's voice was wet and crackly. "No we can't find her."

Holly swayed, but clicked the phone shut. She swallowed back tears as Nick came closer. "Nothing."

Nick's features were taught and pinched. "Fuck, Holly. Where would she go?"

She blinked, her eyes growing wet. She imagined the phone call to Tilly's parents, her heart beat dropping with fear. She imagined the look on their faces when they got the news. Would they ever find her out here in the dark? Holly knew the longer she was missing, the less likely it was they would find her tonight. "Nick..."

"No, Holly. C'mon!" He grabbed her hand, pulling her against him, and she was in his arms, enveloped by his warmth and smell like he'd guessed her train of thought. His arms tightened around her. Listening to his heart thudding through his shirt, she quietened, like he was physically calming her down. "Don't spiral on me. Think...where would she go?"

"I don't know!" Holly fought waves of nausea, the same swelling, throat constriction she'd experienced on the row boat. The tips of her fingers went prickly, then numb, and she couldn't catch her breath, and the world coloured grey. Nick peered at her in the dark and abruptly took her face in his hands.

"Hey, Holly. Look at me." His voice seemed so far away, like she was trapped underground and couldn't find her way to the surface. The pads of his thumbs traced the contour of her cheekbones, the gentle touch slowly pulling her back to reality. What if they never found her? Tilly would forever be a horror story, a mystery, a little girl lost in the woods who vanished because the camp leaders weren't paying attention. She had been distracted. She thought of James's funeral, how they'd sat at the back in the echoey church and how she'd bit back tears, laced with guilt, knowing if she'd had made a different choice, the boy she grew up with might still be here.

"Holly...are you listening?"

"We aren't going to find her. It's my fault."

Her voice sounded muffled in her head, like she was underwater, and no matter how hard she kicked, more waves crashed in, engulfing her till she found she was gripping Nick's shirt. "Holly. Listen to me. None of this is your fault. Breathe."

Weakly, she nodded, sucking in air through her nose. He tilted her chin so he was looking into her eyes. "Just look at me and breathe."

Gasping, feeling returned to her arms and hands, and her heart's thud slowed. She focused on his dark lashes, framing the blue of his eyes, and drew in a breath at a time. She wiped her damp cheeks, Nick's palms warm against her skin. He gave her a crooked smile. "Are you with me?"

"Yes," she said, puffing out air. "I'm sorry."

"It's okay." He let his hands drop and Holly missed the contact. Adrenaline spiked under her skin and she was hot, and shivery at once.

Nick groaned. "That kid has been the bane of my life this trip," he said, though she knew he didn't mean it. He was fond of Tilly. "She's like a little puppy..."

He dropped her like she was on fire, but held her at shoulder distance. "Holly...shit that's it!"

"What?"

Nick grabbed the whistle around her neck, tugging her closer and then blew into it loud and shrill. Holly stared up at him, his chin over her head, wincing as he blew into the silver whistle over and over, his nostrils flaring till he ran out of breath.

Of course!

"Make yourself heard," he said, unwinding the whistle from her neck and letting the ear-splitting screech carry through the dark woodland trails.

Make yourself heard, Holly...

"Yes!" she cried, running ahead with the torch. She threw the beam around the trees. "Tilly! Tilly!" Holly added her voice to the whistle.

Nick blew in the whistle till he couldn't, his face white and drained. He tossed it back to her, and she carried on, heading deeper and deeper.

"Come on, Tilly!" Nick cried into the dark. "Come out!"

Holly thought of James as she blew into the whistle, her eyes pricking, and by the time another slow few minutes crawled by, tears streamed down her face. Silently, she begged for a flash of hope, a moment of relief, to not feel this rock wedged under her ribs. Nick took the whistle back and ran ahead. Holly sagged with exhaustion, letting her beam of light flick over a tall cedar tree. Then she blinked. A flash of red hair caught her eye, and seconds later, Tilly appeared, walking towards them, her face dirty and sweaty and carrying an armful of logs.

Nick dropped to his knees as she ran into his arms. He scooped her up and flung her upward in a hug. "Tilly dragon! Where the hell have you been?"

Tilly dropped her logs, tearfully wiping her snotty nose on his t-shirt. She was dirty and trembling. "I went to get more logs for the fire...but I got so lost."

Holly ran to them and threw her arms around the pair, laughing and crying in a state of near hysteria. "Tilly, we've been so worried!"

"Campfire Joe said he needed more logs, so I went for a walk...." Her voice trailed off, relief and realisation of what she'd done hitting home. She wiped at her eyes. "I couldn't find my way in the dark...but I heard the whistle."

"We found you," Nick said, ruffling her hair. He picked Tilly up in his arms and hugged her almost as if she belonged to him "Don't cry. We found you. And Campfire Joe can get his own fucking logs next time!"

"Nick!" Holly scolded him, but her face cracked in a crazy laugh of relief. She let her head fall on his shoulder. "Oh, thank god. Tilly...don't ever do that to us again!" Wrapping her arms around the little girl, Holly forced away sobs threatening to take over. "You did good, Tills. You found us!"

Holly broke away, hurriedly dialling Martha and giving her the news. Within a few minutes, Joe and Martha rumbled through the dirt paths on the golf buggy. "Go give Martha a hug. I think she may have died a thousand times since you've been gone," Holly whispered to Tilly, and the excitable girl scampered off to Martha, kneeling in the dirt waiting for her. Joe jumped out of the buggy.

"Good work you two," he said in admiration. "I can't imagine what would have happened if we hadn't found her."

Holly's heart seized, but any dark thoughts were forced away by the feel of Nick's hand squeezing hers. She stared up at him in the dark, sweaty, dirty and tired and she decided right them she was so going to kiss him when they were alone. Her heart sped, blood drained from her limbs and she knew whatever she felt, he sensed it. Joe eyed them both curiously, his smile twitched as he said, "I'm not sure there's room in the buggy for all of us...."

"It's fine—" Holly squeaked.

"—we'll walk," Nick said.

"Do you want me to circle back...?"

"We're good!" Nick eyeballed him with a dark look which could only mean get lost, and Joe nodded in understanding, jumping back on the buggy. The moment it rumbled out of the clearing, carrying Martha and Tilly, Nick threw her a look that shattered her mind. He stepped closer as she took a step back. Her spine hit the trunk of a tree, and he closed the gap, closer than he'd ever been to her, their faces inches apart.

This was a terrible plan. Was she going to do this? Kiss Nick Jones, the guy who wouldn't have given her time of day last week. Yet, here he was, pressing her against a tree and making her aware of just how much he noticed her.

Her chest rose and fell against his, and Nick's hands travelled to her nape. He brushed a soft kiss over her eyebrow, and her eyes fluttered closed. "Nick..."

"Are you okay?" he asked, brushing his lips over her cheekbone, and liquid heat pooled in her belly. Nervously her fingers found his elbows, and she realised she never wanted him to stop. Five minutes ago, she was full of bravado, wanting to jump him the second they were alone. Now they were in the dark, with nothing but the moon and the birds in the trees to witness this event. A *life-changing* event. Nick was going to kiss Holly. He brushed his lower lip over hers, and she jerked, going limp.

"Hmm," she managed to reply.

"I really want to kiss you, Hols," he said. Weakly, she nodded, her voice shattered, too afraid she'd say something to break the moment. She grabbed him by the collar and tugged him closer.

Holly gasped, her hands in his hair as he crashed her mouth against hers in a kiss that knocked all sense out of her head. He kissed her so urgently her glasses pressed into the bridge of her nose. She pulled away and yanked them off, holding them between her fingers. Nick's lips moved softly against hers, pushing any thought of dread straight out. It didn't belong here in this moment. As her heart fired rapidly, she breathed in every inch of him. Holly had been kissed before, but not like this, not like life itself depended on it like she'd die if she didn't kiss him again. Nick's hands greedily scoped her body, finding her backside and pulling her tight against him.

"You are driving me insane, Truman," he said against her mouth, running his tongue along her bottom lip, his hands trailing up her hips to her waistline. "Do you know that?"

Holly lost all sense of herself, dropped her glasses, and swept in his kiss as he angled her thigh to wrap around his waist like he wanted to pull her as close as he could, but it wouldn't ever be near enough. He took her hands and pinned them over her head against the tree. "Your tent or mine?"

Holly blinked, brought out of the moment and smiled against his mouth. "Uh, neither!"

"Oh," Nick sulked, pressing his hips into hers, and she couldn't believe it was her who provoked this reaction in him. Out of Nick Jones, her mortal enemy. "Really?"

Slipping her hands free, she fingered his shirt, biting her lip. "It's a little inappropriate—don't you think?"

His brows flew skyward, he was pink-cheeked, breathless. "Shower block?"

"Nick," she laughed, pressing her hands on his chest. "I'm not sleeping with you on a Robin trip. So don't ask me."

He leaned his arm on the tree over her head, gazing down at her with sleepy, hooded eyes burning up with lust. "I guess it would be a little inappropriate." He kissed her again, softly this time, and Holly melted right there, nearly telling him to forget what she said. "Besides, I do have to be good and make it through this trip. If Martha caught us...."

She giggled. "Why do you have to be good?"

"Oh." He waved his hand like he'd suddenly realised he'd let a bomb drop, but it was no big deal. "My trip to France...when this is over..." He scratched the back of his neck, his eyes roaming the woods as if he knew he'd been caught doing something wrong. "My dad promised me I could go if I got through this trip unscathed."

The revelation killed Holly's buoyant mood like a shock of cold water. She hadn't realised he'd been bribed to behave himself this week. Was that why he was making an effort with the kids? Was it just an act so he got to go to France? Had he really changed at all? Her lip trembled, and her thoughts must have betrayed her face because he pinched her chin and tilted her face up to his. "Stop that, busy brain."

She grinned. "Stop what?"

"Thinking. I can see you doing it. Your head went to work, but I want it here with me."

"It is here with you, *believe* me!"

He grinned wolfishly. "Prove it, Truman."

Maybe Nick hadn't changed, but she had—a little, and to prove it, she stood on tiptoe, her palm on his nape as she tugged him closer. She gave him a kiss he wouldn't forget, one to hopefully torture him through the night. Running her tongue along his and biting on his bottom lip, earned a noise of out him that she'd probably replay in her head a hundred times. With the forest wide and open around them, it seemed like they were the only two people in existence.

"That enough proof for you?"

"No," he said with a moan, gripping her backside harder. It only made her giggle. "Don't stop."

"I don't think I'm helping you."

"I'm passed help, Holly. I'm done, lost. You won. You broke me." He brushed back her hair, and she remembered Tess's challenge. He grinned, and it was adorable, and she wondered how she ever missed how even his teeth were, how his eyes creased, and how she never wanted to look at anyone else. She smiled back.

"Really? I won? I broke Nick Jones."

His brow furrowed, and she explained. "Tess and I had a stupid conversation. She bet I could get you to like me in the few days we had together. She called it the breaking Nick challenge. But I didn't expect this."

He ran his hand down her stomach, over her belly, and she shivered in delight. "You've done more than make me like you."

But it wasn't going to last. They couldn't stay in these woods forever. Holly wondered if this was the result of the relief of finding Tilly.

Just shut up. She scolded her inner voice and drew him in for another kiss. This was the guy she'd been living next door to for all these years, the same one who'd made her life a misery, the guy who mocked her, drew her as a nagging cartoon, and the guy who'd painted Wilbur. The same guy was now making it very obvious just how much he liked her.

He drew away, looking earnestly into her eyes. "Well, you've just given us a challenge, Truman."

She trailed kisses along his jaw and neck, and he moaned a strained laugh into her hair. "What's that?" she asked.

"The keep my hands off you for the rest of the trip challenge."

She stifled a laugh into his chest, then craned her neck to look up at him. "I said no sex. I didn't say we couldn't do this."

Nick rolled his eyes playfully. "But I don't want to distract you from the kids...you've got responsibilities, and I don't want to...."

She cut him off, pressing her lips to his and they both laughed. "Walk you back to your tent?"

"Hmm." She kissed him again, then again, and one more time that turned into another delirious ten minutes, until she forgot they were in the middle of dark woods and Campfire Joe would have to look for them eventually. So they walked back hand in hand to the campsite, and Holly reluctantly let her hand drop his, the loss overwhelming as their skin lost contact.

Nineteen

Holly woke grinning from ear to ear, so hard her jaw ached. Had she been smiling in her sleep? She rolled onto her back, hot and stuffy in her sleeping bag, and stared at the thin tent canopy flapping in the breeze above her.

I kissed Nick. She let out a squeal and then pressed her hands over her mouth. She hadn't just kissed him. It was more. Holly scolded herself. She hadn't much experience, she'd kissed a total of two people in her life. But it hadn't ever been that...

Hot. Oh boy. It didn't feel like a drunken fumble at one of Tess's parties. Closing her eyes, she remembered his hands on her backside, her thighs, and in her hair, and she squealed again. He'd wanted more, she'd wanted....

Abruptly, she sat and threw off the blanket, a thin sheen of sweat covering her body. Scrambling in her pack, she grabbed her phone.

She needed Tess. Holly rolled free of the confines of her sleeping bag and unzipped the tent, while her thumb pressed the phone into action. Stuffing her feet in trainers, she hoped no one else was up as she jogged through the clearing. She passed Nick's tent, and saw his massive feet sticking out the end, and had to look away before she burst out laughing. She wondered if he'd had a restless night like her.

She clutched her phone and headed away from the camp, surprised to feel the spit of rain on her skin. It practically fizzled. She was burning and fanned herself. When she got far away enough, she crouched behind a tree and thumbed Tess's number. She couldn't stop grinning. Crouching in a squat and drawing up her knees, Holly planted her bottom in damp leaves. The phone rang, and then Tess's bleary hello came at the other end.

"Are you awake?" Holly beamed.

"Uh, Hols. I am now." She could hear the rustle of Tess's bed covers, and Holly checked her watch. It was early, and the forest was waking up around her at nearly seven am. Something scurried in the bushes and birds darted overhead. "What's up?"

"Tess, Tess!" Holly could barely keep the shrillness out of her voice. "Something *insane* has happened."

Tess moved, grunting as she got comfy. Holly could hear the sound of pillows being shifted and thrown. "This better be good, Holly!"

"I kissed Nick!" She didn't wait for her friend's reply. "I really kissed him. Oh my god, Tess this is insanity!"

"Wait—what?"

Holly glanced over her shoulder to make sure she was still alone and not about to be jumped on by a seven-year-old. "I. Kissed. Nick Jones."

"When?" Tess clearly had just come alive, her voice brittle. "Were you drunk?"

"No," Holly laughed shakily. "I can't explain it."

"Yes you can. Explain. Now!"

Holly giggled into her palm. "I don't know." She gave a helpless shrug. "He's been so different here. *I've* been different here."

"Holly, you *hate* the guy."

"I don't hate him. I don't hate anyone!" She repeated Tess's own statement back to her, something she'd said when they were sitting on the football field before school ended. "I can't explain it. I really...really like him."

Admitting it out loud was cathartic, cleansing. She was giddy, blissed out, and drunk on hormones. This wasn't her, it wasn't the old, sensible Holly.

"But..." Tess stammered. "Okay..."

"It was *you* who said he was cute."

"And it was *you* who said you hated his guts. How have three nights changed that?"

Holly stared skyward, she knotted her fist. This wasn't the conversation she'd been expecting, and the tone of disapproval in Tess's voice made her skin crawl. "I mean...he hasn't changed," she admitted. "But, maybe I've been reading him all wrong? We've misunderstood one another."

"For eighteen years?"

Holly gritted her teeth. "I know...but..."

"Nick is everything you despise. I've lost count of the times you've told me that. I thought you liked my brother, anyway."

"Adam..." Holly blushed. She couldn't imagine Adam throwing her against a tree and kissing her the way Nick had. The memory made her belly flutter, and heat spread down her thighs. Biting her lip, she adjusted her sitting position, pressing her knees together, like she would burst if she didn't.

"Are you still there?"

"Huh? What? Yes!" Holly said, smiling to herself and tracing her fingers through the dirt.

"Oh my god. You are broken. Nick broke you, Holly!"

"Maybe."

"This was supposed to be the breaking Nick challenge, not the other way around."

"Yes, I'm aware of the irony."

"So…" Tess drawled, and she imagined her friend's conspiratorial grin on the other end of the phone. "What was the kiss like?"

Holly chewed the inside of her cheek, hot waves spreading up her chest. "It was…" she breathed. "It was…amazing."

"Oh, my god!"

"What the hell is happening?" Holly melted. "This isn't going to work is it? You said it yourself. We're two different. Besides…"

She didn't want to admit her worst fears aloud, maybe, this was all an act. A charade or a game he was playing to pass the time while he was bored. After all, he was going to France if he made it through this trip unscathed. But she thought of everything they'd shared, every fleeting look or moment between them the past few days. He wasn't the bad boy he pretended to be.

"He's going to France when this trip is done," Holly finally admitted. "So…maybe when he's back…"

"Wait, *Hols!* You aren't serious about a relationship with him?"

Holly drained, again, snarky disapproval was laced in Tess's voice, and she hated it. It made her want to defend him all the more. "I'm…I don't know.…"

"Tell me why the sudden one-eighty," Tess said. "Explain this madness."

Jaw clenched, Holly fought for something to say, hating being put on the spot. "He's amazing with the kids."

Tess scoffed. "Were you planning a family already?"

"No! But...he's great with them. It's like a whole different side to him—shines out. He's artistic and kind...and..." she trailed off, remembering the morning of Lea's asthma attack. "He's...."

"A vandal. He drinks. He stays out late with that loser Davey, not to mention those other friends of his who all look down their noses at us. He barely made it through his A levels...this isn't the guy you hoped for."

Holly hissed inwardly, as if her friend had slapped her down the phone. "I know he isn't what I planned for. My mum... said I should let my guard down. That it didn't hurt to make mistakes."

"And I'm all for you having a good time with some stranger you'll never see again," Tess agreed. "But I know you. If you do this, you'll fall hard. This wouldn't be a mistake. It would be a disaster! One you'd have to see at College and live next door to for the rest of your life."

Holly hated that Tess was fundamentally right. The consequences of having a fling with Nick Jones would be heart-breaking, and after that kiss, she wouldn't be able to forget him. He'd break her into bits, walk away, and then she'd have to live with it forever. How many run-ins had she had with Nick over the years? How many insults and fun were made at her expense?

"I'm sorry," Tess said, her voice flat. "I don't want to say this stuff to you. I want you to fall in love and have fun, more than anyone. But...this scares the hell out of me."

"What if he really has changed?" Holly's eyes pricked with tears. "What if all this time, we've just been reading each other all wrong?"

"Okay..." Tess sighed, resigned. "I want to believe he has. But I can guarantee he'll do something to grind your gears...something that'll piss you off, and that's the *real* Nick. If you can look past that, then go for it. Go at it like rabbits, god knows you deserve it! Remember his goal is to get to France."

Holly swallowed, an awful hollowed-out feeling spreading in her chest. She sniffed, nodded, and then remembered Tess couldn't see her. "Okay."

"When you get back Friday, you've got the party. Maybe you should come together?"

Ice washed her skin. The party. Nick wouldn't go, not with her. He'd have to admit he liked her, to his friends, and everyone in school. There was no way he'd been seen out with her. Holly stared down at her baggy t-shirt, her bare, dirty knees and socks, and trainers. She groaned, thinking of the girls Nick dated in school, all fashionable, pretty with expensive clothes and makeup. None of them owned a hoodie covered in Eagle patches.

"I'll see." Holly already knew it wouldn't work. She wasn't cool, or popular. She didn't fit into the crowd. Nick wouldn't be seen dead with her at a party, she didn't walk in the circles he moved in. At Tess's end, a door creaked open, and someone whispered a hurried goodbye. Tess groaned.

"Who's that at this hour?" Holly frowned. It couldn't be Tess's mother, she was in Italy.

"Ah..." Tess trailed off. "Oh, it's Kit."

"Kit? Why is Kit there?"

The line went oddly silent. "Tess?"

"Well, that's another story," Tess replied. "I better let Adam know she's gone."

"*What's* going on?"

"Um, I better go. Good luck—love you!"

The line went dead and Holly stared at her phone, dumbstruck. Kit and Adam were hanging out? Her brow furrowed as she wandered back to camp, her feet crunching on dry leaves. She ignored a pang of jealousy and laughed it off. She was more confused than anything. How long had she been trying to get Adam Brant to notice her? And Kit had managed in the space of a few days. Maybe Holly should've worn more kohl liner, checked shirts, and battered doc martins?

"Morning," a low voice said from behind her. Holly gasped, too lost in thought to have noticed Nick creeping up behind her. She spun straight into him, and he laughed sleepily, catching her in his arms. She settled there for a moment, fear sticking in her throat. In the morning, now he'd slept on it, did he feel differently? Did he still like her?

"Good morning," she said, and he answered her fears by kissing her right on her smile. Bashfully she sank to her heels, from her tiptoes.

Nick scratched his head, hair mussy, and stuck up at the back, he looked adorable. "The offer to share my tent still stands."

"Shush." She slapped his arm. "The kids are still asleep."

"We can be really quiet."

They kissed under the trees, bathed in the morning light, and Holly wished neither of them had to move. All the negativity of her conversation with Tess dissipated with every touch of his lips, every appreciative noise he made in his throat. He was holding the back of her head, fingers in her hair like he never wanted to let her escape. Finally, when he broke away, he said, "You're up early."

"I was talking to Tess."

Was it her imagination or did his expression darken? Holly knew it must be obvious why she'd gotten up early to talk to her best friend. This kind of thing didn't happen to her often, she wasn't the type to have romantic, passionate moments in a forest under the stars. Of course, she had to tell her best friend. She would've burst if not. Embarrassed, she rushed to fill the silence. "We were talking about the party on Friday."

Nick's brow furrowed, and now he looked distant, which sparked dread in her chest. "Oh, yeah. I'd forgotten about it."

Holly fingered his shirt, trying to look and sound casual. "So...you're coming?"

Nick cleared his throat, blinking, bleary-eyed as if reality had dawned and hit him in the chest. "Oh." Now he was trying to sound nonchalant. "I think Davey and a few of our friends were going together."

Holly's gut sank, and her throat thickened. *A few of our friends...*

She faked a smile. "Well I'll guess I'll see you there. I'll be in the kitchen on snack duty. You can always come and keep me company?"

Nick looked away, awkward, and Holly leaned and kissed his chin, bringing him back to her, to the sweet moments they'd shared only seconds ago. How quickly reality could hurtle through and ruin everything. "Or," she said, her heart thudding. "I mean...we could go together?"

She said it. It was out in the open, the offer lingering between them. He smiled but it didn't quite reach his eyes, and she'd gotten used to those eye crinkling, Nick grins the last few days.

"Uh...sure we could." He stared hard over her shoulder as if the right answer would suddenly spring to his lips. Holly's resolve only wilted.

He'll do something to piss you off...

"Or I could just see you there...?" She raced to fill the chasms. It hadn't been real. The moment they shared, the epic kiss was born out of relief of finding Tilly. She was only here to keep him amused; when they returned, it would be over. Suddenly she hated herself for being so open, too honest, everything she'd told him about James, how she blamed herself. No one knew that. Not even Tess knew the full extent of her grief and guilt, yet she'd spilled it out to Nick last night.

She'd been wrong. So wrong.

Nick stepped away, dropping her arms. "I'll see you there. Davey...you know how edgy he is, and I know a few of the guys he hangs around with—"

Won't like me...I'm not cool enough...I'm too boring...too square. Holly's heart deflated like a balloon.

"I get it." She hugged her waist with her arms. "It was a silly suggestion..."

He broke out of his daze, taking her shoulders and tugging her against him, and she floated to him like a boat on still water. Oh, god, she was in deep trouble. He took her face, grinned, and kissed her nose. "No, no. We'll hang out there. It's just— I'm enjoying it out here, Holly, with you and having you all to myself. It's our last full day here, and I want to enjoy it."

You mean where no one can see you...where your friends can't see you.

"I don't want to think about....reality just yet."

"What's wrong with reality?" she asked. "This is my reality."

Nick looked stumped for words, and she pulled out of his arms, her body rolling in a deep shudder. He still had her hand as she walked away, and she tossed him a weary smile as she let her fingers slip from his. "I better go..." She couldn't think of anything to say, keeping her eyes on the ground, knowing her emotions were rising and she'd likely cry if he kept staring at her with those puppy dog eyes.

"Holly..."

"I've....I'll see you later." She ran to her tent, tears clogging her throat, berating herself for being so stupid, for letting down her walls and him crawl into her heart.

The challenge was over. Nick won, and Holly was well and truly broken.

Twenty

Nick swiftly concluded he may have truly fucked this one up. He could actually pinpoint the moment where any ounce of belief Holly invested in him over the last few days evaporated like droplets in the air. How could something so good have gone south so fast?

Nick admitted he'd been caught in a lusty daze, swept up and lost in the kiss, enjoying himself more than he'd dreamed. She was a good kisser, he'd not expected things to get hot so fast, and she'd felt good right there in his arms. Then she mentioned Tess's party, and reality kicked in like a bulldozer, steamrolling over their blissful bubble.

Stalking back to his tent, he sulked, lying on his back and looking up at the dark blue canopy over his head while the early morning sun beat the top. He questioned why he'd pulled away, why the mention of home railroaded his thoughts.

Why couldn't he take her to a damn party? Why couldn't he prove this thing between them could work?

He exhaled and scrubbed his face.

It just couldn't. With a rock growing in his belly, he hated to imagine what his friends would say if they saw them together. Holly wasn't part of any crowds he knew of.

She stood alone, burning like the sun, blazing her own trail and had since the day he'd met her. That's what he should have drawn for her. A sun, burning bright, throwing light on everything it touched, helping others to grow and shine, pulling the good out of the earth. But it shone alone, untouchable, because it was too hot, and you'd die if you got too close. Nick wondered what the fuck was happening to him. He was thinking in prose.

He squirmed, envisioning what Davey would say, the roasting he'd receive.

And more importantly, how they'd treat her. Hadn't he hurt her enough over the years? He couldn't bear to see her the butt of any more jokes. Holly, no mates. Holly and her Robins—lifelong loser. Nick released his fists, his nails making marks in his palms.

"*You* are a dick," he whispered to himself. "You are the loser."

Avoiding the kids yawning and emerging from their tent, he ran for the shower, washed and dressed, and returned to the camp with damp hair. Holly spotted him heading for the fire and turned her back. Nick's jaw clenched. *Great one*, he thought. *You nailed it. It took less than ten minutes to make a girl you like hate you more than ever.*

Nick jerked as a speck of rain dripped down his neck and looked skyward where dark clouds drew closer. A breakfast of cereal from boxes was being served, and Nick ate slowly, thinking the milk had finally turned sour and he was looking forward to normality again. Holly crunched hers across the camp, making it clear she was avoiding him.

"So, it's our last full day here!" Martha gathered the kids around her feet, looking up at her expectantly. "And we've got lots planned."

Oh goodie. Nick wasn't sure he could stomach another day of crafts, bug hunts, or games in the field where he got attacked by seven-year-olds. He wanted to go home, have an hour-long shower and possibly spend some time alone, working off this crush on Holly. It was slowly eating its way under his skin. Glancing across the top of the kid's heads, he caught her looking at him, and when she quickly looked away, he cursed under his breath.

Martha explained the morning's events. They were going to set up in the field and do some big art with leaves, twigs, and branches. Nick sagged, boredom fully kicking in, but Chloe's fingers linked through his. She bumped his thigh with her elbow. "I'll be your partner."

He held her hand. "I was counting on it." He gave her a wink, and she beamed. Holly cleared her throat and pulled out some cardboard boxes from the supply tent, stalking through the woods ahead of the group. Chloe tugged his hand, and he followed her helplessly.

Holly threw down blankets and set out the art supplies. More rain dripped from the sky, but the group ploughed on undeterred. Nick stuck with Chloe, who was reluctant to let him leave her side, and the wind had turned chilly by lunchtime when they made sandwiches.

Holly hopped around the creations, taking photos, the breeze rustling her hair as she snapped what the kids had created in the grass. Chloe and Nick created a giant oak tree with twigs and stones that were supposed to resemble acorns. When Holly got to their piece, she threw Chloe a pretty smile, making his heart lurch. "This is great!" She grabbed Chloe in a hug. "You worked so hard."

Rain splattered Nick's head, and he shivered. "It was all Chloe's idea."

Holly flung him an acidic stare, *that* look back in her eyes, and in a clipped tone, she said, "Good of you to let her take the credit."

Nick's shoulders fell, and he swallowed back a retort, determined not to let the insults she expected come spewing out of his mouth. She was baiting him, waiting for him to slip up, and he wasn't going to bite. Irritated, he ignored her for the rest of the afternoon, even when she tossed some dangerous looks in his direction. He gritted his teeth and played nice, playing chase with the kids, even when rain threatened them off the field. He knew he'd hurt her about the stupid party.

Nick didn't want to face reality yet and knew if Holly were being truly honest, they weren't a good fit, and her friends might balk at the sight of them together. Dumping himself by a tree, he watched as Chloe and Tilly showed Holly some dance moves, and like a kid herself, she laughed and joined in, red-faced, unembarrassed, and free, not caring if he watched or what he thought.

Damn, he liked spending time with her. He'd enjoyed getting to know the real Holly Truman, and he was slowly becoming more enamoured with the silly cartwheels and dance moves she performed. Holly wasn't uptight. She was free. He was the one in the cage, one he'd locked and bolted himself.

Later, as the afternoon wore on and the sky grew dark with clouds, he chased after her when she dashed off to the toilet block. He didn't want this morning to be the last time he kissed her. "Holly," he called as she rounded the shower block. "Holly, wait."

At first, she pretended she couldn't hear, but her shoulders tensed when he called out a second time.

"What, Nick?"

"Why are you avoiding me?"

Holly shrugged, clapping her hands. "Just going back to what I do best."

Nick's face creased, crestfallen. "Last night....that wasn't nothing. I meant what I said. I do like you, Hols."

She puffed and held her hands in the air. "Not enough to be seen out with me in public, it seems."

Nick scoffed. "Are you serious? You're ruining our last day together because of a dumb party. I'm going, *you're* going. We'll hang out...."

Blinking back tears, she didn't appear to have heard what he'd said. Instead, she looked at him through wet, spiky lashes. "Why does it have to be our last day together?"

Stung, his jaw dropped, unaware he'd even said that. He shook his head as if to clear mental fog. "I don't know. It doesn't."

Holly shook her head, wiping her eyes on her hoodie sleeve. "No, you're right. I can't do things half-assed, Nick. Surely you know that much about me? I can't go back...if we go any further—I won't be able to go back. So we shouldn't start. We are too different and don't fit in each other's worlds."

He took a slow, deliberate step closer as if she were a baby deer requiring a careful approach until she held up her hands for him to stop. His feet sank in the grass. "I've really liked getting to know you. The real you. I'm not sure I can just stop. I don't want to forget this."

She wiped her nose, paced, and folded her arms. "Well, you'll have to. Your friends *don't* like me. My friends don't like you. I saw your face when I asked you to the party. You looked terrified. And even if we moved past it, we are too different. Admit it."

He cleared his throat, desperate to tell her he'd made a mistake, but she continued. "It's okay. I'm letting you off. Nothing really happened, and we can just go back to what we were. When the bus pulls into Willowdale tomorrow, it'll be over, you'll go to France, and I'll...." She looked skyward, wiping away a fat raindrop landing on her forehead. "I'll just be the same as I always was."

She choked out a laugh. "I mean...look at us. We're already fighting. We wouldn't last five minutes together."

Say something, take this back, fix this...

Nick couldn't find the words. Anything he said would be selfish. He wanted her right now because they were alone and they were free. He could be himself with her, laugh, let go and have fun. There was no image to uphold here, no reputation to maintain. So instead of fighting, grabbing her, and holding her like he wanted, he let her go inside and didn't follow.

He went back to camp and started to pack. Angrily he flung his clothes back into his pack. Fuck it, he wasn't staying another night, he didn't want to hurt her any more than he already had. He'd hitchhike the two-hour trip home if he had to. Grumbling, he pushed past Martha, nearly knocking her over with his bag.

"Nick, where are you going?" She clutched a phone to her chest and looked worried, but he ignored her and started across the field.

Nick fought a knot in his throat, wondering if he should say goodbye. Holly was stalking across the field when he ran straight into her. Her eyes went wild as she spotted his pack.

"You're *leaving?*"

"I'm not putting up with another hour of this shit," he snarled, and her face dropped. "You're right, Truman. I can't change, and I can't play pretend any longer—even if it means losing France."

Holly screwed up her face, folding her arms. "Well, it's good to know you're consistent!"

He laughed nastily as he walked backwards, holding out his arms. "No surprises with me, Holly. What you see is what you get, and I'm not playing babysitter anymore. These three days have been torture!"

Holly's eyes filled up, but inside, something snapped, and he thought this was better. It was better to leave now, unbroken and with her feelings as they were, intolerable hatred. "Guess you lost your dumb challenge."

They broke apart as the golf buggy sped across the field toward them, and Nick groaned inwardly, faced with the golden god and his sunny disposition, almost as irritating as

Holly's. The light was fading, the air whipping into a frenzy, and Campfire Joe looked ashen as he jumped off the cart.

"Are you going somewhere?" He cocked a massive bushy brow. Nick looked away.

"Home."

"That won't be possible, I'm afraid."

Nick tossed his glare skyward. "Am I locked in or something?"

Holly appeared by his side and nudged his shoulder to shut him up. "Is something wrong?"

Joe gave them a grim nod, waving his hand skyward. "I'm going to have to move you all into our office space inside," he explained. "There's a huge storm heading this way, it's already hit Willowdale, and half the roads are impassable."

Nick groaned. "What?"

"I'm sorry," Joe said. "It's a high-impact red warning. It's all over the news. You aren't going anywhere."

Holly followed the buggy back to the woods, Nick lagging behind with his pack tossed over his shoulder. Inside her chest her heart was heavy, like a slab of concrete. She thought she might sink if she jumped in a lake right now, weighted and miserable.

He makes you miserable. This is better.

With a beep, the buggy pulled up and Joe jumped off, to find Martha grim-faced. She was already holding her phone. "I've just had several worried parents on the phone. Is it true?"

Joe nodded his blonde head. "Afraid so. It's a storm coming off the coast from Spain, and unfortunately, its caused massive flash flooding inland. We'll have to move all the kids indoors. It'll be fine if you're inside....only...." Joe cast his eyes around the group. "There's not much room. Come on, we better pack up fast."

Holly faced several worried expressions, little voices demanding her attention and for the first time on this trip she sensed her patience wearing thin. Bryony sobbed and wanted to go home, Tilly, unhelpfully, up a tree, refused to behave, and Chloe was whining she'd lost all her special pebbles to take home. Nick rallied them, coaxing Tilly out of her tree and helping Chloe round up all her belongings.

Holly's heart fluttered with real panic, she imagined all the parents at home worrying about their babies, the responsibility of caring for them weighing heavy on her shoulders. Sarah followed her around camp as she tried to pack up, yanking tent pegs from the ground harder than she needed to. The first spots of rain pelted their hair. "Holly...can I call my mum? I want to go home."

"Sarah, its fine." She took the little girl's shoulders and knelt in front of her. "We're going to have a different adventure tonight. We're going to stay in Campfire Joe's office and be nice and cosy in there."

Sarah sniffed and a tear rolled down her cheek. "Please, can't my daddy come and get me?"

"Sarah—"

"Hey, it's fine!" Nick picked her up and tossed her in the air with a grin on his face. "It's only a bit of rain, nothing to panic over. We're going to have fun!"

Holly tossed him grateful look but he glanced away, his gallantry had nothing to do with her. Nick was busy on his knees, chatting with the kids, keeping them occupied as he grabbed up tent pegs and bundled up ground sheets in his arms.

Sheets of rain fell, splattering the leaves and the kids ran around squealing in delight, but Martha threw her a anxious look. "Leave the rest of the tents. We'll have to hope for the best. Let's just get all the non-waterproof gear inside."

Screaming, the children ran after Joe's buggy as it beeped across the field, the lights piercing the grey mist. Holly looked over her shoulder, only her tent and Nick's left in the small camp. The fire pit filled with water and quickly turned to a thick, black tar. Holding a jacket over her head, Holly ran behind Nick, chasing across the field as rain pelted from above. Both breathing hard, they reached Joe's small office cabin and both shared a look of horror.

He hadn't lied about the size. It was tiny.

"Shit," Nick grunted as the kids quickly filled all the remaining space. Inside, the cabin was stuffy, and the windows steamed with condensation. A small coffee machine hummed in the corner and a sink was filled with dirty mugs and plates. Joe pulled back his desk and chair, throwing boxes against the wall as the kids lay out their camp rolls and bedding. There was no room for inflated mattresses. Holly eyed a heavy filing cabinet as Joe pulled off stacks of old paperwork from the top.

"This is grim," Nick whispered in her ear, and she shivered, not expecting him to be standing so close. But there was nowhere else to go. Nowhere else to stand.

"I don't know what to suggest," Holly said, looking about her for available space. There was room for one more on the floor with Martha. Joe gestured to the entrance hall, a dark cobwebby space right in front of the vented door.

"Nick could squeeze in there. He'll just about fit."

By the look on Nick's face, she guessed he'd rather take his chances in his coffin tent. Joe smiled grimly.

"It'll be cosy in here. This is the best I can offer, and you can use the phone to call anyone. I would advise parents to stay away tonight, it's too risky. It should be over by two in the morning."

Martha vanished with her mobile clutched to her chest, and Holly was left to stare about their grim accommodation in horror. A giant spindly spider weaved its way acoss the ceiling and she shuddered. The rain bashed the corrugated tin roof, and Holly threw open a few windows allowing cool air to circulate quickly. The kids didn't seem phased by all the upheaval. To them, it was yet another adventure. Wind hit the thin walls, howling and rattling the glass windows. The lights buzzed on and off as the weather worsened, and the kids laughed hysterically.

"At least they don't seem upset," she said, as Nick unrolled his sleeping bag in the doorway. She eyed the space and grimaced. This was going to be an uncomfortable night. He was well over six foot and wouldn't fit. "Look...maybe I should take the doorway."

Nick chased a hand through his hair, giving her a dark glare from his walk space. "I'll manage." He looked away, whatever civility between them truly over. Holly thought maybe it was better, though her mind raced when she thought of him pressed against her in the dark and the kiss they'd shared.

Why did it have to be over? Why did they have to be so different?

Martha barged through the door behind him, and it bounced off his shoulder. Grumbling he moved out of the way so she could squeeze through. Martha didn't seem to notice or care, as she carefully stepped over make shift camp beds. "I've had several very nervous parents on the phone. Some are desperate to come tonight but I've warned them off. This is such a disaster, Holly!"

Holly put a warm hand on her shoulder. "We'll manage!" she said. "Look—they think this is an adventure. We're undercover, warm, dry, and have light and food. First thing, we'll get packed up, and they can come to collect them."

Grimly, Martha nodded in agreement, determined to keep a neutral expression on her face as she headed for her tiny bit of floor space.

The electricity didn't last long. An hour after everyone ate some hastily made sandwiches, the light sputtered and plunged into darkness. Martha grabbed the camping lights and spread them around the room, and the kids cuddled and told stories. Holly sat with her back against the filing cabinet, knees drawn to her chest, now and then catching glimpses of Nick in his doorway. His back was against the wall, ear buds in and his eyes closed like he was napping. When it got late, Martha instructed the kids to sleep, and Holly bundled a pillow under her head, the carpet scratchy and dirty under her hands. The hard floor was cold, like sleeping on a wooden block.

Trying to doze, Holly picked at her nails, trying to guess the time. Lights blazed through the window, and several kids sat up in the dark. Holly rubbed her eyes. "Is that a car?"

After a few moments, there was a loud knock on the door, and Nick had to scramble to his feet to open it, taking all his bedclothes with him. Outside in the rain was Mr. Grey, Tilly's father, and behind him was a large minibus filled with anxious parents. Rain dripped off his jacket. "I'm sorry—we couldn't wait!"

Tilly and Jack whooped a high pitch squeal of delight and ran for their father, who scooped them up in his arms. Martha met him at the door. "How did you get through?"

"I took the long way. I'm sorry, I know you warned us not to come, but the weather has been so dreadful in Willowdale..."

"It's okay!" Martha smiled. "I'm just glad you're all here in one piece."

Mr. Grey settled Tilly at his feet. "We've got room to take the kids off your hands. I've got a bus full of worried parents."

Holly and Nick exchanged a worried look, simultaneously guessing their parents weren't on the bus. Martha had made the calls, and Holly knew her mother would trust her to be safe.

Martha let out a sigh of relief. "That would be wonderful. We just want them out of this shed."

Mr. Grey peered around her, spotting Holly and Nick standing in the dark. "I'm sorry—I don't think they'll be room for more of you."

"We're fine!" Holly insisted, glad the burden was off her shoulders. Jaw clenched, Nick nodded in agreement.

"We'll manage," he said.

It looked like the three of them were staying put, but inside she melted with relief, glad the kids didn't need to be in this squalor another second.

It took ten minutes of commotion, but eventually Holly and Martha waved the bus off, freezing as rain pelted their skin. Alone in the dingy office, Nick dragged his sleeping bag into the middle of the room and turned over, fixing his earbuds back in place. Holly clambered back to her bed, reluctant to lay back down. She stared at his shoulders and wondered if he could sense the heat of her gaze on him. She wished he would turn over and talk to her, she hated the knotty sensation in her stomach.

Holly's shoulders tightened as the wind battered the walls, the roof creaking and moaning. When it got late, Martha fell asleep, and Holly struggled to get comfy. She was cold, stiff and getting a headache. Her neck throbbed. She tossed and turned for hours while the rain pounded the roof.

A shuffling noise made her blink awake, not that she thought she'd slept, and she craned her neck, spotting Nick rising out of his bag. He grabbed up his pillow and duvet, and she sat up. Martha was snoring gently, deeply asleep.

"Nick," she hissed in a whisper. "Where are you going?"

In the dark, he threw her a scathing stare. "I can't sleep another second in here. It's too hot, it stinks, and I...."

Holly stared at him wide-eyed with panic. "Where—"

"I'm going back to the tent. I'd rather take my chances out there than in here."

"You can't. It probably won't even be there!"

Nick rolled his eyes, huffing as he stuffed on his shoes. "I'm prepared to risk it. Besides, the weather is dying down."

Holly listened to the wail of wind hitting the thin glass. "You're crazy! You'll end up blown away in a field."

"I can't stay in here."

They locked eyes, and she guessed he meant something more. Nick swallowed, miserable, as he turned to leave.

"Wait!" Holly called and he stopped. "If you're so set on doing this then take my tent. Its bigger, sturdier than yours, and the bed is all set up. But I *really* wish you'd stay in here."

Nodding, he mumbled a grudging thanks, his eyes shining in the dark as he opened the door with a soft creak.

"Be careful," she called after him, but he closed the door.

Holly lay back down, staring at the ceiling, chewing the inside of her mouth. Her mind trailed back to the woods, their shared moments, and how they both wanted more. She questioned Tess's warning that no matter what, she couldn't settle for a fling. Her heart was fragile and vulnerable, and she liked him more than ever. Everything would be over once they got back to reality. The knot of worry strangled her insides. He thought she felt so little for him, and she hated it.

A long hour passed, and Holly rolled and turned, hot and worried about him alone.

Make a mistake. Her mother's words haunted her. Somehow, she didn't think her mother meant she should go creeping into a boy's tent in the middle of the night. Holly looked about anxiously, Martha was deeply asleep. It wouldn't hurt if she just checked on him to make sure he was okay, and he'd not been swept away in a gust of wind.

Carefully she peeled out of her sleeping bag, her back creaking as she slowly got to her feet, narrowly missing bumping her elbow on the filing cabinet. She bundled up her pillow in her arms and stepped around Martha.

It was so hot and clammy in here, she longed to feel the cool air on her skin. As she creaked open the door, she was splattered with rain.

Holly stared into the dark, took a breath, and closed the door behind her. She raced across the field, her trainers sinking into boggy grass as she ran.

Holly was probably about to make the biggest mistake of her life.

Twenty-One

Nick dashed across the dark, open field, rain soaking through his clothes in seconds. Holding the pillow over his head was useless as it went limp with rainwater. His feet hit the slippery bark of the woodland trails; moments later, he was in the camp. Looking about, he gasped in horror. His tent was up a tree, the flimsy poles blown away, and the blue material tangled in branches.

"Shit," he grumbled, glad Holly gallantly offered him her tent for the night. As he unzipped it and crawled in, he thought maybe he'd made a huge mistake. The wind rocked the flimsy walls and the ropes pinged. He hoped Holly nailed this thing down tight, but he guessed she had. Holly didn't do things half-arsed. She said so herself.

Nick stripped off his wet clothes and bundled them in a corner. It smelled like Holly in here, heady, floral, whatever the intoxicating smell was on her hair. Nick slipped into his sleeping bag, in his boxer shorts, not in the least bit cold. In the cabin, the heat engulfed him, like boiling alive. A clawing, irritating sensation kept him from sleeping, with the cold air from the vent at his back and the hardwood floor under his body.

Even with the wind howling, this was better.

And he wasn't going to spend another second thinking about her. Not one.

Groaning, he grew hard under the covers and rolled on his stomach, it was difficult not to imagine her, surrounded by her scent, hard not to relive those moments last night and just how much more he'd wanted.

But she was right. What was the point in starting something neither could finish?

He lay there for an hour, drifting in and out of sleep, too uptight and irritated to fully go under. Every time he dozed, the tent would rattle so hard he thought it might lift off the ground, the rain was deafening. Whenever he opened his eyes, he thought of her, and her face when he confronted her by the shower block. She was so used to being hurt by him, she expected nothing less.

Nick wanted to be better. So what if she was different? If his friends didn't like it? He liked her. She was funny, kind, and sexy. Words he never imagined he'd say about Holly Truman. What would Davey think if he confessed the girl he couldn't stop thinking about was Holly the square?

"I don't fucking care," he said aloud, rubbing his eyes, surprising himself. He sat up, hot and clammy. He should just march back over there now and tell her how he felt.

Friends didn't matter did they? Not bad friends, like the ones he had back in Willowdale. They didn't matter if he got to kiss Holly every day and see the dimple in her chin deepen when she grinned. He could get to be the one to make her smile. He wanted to be the one to make her laugh. He didn't want to make her cry or see that sad look in her eyes again.

Nick didn't want to be the cause of any more pain.

"You are an idiot," he said to himself, unzipping the bag. He was going back and flicked on the camping light.

He tussled around in the tent, finding his shoes, tossing some of Holly's belonging aside, some craft supplies she'd left behind. He grabbed his shoes but jerked as behind him, the tent unzipped.

"Nick? Are you awake?" Holly ducked to her knees, his camp light casting a dim glow in the tent. Nick scrambled around in the dark. She spotted him dive into his sleeping bag in his boxers, probably too hot to sleep. The rain rocked the tent as she eased inside and zipped it tight.

"Holly! What are you doing here?"

She bit her lip, crawling in on her knees, dripping water over the ground sheet. She sat back on her haunches, incredibly aware of what she'd done.

This was a mistake. Her skin burned. "I was worried about you."

His lip lifted in a smirk. "You were?"

"Of course! You're out here alone in this weather...."

"What happened to avoiding one another until this trip was over?" His question startled her into silence, and she sat on her knees, slowly stripping off her coat, followed by her hoodie. "Whoa! What are you doing?"

"I'm soaked!" She gestured to her clothes and chucked them in a pile with his. "Is it a problem?"

"No...I mean...whatever..." He averted his eyes as she knelt and slipped her tracksuit bottoms down her thighs and wiggled out of them. Her heart quickened, cheeks rosy pink, sensing the humidity rising in the tent. She sat opposite in nothing but a damp shirt, drawing her legs up to her chest.

"Are you okay?"

"I'm fine." Nick pinched the bridge of his nose, staring at the ceiling, their clothes, literally anywhere but at her. "Did you bring a sleeping bag?"

"Uh, no. I have a pillow, but—" It was ringing wet.

"You shouldn't have come out here."

"Nick...I didn't want to leave things the way they were. When do we get to be alone? Really?"

"So you thought chasing me out into a storm was the best plan?"

"I didn't think it through."

After several beats of silence, she glanced up, and his smirk was back, creasing his eyes in the way that made him adorable, like she'd never stop kissing him if she started.

"It's actually...well..." Nick scratched at his jaw, grinning shyly. "It's kind of romantic."

"Don't get used to it!"

"I won't. So, what did you want to talk about?"

Balling her fists, she looked skyward, not sure what to say, words stuck in her throat. Taking a long gulp of air, she finally looked at him, and he seemed pensive, waiting for her to speak.

"I guess. I'm sorry," she choked out. "Not just for today. But for...everything I've ever said or done to make you think I'm this unapproachable, uptight bitch. The Eagle's motto is literally to treat everyone with kindness and respect, no matter who they are, and to nurture and bring out the good in people. I've tried to stick to that since James died. But for some reason, I've treated you badly."

He went to interrupt, but she held up her hand, shaking and watery-eyed she needed to get this out. "*You* aren't blameless. But I'm sorry if I've ever given you the impression you aren't good enough or intelligent or your lifestyle is wrong...just because it's different from mine. These few days, I've seen this whole other side of you. And you are good, Nick. You're a *good* person. And I'm sorry if I made you feel like you're not."

Rain thundered against the tent canopy, loud enough it nearly drowned out her voice. She shuddered, hugging her knees tightly. Nick unzipped his bag. "Holly."

The way he said her name made her shiver, she realised then she never wanted to stop hearing him say it. But tomorrow it would be over, and they'd return to what they were. A tear escaped under her lashes.

"Holly, come here."

She shook her head. "No, I can't."

"Come here, please." He held out his hands. "You can't say stuff like that and expect me not to want to hug you."

Weak-limbed, she crawled into his bag and snuggled down beside him, stretching out along his long limbs. Her toes touched his. Nick leaned on his elbow, stuffing the pillow under her head and then zipped up the bag around them. It was a snug fit, and she was pressed against his bare chest.

"You're right," he said, his voice rumbling right next to her temple, and she glanced up through her lashes. Propped on his elbow, he gazed down at her, and brushed a curl off her glasses. "I'm not blameless. I've been such a close-minded idiot. I've been awful to you, from day one. I've given you such a hard time all because you dare to be you."

Holly ran her fingertip over his snake tattoo, loving how it intricately coiled around his collarbone. "Being me isn't exactly a turn on though, is it?"

Nick cupped her face, his eyes earnest. "Are you kidding me? You heard me the other night didn't you? I'm completely turned on by you. I've loved spending this time with you. I know how hard you work, how you push yourself and now I know why. Do you remember when we first met?"

Holly scowled at the memory of Wilbur's violation. "Maybe that isn't the best thing to bring up?"

He chuckled against her hair. "I know. But I have a different memory. I remember this little girl walking in on the first day of school. She had a cleaned pressed uniform and a red ribbon in her hair with curly pigtails, and you were holding this perfect—pristine toy bear."

Holly, rolled her eyes, embarrassed, but he pinched her chin. "You. Were perfect. That's what I thought. I thought you looked like a doll, delicate and fragile and *perfect*."

"Right, little miss perfect!"

"No!" Nick insisted. "*Pretty*. I wanted to get to know you then and when you told me no, it sparked something in me. I remember you said something snarky, and I felt dumb. Maybe it was rejection?"

"So you stole Wilbur and painted him?"

Nick laughed into his palm, his chest moving against her head. She couldn't fight the giggle working its way up her throat. After a short beat he said. "I'm sorry. I can't explain why I did that. But I'm sorry."

Holly craned her neck, shifting to get comfortable. "He washed up okay." She grinned. "So you're telling me this feud we've had is because I rejected you when we were five? Way to hold a grudge, Nick."

"Oh, I'm a champion grudge holder. Just ask my dad."

"But you forgive me now?" She was coiling her finger along the snake and she knew it was distracting him by the way his skin was exploding into goosebumps.

"There's nothing to forgive. I'm sorry, for everything." He cleared his throat as she trailed her fingers lower down his chest. "I'm sorry you feel you have to apologise for being you. I like you, Holly. A lot."

"I'm getting that." She let her finger slip lower till it brushed the waist band of his boxers and the quick movement earned a helpless yelp out of him. He took her hand, brought it back to the safe zone, kissed her palm, and tossed her a look that made her melt into the pillow.

"Unless you plan on doing something down there, don't tease me," he warned. "Because I'm seriously turned on right now."

"Okay." She wiggled against him, getting comfy and he groaned. "I'm sorry."

"You aren't a bit sorry, are you?" His hand found her waist, settling nicely on her hip, and she liked it there, itched for him to inch a little higher, squirming under him, till his fingers brushed her ribs. "But," he said, kissing her temple, and playing with the edge of her t-shirt. "You could always take this off? It's pretty damp."

They laughed at his obvious attempt to get her naked, though he wasn't serious, not expecting her to actually do it. The suggestion made her flood with liquid heat, her heart racing as she shifted to give him the access he was desperate for. No one had ever made her this brazen, this free. She wanted to be close to him, to feel his skin brush hers. It was intimate and nice, and she realised he knew more about her than anyone. He knew how she felt about James, the guilt she harboured. She'd been naked with him, just not in the physical sense. She wanted him to see her.

He tugged her t-shirt over her head, and his eyes darkened when he realised she was braless and bare against him. An explosion of nerves danced in her belly, as his eyes landed on her breasts, but didn't dare touch her, just the looking was hot enough. "I wasn't expecting..."

Holly pressed herself against him, her skin breaking out into goose bumps. He was so warm it was delicious after shivering in the rain. "I can surprise you."

She held his bicep, running her fingers up his arm till it stopped at the Gaelic tattoo on his neck. "I love this one." Then she stroked the snake tattoo. "And this one."

"Would you like one?" he said, smiling. "I do recall you asking me to *do* you sometime?"

Holly giggled, recalling how humiliated she'd been. "I didn't think I was the type."

Nick scoffed, keeping his eyes firmly on hers; even though every naked inch of her was pressed against him, she wondered at his self-control. "There is no type. It's art. It's for everyone."

Holly smiled at the beginning of an idea. Holding the shirt to her chest, she rolled out of the bag in her underwear and dived for a damp cardboard box in the corner of the tent. Nick watched with interest, his eyes on her backside as she fumbled in the box and grabbed a black marker pen. She hurried back to the unzipped bag, shivering and handed him the pen. "Go on then."

Nicks brows rose almost to his hairline. "What?"

"Draw on me. Design me something."

Nick sat up, hovering above her as he moved the bag aside for more room. Holly laughed, holding her shirt over her chest, still a little nervous to be completely naked in front of him. Snuggling under the bag was fine, but now he could see her, even if the camp light was dim. With a wicked grin, he unclicked the lid of the pen. "Well...where should I draw it?"

Holly shivered, crossing her bare legs at the knee so one foot dangled near his shoulder. "You pick." She waited for him to shift, his eyes hungrily roaming up and down her body, but then she sat up on her elbows and threw him a playful glare. "I warn you, Nick Jones—make it better than a bee with glasses!"

Nick laughed and took her ankle in his hands. "I can do better than a bee this time." He uncurled her knees so he had her ankle in his palms, running the pads of his fingers over her feverish skin, her painted red toes glinted in the light of the tent. He found her ankle bone, and Holly squealed as the pen hit her skin, the ink cool and drying quickly. When he was done, he stroked it gently.

"Can I look?"

Nick made a face, the tone of his voice husky and teasing. "I'm not sure it's right. I don't feel like it's the right spot."

"Oh?"

"I'm going to try again." Holly shivered in delight as he ran his hand up her bare calf, tickling her behind the knee, till he found a sensitive spot on the inside of her thigh. "How about here?"

Holly went rigid, taught with tension, and she could barely form a reply before the lid was off. Nick scrawled something on her skin, his fingers careful as he lowered his head and kissed over the top once the ink dried. His breath on her thigh sent bolts of electricity up her spine. She was languid, numb, and probably couldn't speak even if she wanted to. "Is that a better place?"

Nick ran his hand over her thigh. "No."

"Oh...okay."

He drew something on the top of her left thigh, and she burst out laughing, but it lodged in her throat the second his lips touched her skin, and her pulse raced frantically. Leaning over her, his gaze heated as he dipped and moved the shirt out of the way and her belly sucked in as he trailed the tip of the pen over her navel, quickly followed by his mouth. "Nick..." she choked out and he lifted his head.

"Shall I stop?" he asked, his fingers on her hips.

Delirious, she met his gaze, unsure why she'd stopped him, only she was burning, her skin practically sizzling, teetering on the brink of it being too much. "No," she whispered, her voice a hushed breath, as she flung away the shirt, completely naked in front of him. "No, don't stop."

He sat above her, eyes shining with a smile, and pushed a strand of hair out of her eyes. Feeling the heat of his gaze on her body, she coiled inward and lost confidence, automatically cradling her arms over her chest, but he stopped her. "You don't have to cover up," he said. "You're perfect."

Holly wiped a tear from the corner of her eye, catching it before it rolled down her cheek onto the pillow, unsure why she was crying and suddenly so emotional. Nick dipped his head and drew on her ribs, which brought her out of her daze and made her laugh. "Haven't you got it yet?"

"Nope." Nick wiggled his brows. "I could be here all night."

He took her arm, extended it, and trailed something all along the underside, then ran his lips over the dry ink, kissing his way down to her pulse point on her wrist. Then he doodled in her palm before administering the same attention to the other arm. Mischievously, he winked, leaning on his hands above her as he traced the pen's nib over her collarbone, followed by his mouth, scorching fire in his wake as he trailed his lips up her neck, reaching her chin.

"No more," she begged when they were face to face. She cupped his cheekbones with her palms and brought her mouth to his in an urgent kiss.

Inch by inch, he lowered his body onto hers till she was flattened, limp and alight at the same time. He kissed every worry or fear out of her head, his hands moving under her, lifting her hips to meet his, angling her thigh, so it wrapped around his waist, their underwear the final barrier. Nick's skin burned against hers, she felt how much he needed her, and she ached, wishing she could give it to him.

But they didn't have protection. Half of Holly's mind was lost, she could just tell him yes, right now, she'd do it, and god she wanted to. But it was him who pulled away, their foreheads touching as he whispered. "This is torture. You're killing me, Holly."

"We could..." Was that her voice? Husky and deep, not her own? He smiled against her mouth and shook his head.

"Thanks but....we can't." He kissed her again and growled as though he were enjoying this self-inflicted torture. "I can wait."

He lay beside her, a thin sheen on sweat on his collarbone. "Though...."

"Though, what?" She rolled into him, face to face, they shared breath and heat. He grabbed the bag and zipped it up around her, dancing his hand down her belly, making her insides flutter. "You want to look at what I drew?"

Holly blinked, half dazed with lust, held up her arm, a grin spreading across her face. "It's the sun."

A streak of red crossed his cheekbones, and he tapped her nose with his before kissing her. "It's what I think of you. You are like the sun, bright, and you do good things to all those you touch. You do good things to me."

Now he was making this difficult. Now she really wanted to have sex with him. "You drew this all over me?"

He winked. "Everywhere."

Locked together in a long, delirious kiss, Holly was aware of his hand traveling down her belly till it sucked in at his touch, his fingers danced around the waist of her underwear, ticking the skin, and she flooded lava hot, his intentions clear. Flooded with nerves, weakly she shook her head and his hand shifted. She blinked away tears. "I just...I'm not ready." She realised thirty seconds ago, she'd been suggesting quite the opposite, but suddenly faced with an act more intimate than anything she'd ever done, her nerves kicked in and her bravado crumpled.

Nick smiled and kissed her nose. "Don't ever be sorry."

She took his hand and pressed it on her chest. "But aren't you disappointed?"

Nick's laugh was light, and his kiss ended her worries. "Disappointed? I'm naked in a sleeping bag with you. What's to be upset about?"

Holly breathed out a sigh of relief, her hands trembling as she looked up at him shyly. "You didn't have to stop kissing me though."

"Hmm. Okay" He pressed a kiss to her lips, his tongue parting her mouth, until she was feverish, alight and breathless. He pulled away, his gaze hooded. "But maybe we better go to sleep?"

Holly wasn't sure she could move, her limbs were weighted, and she was still floating, cresting on the wave that hadn't drawn back out to sea. He kissed her nose. "Close your eyes."

She didn't need to be told twice, her lids fluttered closed, and he cradled her to his chest, the sound of rain pelting the canopy lulling her into a dreamless sleep.

At some point in the night, Nick rolled away onto his back. Holly blinked awake, stiff and numb, licking her dry lips as she slowly sat up and adjusted. Her heart leapt to her throat as reality quickly invaded the dream. They were both naked, in a sleeping bag and she'd fallen asleep.

Holly hadn't intended to sleep the whole night, but after that...

God, she thought she might love him. Just a little bit. But her rational mind told her she was on a hormone coma, still on a strung out high after what they'd done last night. Serotonin could mimic love, right? She leaned over and looked at him, from his dark lashes against his skin, to his dark hair messed up over the pillow. How had she not really seen him before? All the glory he was, head to toe. Then she peeked under the bag.

She flushed, looking at the length of his body under the bag. She ran her fingers over his chest and his skin broke into goose bumps. Coiling nearer, she pressed a kiss right over the snake's head, loving she could garner a reaction out of him, she had power to turn him on. Sleepily he turned his head, catching her lips with his. "Morning, sunshine."

She grinned, glancing down at her tattoos. She was never going to forget this. She snuggled next to his shoulder, willing away an emotional clog in her throat. It was going to be over soon.

Running her hand down his flat abdomen, she fiddled with the waistband of his boxer shorts. She didn't have to touch him to know he was hard, heat pulsed from his groin, and he caught her hand. "I told you...don't tease me if you have no intentions...."

Holly giggled "Sorry." She slid her hands up his chest and pulled him in. He laughed against her neck, and it rumbled down her spine. Then he was kissing her everywhere, her face, her eyes, his hands greedily kneading any exposed flesh he could find before they would both be torn apart. The morning had arrived and rudely shone its way into their little world.

Behind them, Holly's phone was ringing, but she ignored it, pulling Nick on top of her, loving every inch of him pressing her into the mat. Curling her fingers in his hair, she kissed him hard, knowing she was teasing him and dancing dangerously close to fire. "Holly...your phone. Shouldn't you go back to the cabin?"

"Nick, shut up!" She kissed him, running her tongue along his bottom lip. He made a noise that sent her reeling, power flooding her system like a bolt of adrenaline. She wanted him to suffer a little bit, to reduce him to the shaking, blissed-out mess she'd been last night, too shattered to speak or form a thought. He groaned, curling his hands under her hips, like he couldn't get close enough. "Holly..."

The tent flooded with light.

Holly heard the zipper traveling upwards, but it was too late. Panic surged to her chest, her eyes flying wide as she dived under the sleeping bag. Nick swore in her ear, and she grabbed for her shirt, desperately trying to cover her nakedness. "Oh, shit!"

Faces filled the tent flaps, worried, tense and filled with horror. Nick covered his head with his pillow rolling onto his stomach. Holly didn't dare emerge from the bag, cursing against Nick's shoulder as they shared a look of absolute mortification.

"Holly?" Her mother's voice filled the tent. *"Holly?"*

"Oh, my fucking god!" Nick closed his eyes, pulling the bag over his head. Holly peeked her head out, and her stomach fell.

Martha stood motionless in the tent's door and then blocked the path, "Oh dear," she said. "Oh, dear."

"I think we better give them five minutes," Nick's father said.

Twenty-Two

Mrs. Truman followed her daughter into Campfire Joe's office as Martha closed the door behind them. Holly sank in a chair beside her mother, her face so tight she thought she might crack if she spoke. Humiliation washed over her, waves crashing down upon her shoulders repeatedly, making her want to sink into the floor.

Martha folded her arms, shaking her head. "I honestly don't know what to say."

Neither did anyone, it seemed. Holly fiddled with dry skin around her nail beds, casting a glance out of the window where Nick and his father were talking with Joe. The field was a wet grassy bog, potholes filled with murky rainwater, and a couple of the trees had been toppled with the high winds. Leaves scattered and lay in clumpy piles. The office had been cleared of all sleeping bags and pillows, and Holly sat rigid, willing her heart to slow.

What had she done?

"Holly," Martha started. "Can you explain yourself?"

Holly sensed her mother shift next to her in the chair. She finally cleared her throat. "Martha, you know Holly very well. You know this was just a terrible mistake."

A boy mistake... They met eyes, and her mother cast her a thin smile. She didn't even look mad. Holly's mouth was too dry to form words, but somehow she sensed her mother's warmth.

Martha waved her hands. "Look, what you and Nick Jones do in your own time isn't any of my business. I'm angry with how I woke up to find you gone. I was worried. Thank god the kids were gone. Can you imagine if one of them had come looking for you?"

Oh, god.... Holly hung her head. Her eyes filled up with tears. Everything she had worked for the last few years had cumulated in this stupid mistake. What was she thinking?

You weren't thinking. Not about anything else but him.

Holly breathed out an exhale and slumped her shoulders. Mrs. Truman's hand rested on her nape. "Martha, look—I agree with you. Holly and Nick...well, it's a huge surprise. I'm sure neither of them planned...."

To get caught? Holly winced in shame, tossing a glance out of the window, where Nick watched her, biting his lip. She wanted to go out there, and throw her arms around him. How could she forget what she'd done? What they'd shared? Holly never wanted to go back. Watching him standing alone, looking crestfallen with his hands in his pockets on the wet leaves made her heart swell. Maybe she did love him just a tiny bit?

"That's the thing. This isn't like you Holly. To act so irrationally...to go out alone in the middle of the night during a storm? It's just *not* you."

No, it's not. She lifted her chin, her eyes full and wet. "I'm so sorry, Martha. I'm sorry I let you down."

Martha folded her hands across the desk, looking pained, her weepy eyes full of regret. "Holly, do you realise what you've done? Do you have any idea what this means?"

She burst, fat tears rolling down her cheeks. She wasn't an idiot. Of course, she understood. Mrs. Truman grabbed for her daughter's hand. "What are you saying?"

Martha, exasperated, held out her palms and waved to the mess and debris outside the cabin. "This is serious. I'm not sure I can assign Holly the gold award—not after what I saw this morning."

Her insides crumpled, and she sagged, rolling forward in her chair. Tears fell and left damp spots on her tracksuit bottoms. "I didn't mean...I only went to check on him."

"Holly, you did a darn sight more than check on him."

"Wait! Let's not be too hasty!" Mrs. Truman cried. "You can't judge her on one mistake after everything she's done for this group, all her hard work and sacrifice, Martha. *Come on!* Can't you look the other way? She's a good kid."

"Rachel, she left a safe place to go out into a dangerous storm with a boy and do—I don't want to imagine!"

"We didn't do *anything!*" Holly's head snapped up, dark eyes brimming with hot tears. She was drowning, gulping for air that would save her life, while everything she had worked so hard for was about to slip through her fingers like sand. "I didn't sleep with him. I swear to you, we didn't...we couldn't...."

Mrs. Truman squeezed her hand. "You don't have to tell us anything."

"But it's true!" Holly twisted to her mother, who was slowly becoming ashen. "I didn't sleep with him."

"It doesn't matter if you did or not," Martha said across the desk. "You were gone when you were supposed to be *here*. Can you imagine if the kids had been here and one saw you and told their parents? I *trusted* you, Holly. The Eagles is a Willowdale tradition, and one wrong move like this could shut everything down. God, it's an embarrassment."

"Okay, Martha, I think Holly gets it!" Mrs. Truman stood up, yanking Holly with her. Her mother looked wide-eyed and angry, her nostrils flaring, and Holly was surprised that her ire wasn't directed at her. "Holly and I will deal with this alone. I'm not saying she didn't do wrong, but she's a kid, and sometimes they mess up. And if you decide to penalise her after one mistake, that's on you."

Holly's lips parted, hardly able to believe her mother was acting as a human shield, it made her cry all the harder. Mrs. Truman tugged her into the middle of the office, her face blotched up with anger, then she abruptly turned and pointed a finger in Martha's direction.

"But when you need a gofer to do your hard work, to organise craft evenings or parties or whatever dirty work you can't be bothered to do, ask someone else. Oh, *wait!* You can't—because you only have her. Come on, baby."

Fresh air tingled on Holly's skin as she followed her mother out into the cool, damp morning. Mr. Jones sat perched on a damp park bench, scrolling through his phone, and glanced up as their feet crunched over the gravel. Nick hopped off the bonnet of the car, arms folded and dragging the toe of his trainer in the stones. He looked messy, hair all stuck up and sleepy, and Holly clenched at the memory of what they'd been doing, less than an hour ago.

Mrs. Truman nudged her shoulder with a weary sigh. "Go say goodbye. We should get on the road."

Holly folded her arms as she met Nick halfway across the car park, her tongue woolly. She itched to reach for him, like she would explode if he didn't touch her. She was surprised at how much it hurt not to fold herself into his embrace. He shoved his hands deep in his pockets and tried to smile.

"I'm so sorry."

"You didn't do anything wrong. I was the one who followed you out into the storm."

Nick looked over his shoulder, spotting Martha watching them from the office window. "Was she pissed?"

Holly couldn't look up at him, she could barely take a full breath. "You could say that."

Nick's face crumpled, then he slapped his forehead. "Oh, shit. The award? Don't tell me...she wouldn't...."

Holly sniffed. "Probably."

"That's not fair."

"It *is* fair. I screwed up, royally. I don't deserve the award."

"But you worked hard. It'll go on your CV—" He shook his head. "I'll talk to her, I'll explain it was me who asked you to...."

Holly grabbed his elbow. "No, Nick. It's done now."

The wind whipped up around him, and she swayed closer, looking up at him through wet, spiky lashes. "I guess...this is it. Like we said...it's over now. We go back to what we were before."

Heaviness, like a dumbbell, weighted her chest, crushing her insides. She didn't think she could go back, she didn't want to forget what they'd shared. Teetering on the brink of tears, she waited for Nick's response, unsure what she needed to hear. She wanted more, and Tess's warning rang true. She couldn't just forget him.

Say we can make this work...

Nick's fingers brushed hers, and he sniffed as the rain began to fall from grey clouds passing overhead. "I guess we do. I'll see you around, Holly."

Something inside her broke, and she spun before he could see her melt. She jogged to the car, where her mother waited with the engine running. It was warm in the car, and Mrs. Truman wasted no time pulling out of car park, the windscreen wipers swishing frantically as they got on the road.

Silence passed between them, and Holly wiped her tears as they fell, sobbing into her chest. Her mother cast her worried, stricken glances. "Oh, sweetie," she said, reaching for her hand. "Isn't there anyway you two and work this out?"

"No," Holly shook her head. "It just won't work...we don't fit."

"But you like him. Why can't you work around your differences?"

Holly snivelled and stared out the window as the terrain changed from dark forest to open countryside. "You can't change what's always been. The fact is...Nick doesn't like what I am. He hates everything I love...what I stand for."

"I don't know...." Mrs. Truman disagreed. "It seems you two are more alike than I ever guessed. He looked heartbroken, Holly."

"It's over, Mum. I just need to focus on what's important. College and..." she trailed off, everything she thought was important didn't seem so urgent now. It didn't seem important if she didn't get to see Nick smile every day. The award, the one she'd relentlessly chased for years, was gone.

"Okay, okay," Holly's mother relented. "Let's get you home, take a long bath, have a good cry, and we can have hot chocolate. Kit hasn't been around much, so we've got lots of time to talk."

Holly's brow arched, wondering exactly what Kit had been up to these past few days and who she'd been with. Why did she have a feeling it was Adam? Not that she gave a shit anymore. Forlorn, she stared out of the window.

"Can I just ask one question, though?" Her mother gripped the wheel, casting a glance out of the corner of her eye. There was a mischievous twinkle there, and Holly's gut clenched.

"Okay."

Mrs. Truman grinned. "Well...I wanted to ask...why you're covered top to toe in marker pen?"

Twenty-Three

Nick's father wound the car through the windswept back roads, debris from the storm littering the wet, slick tarmac. They drove in silence, and Nick ground his jaw so hard he thought it might seize in place. Staring out of the window, he tried to ignore the looks his father cast him from the corner of his eye. They passed a petrol station, and he threw the car up on the forecourt, whistling jovially as he hopped out. "I need a drink. You want anything?"

Nick didn't answer, worried his voice would crack if he attempted to speak. Inside, his stomach whirled with bubbling acid. He was exhausted, hungry, and defeated. A hollow ache spread in his chest when he dared to picture Holly lying under him in the dark, a berry stain blushing across her cheeks. He'd wanted so much more right then, and part of him was relieved she'd not pushed him. God, he was in so much trouble.

How could they move forward? How could he suddenly introduce Holly as his girlfriend? He'd be laughed out of the group. Davey would never speak to him again. Holly just didn't fit. He exhaled, his breath fogging the glass. The driver's door opening beside him startled Nick from his gloomy train of thought.

Never speaking to them again. Choosing Holly over them. Was it such a bad thing? Heat bloomed up his chest, recalling how she'd pushed the hair out of his eyes, her shyness, how sweet she was. The thought of her going off to college and hooking up with some random guy sickened him. Someone who didn't know or care about her, some nobody who wanted a quick lay and didn't know how amazing she was. It made him gag. She deserved so much more, and he knew, in the end, she'd settle for less because....

She's never been told otherwise. Nick grumbled into his palm as his father tossed him a water bottle. He opened it and glugged it gratefully. He was dehydrated and needed a shower, but he could smell Holly's hair products on his skin.

Nick hated himself. He hated that he'd been so awful to her, ignored her, treated her with indifference all these years. He never wanted her to be with anyone else.

"Are you ever going to speak to me?" his father's voice broke his melancholic thought train, heading down a depressing spiralling track. They were driving, and Nick's father glanced at him with concern. "I knew it, though, didn't I?"

Nick tossed him an acidic stare. "Knew what?"

"You and Holly. You have a thing for her; you always did."

"I don't have a thing," Nick grunted, knowing how petulant he sounded. "We just...got to know one another better."

Mr. Jones smirked. "Looks like you got to know one another *very* well."

"Nothing happened." Both of them knew that was a big lie. "We just...."

"You don't have to tell me. I saw what I saw, and honestly, I wish I could swap eyeballs with a random stranger. No father needs to see their son in that kind of position."

Nick rolled his eyes. "We didn't do anything."

"You were both naked!"

"We slept—as in eyes *closed* sleeping. But....yes...." There was nakedness. Nick's pulse raced at the thought. He was well aware his father knew what they'd been up to, the position Holly had put herself in. Nick's face flamed with humiliation. "Anyway... it's over and I don't want to talk about it. Why were you even there?"

Mr. Jones cleared his throat, undeterred, waving his hand in an open gesture. "Martha called to inform us about the storm, but Rachel already told me. We decided to drive up first thing and collect you both. Summer camping is fun, but camping in the rain is miserable. There is no way to stay dry. Not that you two looked like the storm bothered you much."

"Dad!" Nick pinched the bridge of his nose. "Change the subject, please."

"I got that mess you call art cleaned off the Cricket Pavilion—you're welcome. That'll be coming out of your next pay slip."

Nick muttered, ignoring the jibe and the reminder of why he was in this predicament in the first place. Because he couldn't keep his temper. It turned out he couldn't keep his hands to himself when it came to Holly either.

Mr. Jones whistled. "Well, okay. How about this? I booked your ticket to France."

Nick went hot, his palms prickled as he sprung forward in the seat. "When for?"

"Saturday morning. You've got an eleven o clock ferry from Portsmouth, and your mother will meet you in Calais."

Nick swallowed, his throat dry. Glugging the water, it didn't help, and he rubbed at an errant ache in his temples. The party was tonight and he was going, and Holly was going to be there. It'd be his last chance to see her, to talk to her. There wasn't time to think or breathe. He hadn't realised his breathing had become shallow till his father clapped him on the shoulder with his large hand.

"Something wrong? I thought you'd be jumping for joy at getting out of Willowdale for a couple of weeks. I spoke to

your mother, and she said it was tomorrow or not at all...."
His father looked away, huffing through his nose. "...this was
the only time that fits in with her schedule."

When the silence lapsed into chasms of time, Mr. Jones
said, "Nick...is there a problem?"

"Uh, no. No." Nick waved his hand. "It's just sooner than I
thought, and I'm at a party tonight. But I can make it work."

"I mean..." his father's voice trailed into the void. "After
this morning and what I saw...if you want to cancel...."

"No, I don't!" Nick said. Seeing his mother had been the
only reason he'd come on this damn trip. The promise of being with her kept him focused. He didn't want to disappoint
her after she'd taken time out to be with him.

The reason you don't see her isn't your father's fault. Holly's
words returned to haunt him, the memorable moment in
the bathroom. His thinking had been altered, and derailed
drastically since then. He'd not needed the forced encour-
agement, the incentive of a trip to keep him focussed. Nick
enjoyed being with Holly.

Now he was going away and not going to see her for two
weeks. In that time, she'd realise what a horrible mistake
she'd made, trusting him with her feelings, her heart, and her
body. The fog would clear, and she'd wake up and see what
a huge loser he was, undeserving, a coward and not in her
league. All these years, his friends treated her like she was

below them, but she was far, far above, so high you could barely reach her orbit. She was good, too good.

Holly was the sun.

Nick liked her, he loved her curls, freckles, and the way her glasses perched on the end of her snub nose. He loved her laugh, how kind she was, how hard she worked, and looked after the kids. She'd been nice to him, open and honest, and she didn't hide behind a mask like he did. There was no act, no hidden agenda. She'd never changed to fit in or blend in with the crowd.

Nick smiled into his hand, his breath fogging the glass. He even liked the whistle.

I have to tell her...if I'm going away....

Would she wait around for him? It was only two weeks.

"What's going on in there?" Mr. Jones asked as he finally threw the car in the driveway. "What are you thinking about?"

He pulled on the handbrake, and they sat in silence. Nick glanced to his left. Holly was already inside, probably pacing in her room, reliving the worst moment of her life.

"I'm an idiot, that's all," Nick said, and his father narrowed his eyes.

"Can you fix it?"

A beat of silence passed, and Nick's wet, glossy gaze found his father's.

"It depends. I'm not sure I know how to be a good guy," he said.

Twenty-Four

Holly stepped onto the bath mat, relishing in the feel of hot water running down her legs. Grabbing a towel, she wrapped herself and then surveyed the damage. She hooked a foot onto the edge of the bath and gingerly peered at her pink skin, nearly burned clean from rubbing and scalding water.

"Shit," she grumbled, her knees shaking. "Holy shitty shit!"

"Well?" Tess called down the corridor. Huffing, Holly threw on her foggy glasses, flung open the bathroom door, and exited in a plume of steam. Padding barefoot down the hall, she stopped in her bedroom doorway, where Tess sat on her pristine, white bedsheets, painting her toe nails.

"It won't bloody come off!"

Tess looked up, and hid her grin, her eyes raking over Holly from head to foot, almost as if she were counting the black swirling sun beams Nick drew over her naked body. Despite the heat from the shower, Holly shivered. "Don't you dare laugh!"

"I wasn't going to!" Tess smirked and then turned her head away. "Oh, dear."

"Not, *oh dear*!" Holly yelled, wild-eyed. "This is a disaster."

Tess stretched out her toes and wiggled them, the pink paint gleaming with a wet sheen. "Well, that's what happens when you let a budding tattoo artist draw all over you—with a sharpie!"

Behind Tess, with her knees folded up to her chest, sat Kit, leaning against the headboard. She made a sound vaguely like a snort, and Holly's insides crumbled. "Don't you start!"

"Oh, Hols, come on. It's a look." Kit grinned, brushing a pink strand of hair out of her eyes. "It'll come off—in about a week."

Tess threw her a look of disdain. "She's got the party, re-member? She can't go out looking like one of her Robins scribbled all over her."

Kit yawned, stretching out her long, jean-clad legs. "Then she can wear jeans. It's not the end of the world—it's kind of sweet."

"It's a Nick Jones thing to do. He did this to humiliate her—a prank so she'd have to bleach her skin to get his crap off."

At the mention of Nick's name, Holly's breath hitched, and she unknowingly reached for the doorframe. Words in his defence wanted to form on her lips, but she saw the look on Tess's face. Nick didn't do this to humiliate her. Her heart ached in a sweet throb, remembering every sun he'd drawn over her body. It'd been real, hadn't it? Aimlessly, she wandered to the window and spotted his father's car parked in their drive.

Was he waiting to come over after Tess had gone? Would he come over at all? She imagined him knocking on the door, asking her to come with him to the party, and they'd walk hand in hand, and he'd spend all night talking to her, ignoring his friends, and by the end of the night, he'd kiss her and tell her that his entire life he'd been a deranged idiot not to notice her. And she would kiss him and tell him she had been too.

She had been an idiot not to see him, to judge, to look down on him.

But then none of that would happen because she was Holly Truman, and he was Nick Jones.

"I'm having another shower!"

Stomping into the bathroom, she slammed the door and didn't emerge till her skin was ruby red and sore. Most of it was gone, apart from a faint outline over the pulse point of her right wrist. She kind of liked it there.

"So this Nick *thing*," Tess said as she stepped into the bedroom. "Just how serious did things get in that tent?"

Holly flopped on the bed next to Kit, who smiled down at her with a brief sigh. "It's not a thing. It's not going to be a thing."

"But you spent the night together—alone?"

At Tess's interrogation, Holly sat up and folded her legs under her, blushing. "Yes—nothing happened. Just a lot of...."

"Drawing?" Kit finished with a smirk, and Holly smiled and batted her cousin's thigh. Holly didn't want ro reveal all the intimate details of what happened. Somehow it was private, special, and theirs, and not a subject for idle gossip.

"Lots of drawing—and kissing. It was nice."

"Sounds very PG," Kit said. "He's hot, you know. I know you've spent a lifetime hating him, but you have failed to notice the hotness. *I* would've slept with him."

"Well, I'm not you!" Holly scowled, and a giggle forced its way between her lips. "He was a gentleman. It was all...quite romantic. Only now, Martha is threatening to take away my gold award. God..." Holly rubbed her eyes. "If this gets out...."

"If *what* gets out?" Tess demanded, affronted on her behalf. "Your mother is right, Holly. You've given over every spare second of your free time to that club. You are the only Eagle in Willowdale! Martha should remove the stick from her butt and look the other way."

"She's lucky to have you," Kit agreed, biting at one of her chipped nails. "You didn't do anything wrong, not really.

Everyone was safe and had no idea what happened. Only you, Nick, and Martha know about it. And if she kicks you out...."

Holly cocked a brow. "What? You'll key her car? That's the reason I'm in this mess. This wouldn't have happened if you hadn't damaged Nick's car in the first place."

Tess snorted with laughter. "I think she's had plenty of payback these last few days."

Kit shot Tess a glare that could cut glass, and Holly didn't miss how her friend buttoned her lip. She frowned, clocking the odd silence that fell between them. "What's going on? Has something happened while I've been away?"

Kit grumbled and looked at her hands, and Tess giggled. "I'm sure she'll tell you when she's ready. But Kit might understand your whole predicament more than you think!"

Kit jumped off the bed, edgy and annoyed, and Holly followed her with her gaze. Did Kit look slightly altered? She carried the air of someone with a secret, but she knew her older cousin, and she was deep, ocean floor deep, and would only get pissed if she pushed her.

Holly hugged her knees instead. "I don't have a predicament. Nick and I will go on like before. I won't ever be cool or popular enough to fit in with his friends."

Kit blew air through her teeth in annoyance. "Why should you want to fit in with them? I have a feeling he likes you enough the way you are."

Tess grabbed her friend's ankle, something naughty gleaming in her eye. "Alright, enough is enough. Out with it. I want details—dirty ones!"

Kit grinned devilishly, and sank to the end of the bed, and Holly couldn't fight the rush of warmth exploding up her chest. She told them everything. Recounting every shared moment of laughter, warmth, and friendship. She didn't leave out a detail, finishing with the grand finale, the night of the storm and how he'd drawn pretty sunlight all over because that's how he saw her. Bright, good, and perfect. Holly left out intimate details, still too bashful. By the time she finished, Kit and Tess's mouths were agape.

"And you *didn't* sleep with him?" Tess cried.

Holly burst out laughing. "No—like I said, he was sweet. Nothing happened."

"Well, that's a whole lot of nothing happening!"

Holly fell back on the pillow, laughing. "He isn't the same as he is in school, it was like a whole different person. A person I liked."

Who was always there.

Tess made a face of disbelief. "So, you *do* like him?"

Holly fiddled with her hands, staring at her short stubby nails. "Maybe."

Yes, she wanted to scream. *I like him so much it hurts.* "Maybe?" Tess repeated.

"I mean...yes. He's different, kind, funny, and so unbeliev-ably cute with kids. He didn't moan or complain once the whole time. And he's artistic...."

"We can see that!"

"Shut up," Holly giggled and threw one of her stuffed an-imals at Tess, which she dodged. "But, what's the point? It's over now."

"Why?" Kit piped up beside her. "Why does it have to be over?"

Holly studied her older cousin's usually serious, pale com-plexion, now rosy and fresh. Yeah, she looked different. Tess tapped her foot. "Holly, what do you want? Answer me honestly. What does Holly Truman, Willowdale's resident, do-gooder, want?"

I want Nick. I want him to see me. I can change too. Nerves bubbled in her throat, her skin searing as she kept her eyes low and muttered. "I want him to see me as someone who could be his girlfriend—not Holly the square!"

Kit looked miserable. "Maybe Holly the square is who he *liked* on that trip?"

Holly sat up, frustration building inside. Why did she have to be stuck? She could change, even if it were in small incre-ments. "Maybe I don't like her much—not anymore."

The statement floated between the three of them, and Kit traced the light pattern of Holly's bedding with her fingertip. Kit didn't like change. It took her a long time to trust anyone, it'd taken months for her to settle into this family. The idea of change repelled her. "Holly, I don't think...."

"I know. I've always lived the way James believed I should. I've tried to be a good person, to be selfless and kind, and to make myself heard. And I never minded when kids made fun of me for it, for all the Eagle's stuff. But God...don't I deserve a break?"

She looked up, and Kit was smiling, resigned, and sad. "Of course you do."

Holly nodded with authority. "Right. Then how do I make Nick Jones look at me like I'm girlfriend material?"

Tess straightened as though she'd been called to action, her eyes sparkling with an idea. She held up a finger, authoritative and stern. "Hols, you were *always* girlfriend material. There's nothing you need to change...but if I were you and going to a party where I wanted a certain boy to notice me, I'd probably start with a killer dress."

Kit grinned. "I might have something you can borrow."

Tess hopped off the bed, mission in hand, and tore down the corridor, ready to raid Kit's wardrobe. Alone, the cousins shared a smile, but there was concern deep in Kit's eyes, something lurking that made the twinge in Holly's gut grow tighter. Holly didn't want to read into what Kit might be thinking, she could take a tentative guess, but she was high on adrenaline, ready to squeeze herself into whatever dress might knock Nick's socks off and fall at her feet.

Kit brushed her hand, and Holly paused on the way out of the door. "What is it?" Her throat knotted.

"You deserve love Holly," Kit said, her eyes shining, and for the third time that afternoon, Holly was certain something irrevocable had affected her cousin since she'd been gone. "No matter what you wear, look like, or your interests. You don't have to change to deserve love."

Twenty-Five

Holly wasn't used to cool air wafting around her thighs. Usually in shorts or jeans, wearing a dress so short her underwear was nearly visible, was a new experience. Nervously she tugged the hem of the black slip dress, emerging from the bathroom. Tess was already gone, vanished in a plume of heady perfume as she went to finish the last of the decorations for the party. Inside, Holly bubbled with nerves. Kit sat on the bed, awaiting her entrance, she gave a low, appreciative whistle as Holly stepped into the corridor.

"Nice legs!"

Holly ran to her full-length mirror, turning to inspect her bare shoulders, on show in the thin spaghetti strap dress Tess dragged from Kit's wardrobe. "It's too much skin." She pinched the exposed flesh of her upper arms. "I've never worn anything like this."

Kit clicked her tongue and sloped off the bed. Within seconds she returned with a faded denim jacket covered in old music pins. She helped Holly into it and straightened the collar. "That's more you."

Holly nodded even though she guessed Tess would be annoyed at her back peddling. Two hours ago, she was full of bravado. Now with the sun vanishing behind the trees and the party only an hour away, her resolve wobbled. It didn't help that a battered Ford parked outside Nick's house an hour ago, and his friends went in, including Davey, Tyler, and Casey. Holly's stomach shrank to the size of a walnut when she heard music blaring through the walls.

It was oddly comforting to know Nick was in there, but it made her ache knowing they were separated. Thrash metal shook the bedpost, and Kit rolled her eyes. "Someone has company."

Holly stared at her reflection. "I look like I tried too hard."

"Wasn't that the point?"

She moaned into her cupped hands. "I don't know. Maybe? Is this a bad idea?"

Kit eyed her up and down, and then grabbed Holly's Eagle jacket, lying discarded on a wicker chair. Holly didn't realise what Kit was doing till her cousin pinned a shiny metal badge to the denim jacket. The pin had been given to her the day she'd made her Eagle pledge when she was sixteen. Kit gave her a wink. "Just a reminder. I like *this* Holly, always have."

Holly stared at Kit's green eyes framed with dark kohl liner. "Can you do my eyes like yours?"

Kit grinned. "I'll give you a toned-down version."

A lot of poking and giggling later, Holly's eyes were shiny, dark, and sultry, ringed with dark brown kohl, smudged to perfection. Kit added a tinted lip balm to her plump bottom lip and then made her smack her lips together. Holly eyed herself warily in the mirror and nodded to give herself a speck of confidence. "This will have to do."

"You look good." Kit squeezed her arm. Kit's normally dirty pink hair was yanked back in a messy bun, and she was wearing her usual attire, a ripped pair of jeans and a Nirvana t-shirt, cropped so it showed her belly bar. Holly studied her long and hard.

"So...is something going on with Adam Brant?"

Kit's cheeks went pink, and she looked away. "No, nothing. He's just...I've been helping him out, that's all."

Holly frowned. "Helping him out?"

"It's nothing. I'll tell you another time."

Holly edged closer, treating Kit like a baby deer, prone to flight. "He is cute. If you want to talk—"

"I don't!" Kit snapped, her green eyes flashing. Then she ran a hand through her hair, her top lip sweaty. This was unlike her, Kit was usually so steady, in control, and aloof. "Sorry—I didn't mean to yell. Let's just get this thing over with."

Holly nodded, pulling back. If Kit wanted to talk, she would. She'd gone through hell last year with her mum, and getting anything out of her was like pulling teeth. Holly threw her arms around her cousin in a hug, and Kit squirmed.

Trotting down the stairs, the girls were greeted by Mrs. Truman waiting in the hall. Holly met her mother's eyes, giving her a nod of approval. "You look lovely, baby," she said, and only then Holly noticed her mother cradling a phone to her chest. She offered her the mobile. "Sorry, but Martha wants to talk to you."

Holly took the phone and hurried into the kitchen, holding it to her chest as she closed the glass dividing doors behind her. Her heart quaked as she hopped onto one of the bar stools, leaning her elbows on the kitchen counter. With a shaky breath, she tried to smile into the receiver, "Martha, how are you?"

Martha's voice quavered at the end of the line. "Oh, I'm okay, Holly. Just spent the afternoon unpacking all the equipment. It took hours by myself."

Holly's gut instantly pinched with guilt. Of course, she had been lined up to help Martha unpack all the camping gear and craft equipment. But after the storm and the aftermath, Holly fled. "Uh...I'm so sorry."

"Oh, no, that's okay," Martha breezed, even though Holly sensed it wasn't. "It's all in hand now. I've been thinking a lot about what happened this morning."

Holly trembled, a horrible sick feeling creeping up her gullet. She wasn't used to being told off, it hadn't ever happened before. "Okay." Her mouth was so dry she could barely swallow. The award she'd worked so hard for hung in the balance, and Holly wondered if she even cared.

"Look, I was shocked and surprised by what I saw. That girl isn't the Holly I know," Martha said. "But I'm prepared this time to forget what I saw. Your mother is right. I can't take the award away from you when you've worked so hard this year."

Holly shook with relief, and her eyes filled with tears. "Oh...Martha..."

"I've had several parents on the phone today, complimenting us on a fantastic trip. The kids loved it and can't wait for the next one..." her voice trailed off. "I need you, Holly. I need my best Eagle. The only reason we have this club is because of you. So if I approve the award, I will need you on board. We have lots planned, and I need help...what with the new term and all the activities planned, I need you!"

If I approve the award...

Holly faltered as though her heart thickened in her chest. "Oh...I mean, of course, you'll have me. But I go to college in September, Martha. I'm not sure...."

"We could start right away. I have a lot planned, and I need help, Holly. Lots more Robins are joining from different counties because of the amazing trip we pulled off....despite the little hiccup."

Guilt ate her insides, and Holly found herself nodding, imagining the piles of assignments accumulating while she spent her free time planning the next big Robin event. Her mind raced at the thought of firework gatherings, the annual bonfire, Halloween parties, and Christmas crafts. Four days ago, this was her life, and she'd never seen a different path, but now she wanted to spend some of those nights with people who were important. With her friends, her mother...with Kit. And Nick. Where did Nick fit into this? Where did *Holly* fit?

"Look, Martha...I'm heading out now...."

"...Oh..."

"So I'll call you in the morning with my decision, okay?"

Martha balked. "Decision?"

Don't throw everything away... a little voice screamed in her ear.

I'm not throwing it away, she argued. *I can be more than the kid in the square box.*

Holly's eyes welled up again. "Things have changed." She caught her reflection in the mirror below the clock on the wall. "I need to think. Bye, Martha."

"Holly—"

Holly slid the phone shut and puffed out a long exhale. God, what had she done? Hurrying to the front door, she met her mother and Kit. Kit pulled on her long wool cardigan which brushed the floor. "You done?"

Holly's eyes met her mother's, and she nodded weakly. "I think I might be."

Twenty-Six

Davey Thomas kicked a can across the supermarket car park. It clattered loudly under a parked blue Volvo. A woman pushing a baby in a pram stopped a metre away, fiddling with the keys in her bag before she pressed the key for the boot to unlock. Davey did a run-up and sideswiped another empty can with his trainer, which landed under the pram. The woman glanced up sharply and threw the group a glare before shaking her head.

Davey laughed, and Nick groaned inwardly. When was the guy going to grow up? "Nice one," he muttered.

"Would you prefer I help her with her shopping? Jesus, that loser did a number on you."

Nick perched on a low brick wall, casting his eye across the town supermarket, hands in his jean pockets. The sky was dull and as grey as his mood. He was every inch a loser. When Davey and his friends called for him at the house, Nick had no choice but to slope off and join them. He sensed every ounce of the pressure they placed on him right then. Pressure to be aloof, cool, like they didn't care about anything or anyone. They grilled him about the camping trip and Holly. But Nick remained close-lipped.

The joke was Nick knew none of them were as unkind or hateful as they pretended to be. Casey wasn't awful. She spent weekends with her grandma, helping her in the garden. Tyler spent every evening babysitting his kid brother. So why the pretence?

We don't get hurt if we don't let anyone close, Nick thought miserably. *We've been through it before.*

His thoughts dallied to his mother and the trip to France, and he wondered if what Holly said was true. Davey was a different matter; he was just—rotten. And now Nick saw it clearly for the first time.

Raking his hands through his hair, he hopped off the wall. "What are we waiting for? The party started two hours ago."

"Someone keen?" Casey teased, an ugly smirk on her lips. "You planning on seeing someone there?"

Something dark shone in her eyes, jealousy, and spite. He once thought she was pretty, they'd even shared a couple of drunken kisses, but now, her mask was on, and she looked every inch the mean, acidic seventeen-year-old she pretended to be. Casey would railroad someone like Holly. Nick scratched at his neck, trying to buoy himself, he was going to France tomorrow, and these were his friends, people he used to enjoy spending time with. Up until four days ago.

"I think we've dragged out being fashionably late long enough."

Davey threw a can at a Golf, and it bounced off the windscreen. Nick winced. "We have to wait for Tyler, he's getting the vodka."

"They'll be drink at Tess's party," Nick argued. His palms itched. God, he wanted to ditch them. He wanted to see Holly. He had to explain he was leaving in the morning. That's if she ever wanted to set eyes on him again, and if she'd lost that damn award, he doubted it. He cast a withering glance around his group of friends and exhaled. He couldn't blame her, not really.

Another boy joined them, tall and wiry with a mop of blonde hair. Tyler Moore flashed a bottle of Smirnoff and Casey grinned in appreciation. She unscrewed the cap and swigged from the neck, then passed it to Nick. He waved it away. "No thanks."

"Jesus, what is the matter with you? You've come back neutered. Did the little sparrow cut your dick off?"

He glared at her. "No, of course not. God, you're such a bitch!" Nick swiped the bottle out of her hand and took a few mouthfuls, the alcohol burning his throat. "And she's an Eagle, not a fucking sparrow. You ought to know, you were a Hawk once!"

Casey wiggled her dark brows. "That was when I was ten, Nick. Then I grew up and stopped playing make-believe with kids."

Nick took another long glug, and Casey grinned in triumph. When he glanced up, Davey was staring at him with his fathomless black eyes. His friend was unreadable and unpredictable, and right now, Nick had the sense of being studied like a bug in a Petri dish, like Davey might take a stick and poke him. "What are you staring at?"

Davey swiped the bottle out of his hand. "You look different—weird different."

"You mean he has a tan?" Tyler said with a wink, brushing his long swathes of blonde hair out of his eyes. "He looks better if you ask me."

"I wasn't," Davey snarled. "It's not just the tan. You don't look like the old Nick."

Nick met his eyes, longing to be out of Davey's gaze. He swallowed but tried not to show his nerves. Davey didn't waste time with words. He was a barrel of a kid, large, like an immovable boulder. Nick thanked god he would be out of here tomorrow. Why had he wasted so much time with this loser? Davey was a parasite who'd hooked onto him years ago. Both lonely outcasts, Nick tolerated Davey's behaviour, but now he couldn't stand to look at him.

"I'm the same guy who left here four days ago."

"Did you have sex with her?"

Nick's eyes went wide, and next to him, Casey let out a shrill laugh.

"What? No!"

"Of course, he didn't!" Casey cried. "Nick wouldn't be caught dead with that little nobody."

Davey licked his lips. "I'm not so sure."

Nick didn't break the intensity of his gaze. To look away would be fatal. Instead, he smiled his practiced grin. "You're joking, right? Holly Truman. The girl I've been at war with since I was five. No, we did not have sex."

Davey flipped his dark hair, shrugging. "Okay, so you won't mind if I ask her out?"

Nick's smile slipped. "What?"

"You heard. She's bound to be there at the party. She's one of that rich bitch Tess's friends. You won't mind if I have a go?"

A strangled sound left Nick's throat, it was meant to sound like a laugh, but it stuttered. Keenly aware of Casey eye-balling him, Nick fought to keep a neutral expression. "I mean...if you think you stand a chance. I warn you though, she's a block of ice."

Davey shrugged. "I don't mind a challenge—and you know, she isn't bad looking. She has a great pair of legs. Maybe I could crack the ice queen?" His lip curled. "All that time alone, you didn't notice her backside in those shorts?"

Nick paced, sweat dampening the base of his spine. "Whatever. Can we stop talking about Holly? Let's go to this party."

Wiping water off his top lip, he started ahead, Davey's gaze hot on his back. He knew, he was testing. Nick hated him right then. He needed to get there first and make her leave by any means necessary. Davey dragged behind, hands like two slabs of meat, all muscle, and bone. If he cornered her...Nick's gut twinged. He didn't want to imagine him overpowering her.

"You're speeding up all of a sudden?" Davey teased from behind. "Someone you want to see?"

God, you fucking bastard. Why had he ever hung around with this guy? With any of them.

Nick had to make Holly leave the party. And he hoped it would be with him.

Holly sloped about Tess's massive kitchen, her worried reflection beaming off the polished marble surfaces. Her heart skipped every time she heard the sound of front door opening and feet shuffling over the wooden hall floor. Coats and jackets were hauled into Tess's utility room, and laughter filtered from the living room. Holly brushed the hair out of her eyes and filled chip bowls. She topped up the dip and ran around with a black bin bag collecting discarded cans.

When she looked nervously at the clock in the kitchen and saw it tick to ten o clock, her heart sank, and like her small bubble of hope, she plopped onto a comfy chair in the kitchen.

Nick wasn't coming.

As she tried to sit, the hem of her dress rose up her thighs, and she suddenly hated the outfit she'd chosen with a venomous passion. Kit wandered in from the living room and landed on the sofa next to her. She handed her a beer, but Holly pushed it away. "No thanks."

"I think you need to relax," Kit said, narrowing her darkly lined green eyes. "You look wired."

Holly's eyes filled up. "He isn't going to come."

"He'll be here." Kit twisted towards her, resting her chin on her fist. "What do you even plan on saying when you see him?"

Holly's mouth dried up, hating to admit she had no idea. She always had a plan, but Nick derailed her. This wasn't supposed to be how she spent this summer before college. Not pining over a guy she'd spent the last eighteen years hating. "I don't know. I just...want to talk to him."

Kit frowned, but her lips curled in a teasing smile. "I thought you said nothing happened in that tent."

Holly blinked. "I told you what happened."

Kit chuckled. "You said you kissed. It sounds like a whole lot more happened than just kissing, and I'm not talking physically. Holly—you're completely smitten. It's so cute."

Over the last few hours, Holly had mulled over every detail of the trip. More had happened, and not in the physical sense. Nick got her, he listened. He was the calming influence she never knew she needed. Holly puffed out a long breath. Now wasn't the time to talk about James. Other than the humiliating end to the trip, one good thing had risen to the surface. Holly needed to face ghosts of the past, she couldn't hold onto guilt any longer, in a state of purgatory, relentless guilt she'd allowed to live in her heart. It had to be over.

A blush travelled up her neck, and she fiddled with the neckline of the dress, a little too low for her liking. "Do I look like a moron in this thing?"

"You look pretty," Kit said, brushing a stray curl out of her eyes. "My pretty little cousin."

Holly scoffed. "I'm one year younger than you."

Kit pulled her knees under her, her eyes traveling to the sounds of music and laughter booming from the living room. Tess's parents were away on their annual Italian trip, and Holly was always on hand for clean-up duty after an epic party. Outside there were a few kids in the pool, splashing and screaming. It had gotten dark, and the back patio was lit up with fairy lights. Kit looked edgy and yawned, stretching her arms.

"I don't feel one year older—sometimes I feel ancient," she admitted, far off and sad, and Holly studied her profile. Right then, Adam wandered in and stopped dead in his tracks. He spotted the two girls on the sofa and awkwardly cleared his throat.

Holly spotted his throat bobbing, swallowing nervously as he took a seat at the kitchen counter, pulling out his kindle. Holly wondered how on earth he could read with all the commotion, but that was Adam, stoic, gorgeous, and the epitome of the strong silent type. Next to her, Kit visibly stiffened and glugged her beer. Okay, there was definitely something going on.

The front door opened, and Holly jumped, her heart flipping, but sagged when it was only Eddie and his girlfriend Violet. Kit poked her arm. "You really need a drink."

"I need to go home," Holly said miserably. She shuffled to her feet, defeated. The party started hours ago, and Nick wasn't here. He wasn't coming. She'd seen him with Davey earlier, and her nerves bubbled, wondering what Nick had told them.

Her cheeks flamed. What if he told them what had happened? What if he embellished or laughed about her? The horrifying possibilities spread out before her eyes, and she turned to go get her jacket from the utility room. No, it was too much. She couldn't face him right now, not in this dress, not feeling like an idiot, looking like she'd tried.

Why had she bothered?

"I'm going," she said, and Kit's eyes widened as the front door opened behind them.

"You might want to wait—he's here!"

Holly spun, her heart dissolving, and any courage she may have built up quickly dribbled into her converse shoes. Nick stood in the door, messy-haired like he's walked a long way, shrugging out of his denim jacket. Behind him, Davey, Casey, and Tyler were at his back, and she thought she saw Davey mumble something about Tess.

Davey's black eyes roamed the walls and expensive furnishing and upholstery. Nick looked about, and then their eyes met. He spotted her gawking, and Holly shook herself, telling herself she had to calm down. Nick's mouth went slack. His gaze wandered from her shoes up her legs and landed on the short dress she was wearing. Maybe it was her imagination, but she swore his jaw tightened.

Her mouth went to form his name, she thought she said it, but music blared from the speakers. She stepped into the dark, bustling hall, but someone crossed her path, blocking her view. Eddie bumped her shoulder, mumbled a sorry, and then got out of her way.

Holly's heart fell when she saw Nick was gone.

Twenty-Seven

Nick swallowed another glug of vodka, his vision a little blurred as he landed a hand on Tess's front door. Heat crept up his neck, and he paused, that fuzzy, tipsy feeling making him numb.

"What are you waiting for?" Davey said from behind.

He could do this, Nick told himself. He had to do this. He didn't want Davey's filthy hands anywhere near Holly. Pressure built in his skull, his temples throbbing. If he walked out of here with Holly, then the life he'd been comfortably numb in for the last few years would be over.

Nick didn't want to be numb anymore. He wanted to admit what he liked, who he liked, and what his interests were. He wanted to share them with her.

Nick barged through the door, hating he was doing this slightly drunk. He should have spat it on the pavement when Casey offered it to him. Inside, the house throbbed with music. It was dark, dimly lit, and it smelled like spilt beer. Nick's eyes roamed the halls, admitting Tess's home was beautiful. The staircase swept into a grand landing, where a crystal chandelier hung over their heads. A couple kissed on the stairs, completely oblivious as people stepped over them to reach the bathroom.

Nick sensed Davey's eyes on his back and his breath on his neck. "Wow, I knew the bitch had a rich daddy...."

"Fuck you, Davey," Nick barked out of the corner of his mouth. "Don't call her that."

"What flew up your backside?" Davey muttered, shrugging out of his jacket and tossing it on a nearby chair. "You should have another drink."

Casey practically drooled with envy, her eyes everywhere, and Nick hoped they would all behave. Tess had been kind enough to invite them, she didn't have to do shit for any of them. He hoped they'd be a little gracious.

Davey sounded a low whistle above his head and rustled Nick's hair. "I was going to say I needed to find the ice queen—but I don't have to go far. She's right there."

Nick's heart snapped in his chest, and he looked up, startled when he spotted the dark, wavy-haired vision standing in the kitchen door watching him. Blood drained from his limbs. Weak and heavy, he swayed, unable to take her in from head to foot. What was she wearing? He'd never seen her in a dress, the full length of her legs, bare shoulders gleaming under the light. A small, hopeful smile played on her lips, her dark eyes meeting his across the room, and his gut tugged.

His heart sank. She'd done this for him. She was trying to change—for him. Anger boiled in the pit of his belly, and he didn't fully understand why Holly standing there looking radiantly stunning in a black slip dress enraged him. He never wanted her to change. Didn't she know that?

God, she did look beautiful. The smack of Davey's lips in his ear left him with a sense of disgust and loathing. No way in hell was he going within a foot of her now. Suddenly Eddie blocked his view, so Nick had to stand on tiptoe while the oaf lumbered and bumped Holly's shoulder.

"Let's get out of here," Nick suggested, throwing his arm around Davey's shoulder and steering him towards the dark living room, humming with music.

The first person he met was Tess, impeccably dressed in a sparkly black halter neck. Her blonde hair was piled up in a high bun, and in the dark her cheekbones shimmered. Her features tensed as she spotted him. "Hey, you came—eventually."

Nick smiled. "Thanks for the invitation." Tess peered around Nick's shoulder at his bedraggled crew, her expression neutral even though Nick guessed she'd rather they be a million miles away.

"You're all very welcome," Tess said, her smile bright. "Help yourself to a drink."

Davey grinned and held up his plastic cup, glugging it in one. "Already did."

"Well, great. There's food in the kitchen, and the pizza will be here around midnight."

Nick, nervous and edgy, mumbled a grudging thanks. Davey barged past Tess, nearly knocking her off her feet with his bulk. "So," he drawled drunkenly, and Tess recoiled. "Who did your dad have to screw over to get a mansion like this?"

Tess frowned, and Nick's insides crumpled. "Davey..."

"What do you mean?" she said with a sweet smile. He lurched closer; this time, she didn't blink or flinch at his closeness. Nick admired her guts and guessed she'd had to endure thoughtless, jealous remarks all her life.

"I mean...where'd he hide the bodies? What bank did he rob?"

"Of course," she simpered. "I should have guessed someone like *you* would think a man like my father only got where he is today because he hurt someone to get it. Not because he worked hard, and studied and earned every brick of this house. My mother gave up her career to raise us while he did it. Of course, *you* would assume, Davey. I don't blame you. It's just what you are."

She was so breezy, so kind in her delivery that Davey stuttered and spat, "What do you mean by that?"

"I mean..." Tess looked thoughtful while choosing her words, though Nick guessed she was about to make a killing blow to his ego. "All *you* see is what the person you envy has. You don't see the journey it took to get there."

"*Excuse* me?"

Tess grinned in his face. "Enjoy the party."

Nick laughed, and behind them, Casey cackled. "Can you please maybe not insult the host for five minutes, Davey? I want to stay and not get kicked out just yet."

"Bitch," Davey grumbled, scratching his head and stalking away. Nick's chest fluttered, darting to keep an eye on him. He didn't want to let Davey out of his sight, but as he went to follow, Tess caught his arm.

"Nick...can we talk?"

Nick craned his neck as Davey vanished into the sea of bodies on the dancefloor. "Uh..."

"Please, just for a minute?" She tugged him by the hand through the hall, and he followed her until she opened a locked room with a key from her pocket and closed the door behind them. Nick's eyes adjusted to the light flicking on overhead. They were in a small office, Mr. Brant's study, with several monitors, set up under a window desk. Nick sank into a leather reclining chair, and Tess took one opposite. It was nice and smelled like leather, the walls covered in family photos of Tess and Adam through the years.

"What is it?" He folded his arms uncomfortably. Tess leaned forward on her knees, narrowing her piercing blue stare.

"I feel as the best friend, I need to ask what you plan to do about Holly?"

Nick balked. "Excuse me?"

"Holly. You've well and truly rocked the boat. Whatever happened in that tent has broken her, and now she suddenly thinks she's fallen for you...but I know this isn't her."

Two things happened. One, Nick's heart leapt, and the stupidest, soppiest grin threatened to spread over his face, but he kept it in check. Two, his eyes narrowed at the suggestion he was wrong for her.

"Are you saying I'm trouble? Or bad news?"

Tess looked skyward and groaned. "No. I don't think you're any of those things. But judging by the company you keep, Nick...you'll wind up hurting her. I'm scared you'll break her heart. She's so vulnerable, and she acts like she has everything handled."

"I know. I know a hell of a lot more than what you think," he rushed to defend himself, even though he knew part of what she was saying was true. How could he defend himself when Davey acted so openly vile? He'd turned his eyes away and gone along with the crowd for so long.

"Something like this hasn't happened to Holly before," Tess worried aloud. "She'll fall for you, and then you'll do something stupid. Like tonight. Why the hell didn't you just knock for her? Ask her here yourself?"

Nick had no choice but to splutter. "I was...going to...."

"I'll tell you why. She isn't cool enough for you, she's too square, too boring. You had fun while you were away, and now it's like she doesn't exist. She's been waiting for you all night, Nick!"

"I know!" Nick snapped, his head throbbing. "I know I should've acted differently. I know I'm not good enough for her."

Tess shook her head. "I didn't say that. She thinks you're good for her and that's enough for me. But you better *prove* it, Nick Jones!"

Wilting under her acidic stare, Nick deflated. "It doesn't matter. I'm leaving in the morning."

Tess's eyes went saucer wide. "What?"

"I'm going to France for a couple of weeks to see my mum. I was going to tell her tonight."

Tess stood, looming over him, her nostrils flaring angrily. "Then you better get out there and do it! Right now. I won't see her cry over you."

Tess stormed out of the office, leaving him in the chair alone, swinging left and right. He rubbed his eyes and groaned. This was a mess. With a sorrowful weight pressing on his chest, he heaved himself out of the chair and cracked open the door, peering into the dark empty hall. Music blared from the speakers, heady and loud, and as he headed back to the party, the sound crushed his skull.

Abruptly the music shut off, and the air was filled with voices and hushed whispers. Something crashed to the floor somewhere, and he heard a girl scream.

Nick's blood froze, and his feet moved like lightning. He should have never taken his eyes off Davey.

Twenty-Eight

Holly waited in the frame of the door, prickles of fear gathering on the back of her neck. Disappointment washed through her, and she licked at her dry lips. Did Nick just turn and walk away from her?

Hot tears formed in her eyes, and she wiped them back. What had she been thinking? That Nick could change? He could be different from the boy who'd been a pain in her side all these years? Who was she kidding?

Stalking into the downstairs bathroom, she locked the door and sagged against the wall, staring at her reflection.

You can't change, she told herself. *You'll always be a nobody to him, never good enough*. Holly wiped away the smudged dark liner under her eyes, hating herself for trying to be something she wasn't.

James's voice filled her head. *Make yourself heard, Holly*, he told her. Holly Truman was a square. She liked crafts and campfires, making paper lanterns and spending time with the kids. She loved watching their faces light up when they achieved something amazing when they confronted fear and conquered it, leaving fear to quake in their dust.

Holly was an *Eagle*. Something a few hours ago, she was prepared to chuck out the window.

Holly liked Nick, but she couldn't have both and couldn't change herself to fit in his world. So like the sun and moon, their worlds would pass, on their separate courses, never to meet, never to fit together, always on opposite sides of the planet.

Straightening her spine with an imaginary shiver of steel, Holly exited the bathroom and headed back to the kitchen, where she stopped dead in her tracks. Her squeal of delight left her lips before she could stop herself.

Kit had Adam pinned against the kitchen counter, both lip locked in a kiss devouring them both. Neither seemingly able to come up for air until Holly's shrill cry tore them apart. Kit groaned and wiped her red mouth while Holly grinned, her heart filling for her cousin.

"Oh my god!" she squeaked. *"You two!"*

Adam went a flustered shade of berry red, wiping his sweaty palms on his hoodie as he slipped away. "This is so embarrassing," he grunted, probably the first actual sentence he'd uttered all night. He squirmed as he edged past Kit, who was huffing.

"I knew something was off with you!" Holly pointed her finger in triumph. "There's no way you aren't telling me every *single* detail later in bed."

Kit groaned, hands tracking through her pink, dirty locks. Her lips pursed, but after a while, she broke into a grin right as Adam wound his arm around her waist. With a shriek, Kit shoved him off, disgusted. Adam went stiff and turned his eyes at Holly.

"*This* is the issue," he said. "This is all she wants. She doesn't want to actually date me."

"Quit whining," Kit threw at him. "Or that'll never happen. You're so needy—like a dog or something."

"Oh my god," Holly said with a laugh. "Kit—I never realised you were so mean."

Kit growled and broke away from Adam, who stared after her like a lost pup. Holly looked skyward, wondering if Kit ever knew how long she'd crushed on Adam, the unreachable and completely gorgeous brother of her best friend, for years. Holly didn't mind a bit. Weirdly, they fit in a way she guessed she and Nick never would.

Kit would give Adam a hard time, and something about how she looked at him, slyly, out of the corner of her eye, she guessed Kit already had given him a hard time. But he was hooked, smitten, and followed her out of the door, leaving Holly alone in the massive kitchen.

Twenty minutes ago, Holly was ready to vacate and leave this party behind, but now as she surveyed the carnage in the kitchen, she didn't think it was right to leave Tess with all the clean-up, even though she would be the first to understand why she'd left.

Sighing, she dragged a fresh empty bin bag out of the cupboard and thrashed it open. She spent time trawling the lower floor, picking up discarded plastic cups and empty packets of crisps lying on the ground. Beer cans clattered into the bag, and she swiped up as much trash as she could find, even though the music pounded in her ears. Standing on tiptoe, she spotted Tyler and Casey, but Davey was absent, and with a churning gut, she wondered where Nick was. Maybe he'd left? And perhaps that was a good thing.

The air was thick with the smell of sweat, and Holly dodged bodies on the dance floor, picking up empty cans as she went. Her mind ticked relentlessly, and she wondered what answer she would give Martha when she called tomorrow. She didn't want to give up the kids, she didn't want to give up a way of life she loved. However, she would be damned if she would spend every waking minute earning back Martha's good opinion, holding the award over her as leverage.

James told her to make herself heard, and that was what she would do. Smiling to herself, she thought Nick would approve. Not that it mattered now. The kitchen was bright when she went back in, and her feet skidded, spotting the hulking figure by the sink.

There wasn't time to quietly back out of the room. Davey's black gaze snapped up and met hers. His face, which wasn't ugly when he didn't look so irritated, lifted, and his eyes hotly grazed her legs under the dress. Bashfully, Holly ducked behind the central island. "Hey," she said meekly, hating his eyes on her.

There was a plunging noise and a pop, and golden champagne spurted from the neck of the bottle Davey was holding. Holly instantly stiffened. "Where'd you get that?"

Davey chuckled darkly and took a long swig. "The hostess is very generous."

Holly frowned, folding her arms. "I don't think Tess is giving out champagne, Davey."

Davey ignored her and tipped some into an empty cup, thrusting it in her direction. "Relax, I found it in the study, tucked away, probably for Christmas. The room was unlocked—don't look at me like that."

Holly looked over her shoulder, certain Tess would have locked her father's office. "I'm pretty sure the study was a locked room. And the champagne isn't for party guests."

It would have cost a fortune, Holly was sure of it. The Brant family didn't skimp on alcohol, and Holly's fear mounted in increments, hating to imagine Davey poking around in there. What else had he discovered? She skirted around the island, but Davey moved quicker, blocking her path, and she had no choice but to look up at him. "I'm just going back to the party," she said, but Davey sneered.

"You're going to check I haven't stolen anything else," he accused, which wasn't entirely wrong. What Holly wanted to do was find her friend and make sure she locked the room.

Holly kept her smile flat, even when he pressed closer and she could smell vodka on his breath. "Leave me alone, Davey."

"Check my pockets if you want, Truman." He wiggled his brows suggestively. "If you think I've stolen something?"

Holly snorted. "You did steal something. *That!*" She pointed to the near-empty bottle. "Can you please get out of my way?"

He brought his face closer, and she recoiled. "So you can get me kicked out? Why? Because I happened to pick up a bottle of booze that happened to be lying around?"

"It wasn't lying around...." It was hard to maintain her bravado when he was close to her. Wildly she looked about for help, but she was alone in the kitchen while outside in the hall, the music only seemed to get louder.

"You're still so high and mighty, aren't you, Truman? Such a good girl, right to your core. I wondered if Nick wouldn't have screwed that right out of you while he had you alone."

Holly choked, the words stinging like a real, hard slap. Her lip wobbled, and the brief flash of pain crossing her face was enough for him to find his *in* and advance. "I knew it! It's written all over your face. You did screw him on that trip...wow who would have thought you'd be such an *easy* lay?"

"Leave me alone!"

"What was it? Four days? *Four* days for you to drop your underwear...what did he say to you? That you were special, that he liked you? You know he's a liar, right? He didn't even want to come here tonight...the thought of having to bump into you accidentally...."

"Shut...up!" Holly's eyes filled with hot tears. Her fist balled, and her right hand inched towards the bottle of champagne Davey discarded next to him on the countertop. He breathed vodka fumes in her face, a horrible mix of bile, alcohol, and sweat rising off his body.

"... he thought he might be doing you a massive favour. I don't think even he knew how *easily* you'd put out...."

Humiliated, she squirmed in his grip. "We didn't have...."

Davey snarled. "He told us everything...and here you are all dressed up for him. It's pathetic."

Holly's fingers closed around the neck of the bottle, and the red mist of anger descended like a filmy curtain. Her vision whited as she flung the bottle in his direction. It bounced off his shoulder and then shattered against the tiled floor. Holly let out a high-pitched scream, loud enough to attract some attention. Davey stared angrily at the shattered glass. "What the fuck is your problem? Can't take a joke?"

But then his expression changed, and he stared up at her from the flat of his back. In those moments before he fell, Nick caught his collar, spun him, and landed Davey with a smack in the jaw that sent a spray of blood droplets flying through the air.

Nick flexed his knuckles, stalking out of the front door, leaving it to clang behind him. Cradling his bruised fist to his side, he longed to feel the cool air on his skin and didn't stop till he reached the lawn. Bending double, he rubbed at his eyes. The full reality of what he'd done hit him like a bulldozer in the chest. He heaved and saw stars.

He shouldn't have come here tonight. Behind him, the party guests filtered onto the porch steps, interest gathering. Inside, the music died, and hushed whispers floated out to follow him in his darkest moment.

Oh, shit. Shit. He'd hit Davey. His friend. He'd seen red, anger, and defiance boiling like a geyser, exploding when he'd stalked into the kitchen and witnessed him towering over Holly.

"Nick, wait!" Her voice followed him, but he didn't look back, barely breathing as his feet hit the pavement. He needed to get as far away as possible before doing anything else stupid.

"Nick!" She caught the sleeve of his jacket. "You can't just leave."

Shoulders slumping, he stopped so abruptly she nearly careered into his back. Slowly he turned, inches away, wanting to be closer, but the tears in her eyes told him he'd blown it.

It was the final disappointment. She balled up those little fists, and standing under a street lamp, she looked dishevelled, wrung out, and he wanted to kiss her. She really had broken him this week. Miserably, he huffed. "What?"

"You shouldn't have hit him, Nick."

Nick raised his arms in a shrug. "Are you surprised? You know me, Holly. Take me as I am, or leave me."

Holly stuttered and took a timid step forward. "I don't want to leave you. I've waited for you—all night. Why didn't you come to find me?"

Nick spluttered helplessly, waving a hand between them. "Because of this. This will never work. I'm...just not good enough. Not for you. You need someone like...Adam...good, studious, a match for you. We aren't matched."

Her eyes welled up. "You won't even try. But I'm starting to believe you."

"It's about time," he said. Nick's chest tightened, fully aware they had a captive audience. There were even kids hanging out of the upstairs window. Holly's older cousin Kit lingered nearby, arms folded and a bitter look of disappointment on her face.

Holly burst, her eyes leaking as she nodded. "Maybe you are right? I was so stupid to think this might work out. You can't change what's always been, right?"

"I'm leaving anyway," he said, and her face fell. "First thing tomorrow. It wouldn't have ever worked. I need to go and be with someone who knows me. Who gets me...."

She swatted at her face, her chest heaving as she barely caught her breath. "Were you even going to tell me?"

"I was going to."

"I've been in the kitchen all night... waiting for you. I wasn't hard to find."

Nick stumbled over his words. "I was trying to find the right moment. And then..."

"Then what?"

"I saw you in that dress." He gestured to her figure, her skin goose-pimply in the cool night breeze. She fingered the hem.

"It's just a stupid dress."

"You didn't have to change who you are—not for me. I don't deserve you."

She lifted her chin. "No, you don't," she spat. "You're right about one thing. No surprises, hey?"

He smiled grimly, aware Tess had crept onto the lawn. Adam and Kit huddled closer by a tree, and Nick thought they might be holding hands. He was wretched, tired, and wanted to be out of her sight, out of everyone's sight. "I'll see you around, Holly."

He turned, wetness gathering on his lashes, ready to run back and beg forgiveness for being an idiot, for keeping her at arm's length. Sorry for making her feel like she had to be different, to change to fit in, or to keep him. God, he needed to get on the ferry and get away from this town.

"Nick." She jogged after him, light tangling in her hair. People gradually filtered back inside, and all the lights went on in the house. The party was over.

"Nick, wait."

He stopped and turned. Her eyeliner was smudged and tracking down her cheeks.

"I would have taken you as you are," she said, her voice choked. "I would have taken *everything* you are."

He sniffed, awaiting her killing blow. His shoulders were heavy, like blocks of wood, his neck muscles aching. She stepped closer, and he could smell the familiar scent in her hair.

"Davey said you told him private things we did while we were away...but I never believed him, not once," she whispered, taking his hand and running her thumb over the graze on his knuckles. Somewhere in the house, Davey was probably still nursing his bloodied nose. That relationship was dead, and he didn't care. He imagined what he must have said to her while he'd had her cornered. It made him sick.

"I would have never told him about that night...I wouldn't."

Holly wiped wet strands of hair out of her way, lifting her swollen eyes to his. "I know you wouldn't. And that's just it. You could have just told him the truth—about me. If I meant anything to you, you could have told him right then, but you didn't."

"Holly...I was going to...my friends are difficult."

Holly sniffed up tears. "It isn't difficult. You were embarrassed to tell them because it's me. You weren't brave enough to admit how you feel. You could have told Davey the truth, what really happened...but you never said a word. And that's why I could never be with you. That's why you aren't good enough."

Twenty-Nine

Holly woke with her right eye welded shut with mascara and her face stuck to the pillow. Blinking rapidly, she sat in her bed, her cheeks hot and swollen. Smacking her lips, she reached for the water, and after glugging it greedily, it hydrated her parched throat. There was a soft body in bed next to her, and when Holly poked Tess's backside, she groaned and swatted Holly's hand away.

Holly was thankful for many things. Firstly, she was thankful Kit convinced a very bewildered and sober Adam to drive them all home, after she left Nick gaping after her on the pavement.

Secondly, she was thankful her best friend abandoned her own house party to come home with her and pile her under a duvet, where they both ate ice cream and cried. Tess seemed to sense Holly's abysmal sense of loss and defeat and insisted on sleeping beside her in her double bed.

It even hurt when Nick's music blared through the walls later that night. Holly sobbed into her pillow, wishing the inches between them were gone and she could take back what she said.

Sitting up in bed, she jerked, her eyes struggling to adjust to the light streaming through the curtain. What time was it? She ran to the window, her heart in her chest pounding when she saw the empty space in Nick's driveway. Holly glanced at the clock, it was nearly nine in the morning, and by now, Nick would be on the road to the coast with his father.

Sinking on the bed, Tess stirred and opened her eyes. She smiled warily. "Hey."

Holly drew her knees up to her chest. "Hey."

"How are you feeling?"

Holly swallowed a lump in her throat. "Dreadful."

Gingerly, Tess sat up, bleary-eyed, with the greenish tinge of a hangover. "Not as dreadful as I feel."

"I meant about Nick," Holly said with a weary sigh, even though she knew Tess knew what she meant. "I didn't drink."

"Uh." Tess held her head. "Might have gone better if you had. You still hate his guts?"

"I've never hated his guts."

Tess laughed. "Are you serious? It's all I've ever heard come out of your mouth when it concerns Nick Jones. I mean, the guy ignored you all night at the party and didn't have the decency to tell you he was leaving first thing in the morning. Now more than ever, you have a right to hate him."

"Hate is too strong," Holly said. "I just wish I could start over."

Tess frowned and twisted in her direction under the covers. "Nothing has changed, Hols. Even if you two spent hours talking it out—the basic differences are still the same."

Holly nodded. "You're right."

"Although," Tess drawled, tilting her head with a wicked grin. "The guy did look pretty broken. I mean, when you said...you're not good enough for me—ouch!"

Holly winced. "I'm such a bitch. Maybe they are right? I am such a..." She sighed and hung her head. "...a square. No wonder they all hate me."

Tess rolled her eyes. "Oh, you mean the *delightful* Davey and his band of misfits. *Huge* loss, Holly. Though...Nick did knock him clean off his feet. I think he might have broken his nose. It might make him cuter."

Holly chuckled sadly. "Ah yes, the manly display of testosterone. Nick *must* love me!"

They both giggled, and Tess shifted on her pillow, nudging her elbow. "What do you want him to do? Get a personality transplant?"

"No," Holly said. "But rather than flying in at the last possible second to defend my honour...I would have far preferred he just tell his friends the truth."

Tess wagged a finger. "Of course, the simple option. Far too easy for someone like Nick."

Holly let out a sad chuckle, leaning her head on Tess's shoulder. Tess wrapped her in a warm hug. "Never change, Holly. We love you as you are. And I have a sneaky suspicion, he did too."

Tess kissed her forehead. "Go get showered, and I'll take you to breakfast. I need something fattening to get rid of this hangover."

Holly looked up and grinned. "And then I'll help you clear up your house."

"Oh, I have a feeling Adam might already be on it. Speaking of my mysterious older brother, what is going on with him and Kit?"

Jumping out of bed, Holly grabbed a clean towel, throwing her hands in a shrug. "I plan on torture to get it out of her."

"Ooh, can we use pliers?" Tess wiggled her brows.

Holly threw a cushion at her and spent the next ten minutes standing under the hot spray. She lathered her hair and soaped her skin, leaning her forehead against the tiles and finally letting herself have a good, cleansing cry out, where Tess couldn't hear her. Her eyes stung she cried so hard. She wished she could've taken back what she said, a knot was growing in her stomach as she imagined his face crumpling.

She didn't even have his number to call him. Holly did know friends who would have his number. And if she called, what then? This little back and forth wouldn't ever be done. The knot tightened even as she dried herself and pulled on fresh clothes. Her faithful old shirts and tattered hoodie, then looked at her reflection, slipping on her glasses.

Good old, Holly. The same as she ever was, only now, inside, she was utterly changed. She'd tasted lust and longing and wanted it back. She wanted Nick back, remembering his weight on her as he'd kissed her senselessly in the tent.

She opened the bathroom door to her phone ringing on her bedside cabinet. Tess tossed it to her, sauntering by as she ducked into the shower. Martha's number flashed on the screen, and Holly groaned.

Time to face the music.

"Hello!" she said as brightly as she could manage. "How are you?"

"Holly! I caught you up and about. I was sure you'd still be asleep." Martha sounded marginally cheerier than she had yesterday. But Holly was sure that wouldn't last, not when she'd revealed what she planned to say to the older Eagle leader. "Have you had a little time to think about what I proposed yesterday?"

Holly gathered her courage, sitting cross-legged on the bed, her insides spiralling as she prepared to do one of the bravest things she'd ever done. "I have," she replied, nervously licking her lips.

"And what did you decide?"

"I can't...." She swallowed, blowing out a long breath as the other end went very quiet. "I can't do everything you want me to do, Martha. I know you have a lot of pressure on you, being the only Eagle leader in the town. But..." She closed her fists. Telling the truth was hard. "I need a break. I'm eighteen, and this is my last summer before college starts, and then I'll be swamped. I want to help you, and I *will* make time. But I can't be there for every event, every fundraiser, every trip with the kids...I just can't."

"Holly..."

"And if it means I don't get my award, if all I've done over the years isn't enough, and you somehow want me to earn it back...then I can't. I'm done. You can keep the award. I've given you enough. I..." She closed her eyes. "I'm *enough*."

Make yourself heard...

Holly let out a breath of relief, and she was sure at the other end, Martha clicked her nails. When she didn't speak for a long time, she wondered if Martha had hung up, but then she heard her voice.

"Holly. I never meant to make you feel like I was going to hold the award hostage—because of one silly..." she paused. "I was going to say mistake. But that's wrong. Nick Jones is...a *good* match for you."

It was Holly's turn to go silent, and then she let out a choked laugh. "Are you serious?"

"Deadly."

Holly blinked, but Martha rushed on.

"I've had a very interesting telephone conversation with him this morning."

Holly's pulse spiked, and she sat stiffly on the bed. Tess appeared from the shower, damp and wrapped in a towel. She mouthed 'what?' to Holly, but she waved her away, her blood flooding hot.

"Nick phoned me and insisted I give you the award. He actually gave me quite an earful. Said I was being unfair and a hypocrite—which maybe I was a little." Holly silently scoffed at Martha's reluctance to admit her wrongdoing. "He fought for you, Holly."

The world went slightly grey at the edges, and Holly had the sense of being sucked out to sea, waves crashing and clawing at her ankles. Her vision swam, and she struggled to hold the phone to her ear. Nick fought for her? "W-what else did he say?"

"Well, that's the thing, and I'll get to it. But firstly, Holly, the award is yours, fair and square. You've earned it, and I wish you every success, even if you never returned to the club, which I sincerely hope you do. But don't feel any pressure on my account—as of this morning, a new member signed up."

Holly gasped, her mouth hanging wide, which only made Tess wave her hands frantically for attention. Holly shushed her. "What?"

"Nick signed up as a volunteer. He's going to train to be a leader like you; honestly, I couldn't be happier. He was wonderful with the kids, they adore him, and he is a great extra pair of hands. So...you're free, Holly, if you want to be."

"I don't know what to say. You know I could never leave you all."

Now, how could she leave? Nick was going to be an Eagle. He was volunteering his free time, to work with kids, to prove he was better. He was good enough.

Good enough for her.

"I have to go, Martha!" Suddenly, a fire lit under her backside, and panic flooded her system. How could she let him leave without telling him how she felt? She had to tell him he *was* good enough. She was crazy about this cute, tattooed grump who used to eat crayons and painted all over her favourite stuffed toy when they were kids.

Holly beamed. "I'll see you soon, Martha. I promise! Thank you so much for calling me."

Promptly she hung up and faced Tess, who was waiting with her jaw sagging. "What?"

"Nick signed up to be an Eagle!" she spluttered. "I have to find him. I can't let him go off without telling him how I feel. Two weeks is too long to wait, and who knows, after last night, he might stay all summer in France!"

Tess spluttered. "Call him. I'll find someone who has his number."

Holly paced and wrung her hands. "What if he sees it's me and won't answer?"

Kit, disturbed by the yelling and flapping, fell through the door, and slumped sleepily on Holly's bed. "What's going on?"

"Nick has joined the Eagles, and Holly has had an epiphany and thinks she needs to chase him to the coast before he sails out of her life for two weeks." Tess filled Kit in, and Holly's gut whirled. She grabbed at her hair.

"I have to find him!"

Kit shrugged and then yawned. "Call him. Facebook him. Instagram or Whatsapp. There are literally a million ways you can get in touch."

Holly dramatically fell on the bed, clutching Kit's hands and throwing her a watery, imploring stare. "I was a complete bitch to him last night. I all but called him a loser...."

"You kind of did," Tess said.

"What if he meets a beautiful French girl and stays for the rest of the summer? I can't let him leave without telling him I'm sorry."

Kit stood, her eyes teary and bright. Gone was her cynical smirk, her features soft and pretty. She understood. "I'll call Adam. We'll look up the ferry times on the way!"

Holly grinned. "Really?"

"It's kind of my fault you fell for him in the first place. I did key his car."

Kit stood and pulled Holly to her feet. Tess folded her arms. "This is all very dramatic."

"That's because it's love—or very nearly," Kit said, throwing an arm around Holly's shoulders. "And don't pretend you aren't coming!"

"Oh, I'm coming," Tess said with a wicked grin. Holly skipped down the stairs, grabbing her coat and praying she wouldn't be too late.

Thirty

The car wound through the busy streets of Portsmouth, the tall buildings looming over the vehicle. They drove in silence and every minute that ticked by was a moment Nick tried not to think about Holly. Resting his chin on his fist, his elbow crooked on the doorframe, he stared relentlessly out at the grey, leaden sky as a few spots of rain dripped down the window.

So much for summer, he thought, his mood darkening like the clouds above them. It was still early, unreasonably so for a Saturday morning, and usually, Nick would be in bed, with his head under his pillow, nursing a hangover. But his father woke him military style, yanking the duvet off him at six, and announced they would have to move to make the hour trip.

Dry-mouthed, Nick sipped at his water, wishing he still couldn't see her face staring up at him tearfully under the street lamp's glare. She had been so pretty in the black dress. Nick's chest stung, and so did his knuckles.

"Are you going to say anything?" his father asked, glancing at his profile as they drove. "I'm tired of all these silent car trips we keep taking."

Nick huffed, tired and wrung out. "What do you want me to say?"

Mr. Jones tutted. "I don't know. Are you excited? You've wanted to visit your mother in France for years."

Nick rolled his shoulders in a shrug, and Mr. Jones muttered under his breath something like 'teenagers' and Nick boiled, and like a geyser erupted. "I'm happy, okay? I'm psyched to be seeing her."

"You don't look it...you look in fact...quite the opposite."

"Sorry, I'm not animated enough for you."

Mr. Jones flicked his chin toward Nick's battered right hand, lying on his knee. Nick noticed and instantly curled his fist. "You've been fighting."

Nick opened his mouth, his brain barely functioning at a level to cook up a good lie, so instead, he went for the truth. "It wasn't a fight. I punched Davey."

He flexed his fist, and his knuckles throbbed. There was a tiny gash in the skin and sickly, he suspected it might be from Davey's teeth. Casey and Tyler had both texted him independently and said Davey was shaken but okay, and sloped off nursing a bloodied top lip. Tyler proclaimed he deserved it, and Casey stayed to help clean up. Nick's brows rose. Maybe people were capable of change?

"Why did you hit him?"

"What do you care? You've made it very clear how you feel about Davey."

His father scoffed. "I don't want you fighting—and stop being so petulant. I'm here for you, remember? No surprise, I don't like the guy, but I don't want you thinking it's okay to smash his teeth in."

Nick stared out of the window, his blood coursing at the memory of the thirty seconds he'd witnessed before he'd grabbed Davey's collar. All he saw through the fiery mist of his temper was Holly pressed against the counter and Davey holding her, his meaty fingers digging into her skin, towering over her.

Nick didn't think, and that was his problem. It had always been his problem. He found his temper, rage, and irritable streak so hard to control. She looked so tiny compared to Davey, and Nick reacted. Badly.

And the worst part was it earned him zero hero points with Holly. It had the opposite effect, she looked at him...

Like you're the same loser she always thought you were.

"I don't think it's okay to use my fists. But you didn't hear..." his voice trailed off, and his father's head snapped in his direction. They joined a queue to park in a visitor centre of Portsmouth Ferry Terminal, where Nick could walk on the pedestrian gangway. He found a space and pulled on the brake.

"Didn't hear what?"

"What he said to Holly."

Mr. Jones's eyes creased with a wane smile. "Oh."

"Don't start—okay? It isn't going to work, and she hates my guts now anyway. I didn't come through when I should have. I should have fought for her."

"Kind of sounds like you did."

"Not the physical kind of fighting, Dad." Nick rubbed his aching brows, his hangover making his temples throb. "I should have been better."

They sat in silence, and Mr. Jones clicked his tongue and then finally threw open the door. Salty sea air wafted into the car, and Nick turned his face, seeking out fresh air like it would clear the fog. He popped the boot and grabbed Nick's bags, throwing them over his broad shoulder. They crossed to the ferry terminal, where Nick flashed his passport and ticket, and they hung around in the waiting area.

Mr. Jones beckoned him outside, where the gulls flew low, and the massive white ferries groaned as they docked. Nick's was already in, and slowly cars were being ushered on. "You've got ten minutes before it leaves."

Nick sighed. "I'll board—you get going."

His father handed him his luggage, and Nick groaned under the weight, not as well built as his ex-army father.

"I could take you home—right now." The suggestion made him pause and stare up at his father in surprise.

"What? No. What about Mum?"

He smiled sadly. "She'd understand, Nick. All I'm saying is...if you want to go home, we can."

Nick thought of his mother, probably already making her long journey to Calais, and his stomach twisted at the thought of disappointing her. Right now, all he wanted was to go home and bang on Holly's door. But he couldn't stand to see that look on her face. He'd let her down.

He could have been honest, he could have made a stand.

This is the real me, this is what I want. Holly is who I want.

He half wondered if she knew he'd signed up for Eagle duty when he returned. If nothing else, Holly was free now, she didn't need the pressure of the club, and she could rest knowing the weight was off her shoulders. She could fly free, and even if she never spoke to him again, he was glad. Part of Nick kind of missed the kids.

He shouldn't have smacked Davey, it wasn't an attractive quality, and he didn't blame Holly for her reaction. Longing settled in his chest, and he hoped it wasn't over.

Nick wanted to be better, and this was the only way he knew how.

"I can't let Mum down...but thanks." Awkwardly he went in for a hug, and his father choked in surprise. It took him a moment, but the older man tightened his hold and squeezed hard. Nick thought of what Holly said in the shower block, and his throat thickened. "Love you, Dad."

Mr. Jones's chuckle rumbled through his chest, and he held his son tighter. "God, Nick, what did that girl do to you? I love her already—and I love you, too."

Nick didn't want to let him go. Was going away a huge mistake?

"She's good for you," he said in Nick's ear. "And I hope you can work it out when you get home. Have a great time with your mother."

Nick's knees quivered as he hauled his bags over his shoulder and went through the turnstile to the pedestrian gangway. The ship was massive, already filling up, and his hand found the rail, tracing its path as he boarded the ferry. Inside it was stuffy, and he immediately went up top, throwing his bags by a bench, the sea breeze blasting through his hair as he leaned against the rail. A lump formed in his throat as he spotted his dad by the entrance, waving.

Nick tried to smile and lifted his hand in a wave. An announcement from the captain sounded over the tannoy, and the last of the cars were ushered on. Jacketed crew members closed the gate, and the folding ramp lifted with a clunk and a buzz of machinery. Nick's heart fluttered.

Something buzzed in his jean pocket, and he pulled out his phone, his mother's photo flashing on the caller screen. Nick grinned, a rush of warmth filling his chest as he slid the phone open.

"Mum...hey, we're about to pull away."

The line was crackly and muffled, but he heard his mother's bright, breezy voice. She always sounded like she was late or walking somewhere in a hurry, a little ditzy, but he loved her for it.

"Hey, sweetie pie," she cooed. "So...don't be mad at me...."

Nick frowned into the receiver, his hands prickling. "What?" He tried to sound as breezy as her. The wind was whipping up, and he stepped inside the cabin door as passengers rushed past with their kids onto the viewing deck. A little girl dropped her bear by his feet, and he knelt to give it to her. She gave him a pretty smile, and he grinned, reminded of Chloe.

He actually missed the Robins!

"What is it?"

"I fucked up. My gallery was having a huge showing last night, and I forgot I was supposed to collect you. I slept in and missed the train....is there any way you can make your own way to the town?"

Nick's brow furrowed, and the phone suddenly heavy in his hand. He looked up and spotted his father waving manically, and his eyes welled with hot tears. What the hell was he doing? Panic exploded in his chest.

"Nick? I'm sorry okay? I messed up, but I promise I'll make it up to you when you get here." She yawned sleepily. "I'll message you the address and all the directions. But you'll be okay, right?"

Time slowed to a crawl, and he couldn't breathe. He had to get off this ferry!

A horn sounded overhead, and waves lapped at the bow. Nick ran, and the phone slipped. He hung up and tossed it in his pocket.

Grabbing the rail, he hurtled down the narrow galley steps, bags tossed over his shoulder. He ran till a stitch formed under his ribs and jumped the small rail to where crew members were locking up the car loading bay.

One of them in a high-vis jacket spotted him and waved. "What the hell are you doing? We're about to depart!"

"Let me off!" Nick yelled. "Please, *please*, let me off this boat!"

Thirty-One

"Adam...you drive like a pensioner!" Kit cried from the front seat. "Speed up!"

In the back, Holly's nails gripped the faded, scratchy material of the seat. She tried to mentally untangle the knot in her stomach, her pulse spiking as they joined another long, snarled queue of traffic trying to exit towards Southampton.

Adam shot Kit a withering glance. "Do you think you could do better? What do you suggest I do?"

"Overtake this idiot!" Kit wailed, waving her hand to the large, packed people carrier blocking their path. "He's got lots of room to move over."

"Kit, it's no good if we end up having an accident—we'll never find him," Tess chimed in, her feet up on the seat as she thumbed through her phone. "It's saying here the 11.20 is on time. We have twenty minutes!"

Holly sagged in her seat, stressed but grateful she wasn't alone right now. Anxiety made her heart thump, and she stared out at the dismal rows of traffic. "I think it's clearing."

Tess gripped her hand and squeezed it, and their eyes met in a reassuring smile. "We'll find him."

"Doesn't anyone you know have his number?" Kit twisted to look at the friends huddled in the back of Adam's Volvo. "Or anyone on Facebook?"

Tess bit her lip, looked skyward, and groaned. "I might know someone...."

"Then do it, please!" Holly begged, and Tess reluctantly took out her phone and pulled up Instagram, her pink nails shining as she flicked through. Davey's profile popped up, and Holly made a face.

"You're following him?"

Tess snorted. "Uh, *no*. As of last night, he followed *me*." A rosy blush appeared on her skin. "Maybe he liked me telling him off?"

"That's just—weird." Holly pursed her lips. The thought of Davey Thomas following Tess after he'd acted like a complete idiot and hot head, then humiliated by Nick was all too fresh. "I think he's awful."

"He is awful!" Tess agreed. "But he'll have Nick's number. And after the way he spoke to you, he owes me."

Holly watched, fascinated, as Tess typed in a lightning-fast message, and with equally quick speed, Davey replied with

Nick's number. She gasped, "Wow, you might have a fan, Tess."

Tess effortlessly pulled up Nick's number. "I'm calling him. He may not answer...."

If he knows it's me...

The ache in her chest tightened like a rope. God, she hoped he wouldn't laugh in her face. Traffic cleared, and Adam sped through the historic market town of Southhampton. Stalls lined the streets, and in the distance, the sea twinkled as they neared the port. Holly dived between the seats, pointing to the terminal signs. "There, Terminal B!"

"I see it," Adam snapped through gritted teeth. Holly grabbed his shoulder and squeezed it gratefully, and from the passenger, seat Kit gave her a grin.

"Thanks, Adam!"

"It's engaged," Tess wailed. "I'll keep trying."

Holly sat back as they joined another long queue, mountains of cars all joining the Ferry terminal lane to board the boat. She wound down the window, letting in the fresh salty air.

What would she say when she saw him? *I'm sorry. Don't go. Don't fall in love with anyone else because I've been an idiot, so preoccupied with rules and routine, I never saw how amazing you were.*

She thought of the day he'd stolen Wilbur and smiled. Tess hung up, shrugging helplessly.

"It's either engaged or going straight to voice mail—do you want to leave a message?"

Holly shook her head, hoping they still had time, even if the clock on Adam's dashboard was counting down. The queue snarled to a halt, and Kit craned her neck. "Think they're holding us."

The car rolled to a stop, and Holly peered over her friend's heads. She took the phone and darted out of the car. Her heels slapped the cobbles as she ran frantically down the bustling pavement to the pedestrian boarding area, a small white cabin. A man in a orange high vis bib held up his hand as she breathlessly grabbed the rail. "I need to get in!"

"Not without a ticket, love." He sauntered to the gate, one hand deep in his pocket and the other holding a clipboard. "You looking for someone?"

Holly's chest was tight, full of cold air. She bent double and heaved. "Please. I need to speak to a passenger who might have boarded."

The man made a disgruntled noise and peered over his clipboard. "Name?"

Holly panted with relief, and sweat beaded her top lip. "Nick—Nicholas Jones."

A beat of silence passed, his brow furrowed, red skin worsening. He ducked into the cabin, checking the computer, but emerged seconds later. "There's no one by that name for this crossing to the Isle of Wight. Maybe it's the next one?"

Holly's gut rolled, and ice washed her palms. She stuttered, "Isn't this the ferry to Calais?"

He studied her, his older eyes creasing at her confusion. "No, love. This is the 11.20 to the Isle of Wight. Our Calais crossings don't start till this afternoon. But Portsmouth had a crossing at 11am—which would have likely gone now."

Her knees buckled, and she went white. Gripping the rail, she tried to give him a vague smile but burst into tears. "Thank you."

Weakly, he nodded, and she turned, hugging her waistline as she trudged back to the car, where Adam was still at the wheel and Kit, and Tess waited on the pavement. Kit held out her arms and Holly collapsed into them. "We're in the wrong port," she wailed into Kit's hair. "We were supposed to go to Portsmouth."

Kit wrapped her in a tight hug. "I'm so sorry, Holly." Tess's warm hand found her shoulder and then all three stood on the pavement in a group hug while disgruntled passengers wove by pulling their luggage. "Let's get you home."

Holly pulled out Tess's phone. "Can I use this? I want to leave him a message."

Tess nodded, and they both stepped away, allowing her some privacy as she found a seat on a low brick wall, her chest heaving as she stared out over the bustling port. In the distance, ferries weaved through the estuary, waves lapping at the bows, their horns sounding above the cry of gulls.

Holly dialed his number and waited, her lungs caged, hoping maybe he'd pick up. When he didn't, and it went to voice mail, she took a reedy breath before speaking.

"Nick...." She closed her eyes against the sun beating on her lids. "If you get this...I'm so sorry. I tried to find you, I wanted to tell you this in person. I should never have said those awful things last night. We've both made such a mess of things, but if you ever want to try, I would take you as you are. I still would. You are good enough—you're perfect."

The lump in her throat dissolved, and she laughed. "Okay, maybe not perfect, but neither am I. I just wanted to tell you that. I never ask anything for myself. I tend to forget I want things too. But this time, I want to ask you...don't fall in love with anyone else while you're gone. I just want it to be me."

She clicked the phone shut, and with a heavy, wearied step, she headed to her friends, who waited with open arms.

The skies cleared of their grey cloud, and by the time Adam drove back into Willowdale, it was fresh and sunny, and children littered the playgrounds. Summer was here, and Holly had weeks of rest to look forward to. But somehow, it felt hollow without Nick. Her thoughts returned to the camp and him piggybacking her across the meadow after she'd stung her leg. She thought of him decorating jars and rowing the boat.

She wished she could go back. Tess squeezed her hand, and Holly pulled her arm around her shoulders in a hug, resting her head on Tess's shoulder. "How about a shopping trip?" she suggested.

Holly looked up at her oldest friend. "I want to talk to you soon," she said, her voice wavering. "About James."

Tess gave her a sad smile and a kiss on her forehead. "It's about time."

Nick, unknowingly opened a conduit between now and the lost fourteen-year-old buried with guilt. Guilt she now saw in stark reality. It was time to share the burden, with her mother, with Tess and finally lay James to rest. No matter if she chose to continue to be an Eagle, or she flew free for a while, the weight had lifted. Nick had given her that.

"Or...we could go to the pub?" Kit suggested from the front with a wink. Tess made a face.

"Ooh, how about a sleepover at mine, and we give you a makeover?" she said with a wicked laugh and Kit scowled. "We could reveal what your actual hair colour is under that dye."

"I like the pink," Adam chirped up. "I don't want anything to change."

Kit blushed and gave him a shy smile, and despite the horrible, achy feeling in the pit of her belly, Holly found herself grinning at them.

"Oh, we are so going to torture the truth out of her," Tess whispered, and Holly giggled. Adam pulled the car into Holly's road, slowing as they approached the house. She didn't know what she would do first. This was the first time Holly Truman had nothing planned. No club activities, no adventures, just alone time with herself.

A long bath, she thought miserably. *And then maybe cake.* She rolled up her sleeve and gazed at the faded print of the sun Nick drew on her wrist, remembering the kiss he pressed to her skin afterwards.

"Holly," Adam said, his voice strained as he stopped at the curb and yanked on the brake. "I think..."

"Oh my god!" Tess squealed. Holly jerked into a sitting position, her face breaking into a massive grin. She threw open the car door, and her feet hit the pavement.

Nick sat perched on his bonnet, hoodie wrapped around his waist, his arms folded across his broad chest. His face looked cold, stern, but when he saw her, it broke, his eyes creasing and the dimple in his cheek deepening.

"Nick!" She didn't care if she sounded like a moron as she ran down the street. He hopped off the bonnet and gathered her in his arms, kissing her hair. She wrapped her arms around his neck, grinning at him. "You didn't go!"

Nick's expression soured as she let out a long exhale. "I had a little wake-up call. My mother called and let me know how unconcerned she was about me joining her for two weeks, and I realised what I was leaving behind. Or who I was leaving behind."

She took his hand and kissed the back of it, sad he'd come to that realisation, her heart hurt for him, the perfect image of his mother, shattered. But she was grateful he was with her. "I want you here."

Nick leaned back, thumbs grazing her cheekbones. Holly stood on her toes and kissed him, relief and sunshine washing through her. She stared up at him tearfully. "Nick, I'm so sorry."

His eyes darkened. "I'm sorry. I should have been honest. I should have....been better. You deserve better, Holly." He cocked his brow. "I got your message, by the way. Perfect, am I?"

She giggled and poked his shoulder. "You're perfect for me. I think we fit, and I want to try."

"I was hoping." He grinned bashfully, and her insides melted. "If it's okay with you...I'd like to spend every waking moment this summer...with you. If I don't drive you insane before then."

She kissed his smile, flooded with longing. "Deal."

"You have me, Holly, entirely. You won your challenge. You broke me."

She took his hand, linked fingers, and leaned on the bonnet with him. Adam pulled the car away, driving Tess and Kit so they could be alone. The sun beamed off the car with the promise of summer for the two of them, and she couldn't wait to be alone with him.

The pad of her thumb grazed his knuckles. "I think we both broke a little."

Nick swept her up in a long kiss, hands tangling in her hair as if he would never be close enough. His mouth warm and needy on hers. She grabbed his collar, tugging him closer, smiling against his mouth as his hands found her backside, and he made a happy noise in his throat.

Holly didn't have time to come up for air until he eventually pulled away, kissing the end of her nose. He rose his brows suggestively.

"So....We still have the camping equipment packed up. I wouldn't mind going back to the tent and starting where we left off."

Holly went hot, head to toe, looking up at him through heavy-lidded eyes. "Sounds like a plan. Though, you like a lot of cuddling, right?"

"Fine by me." The smile he gave her washed away the last eighteen years. He pressed a kiss to her temple, fiddling around with something in his pocket, and to her surprise, he pulled out a black sharpie.

Holly laughed, tugging him down for one more kiss. "And what's that for?"

Nick smiled, mischief shining in the blue of his eyes. "I never did find the perfect spot for the tattoo."

Acknowledgments

Hello, dear readers. Thank you so much for reading Nick and Holly's story. I do hope you enjoyed going on this journey with them. I loved every minuite of crafting their love story. It is always a little emotional writing an acknowledgment, but my biggest thanks in writing this book must go to my friend and fellow author, Chris Kenny. Thank you for your time, and support and for keeping me on track.

For every book I write, I must thank my husband for his unwavering belief and support. One day I'll write our story. Also I need to thank my two daughters, who make me whole hearted.

If you would like to connect with me, I'd love to hear from you! You'll find me over on the clock app, and look for @evelyngraceauthor. Thank you!

About Sammy

Sammy Rose Taylor is an author of teen and new adult fiction and lives in the Essex countryside with her husband and daughters. You will find her writing, reading, going on long walks, and caring for her fur baby, a rescued Bengal named Benz.

She wrote her first book when she was thirteen and has always dreamed of living life as a full-time author. Sammy also writes Paranormal fantasy and romance under the pen name Victoria Wren, and has published a YA contemporary paranormal series.

Bad Elves

After two years, Tess Brant returns to Willowdale at Christmas, alone and newly single, after being dumped by her college boyfriend. All she wants is a warm, comforting family Christmas around a log fire in her parent's cosy country house. Instead, she comes home to find the lights off, and the Thermostat switched to zero. The Brants are bankrupt, and in a humiliating turn of events, Tess is forced to apply for a job at her local department store. As a Christmas Elf!

Not only that, but Davey Thomas is back in town. The former young offender has been away on his uncle's farm, and is home for Christmas. Rude, cocky and smoking hot, Tess never expects him to apply for the same job! Broke, Davey is hired as an Elf. Can the former rich girl and Willowdale's former bad boy ever see eye to eye? Especially as they make life miserable for one another. Pranks turn to mischief, and soon neither can fight their growing attraction to one another.

Opposites do attract, and both fights to keep their lust in check. It's the magic of Christmas, right? No one wants to be alone at this time of year. Or can Davey prove to Tess that change is possible and, sometimes, magic is real?

Printed in Great Britain
by Amazon

11277982R00197